RUN JANE RUN

By

Celeste Charlene

April 1, 2017

Marie,

So nice to meet you at the women's retreat God bless you

Celeste

Copyright © 2015 Celeste Charlene. All rights reserved. No part of this publication may be reproduced, stored in a retrieval system or transmitted in any form or by any means, electronic, mechanical, photocopying, recording or otherwise without the prior written permission of the copyright holder, except for brief quotations used in a review.

This is a work of fiction, and is produced from the author's imagination. People, places and things mentioned in this novel are used in a fictional manner.

To Kathryn Page Camp, my faithful friend and critique partner. Thank you.

CHAPTER ONE

Megan Jane clutched the steering wheel tighter. She glanced in the rearview mirror. No one followed.

Her husband had given her a list of errands that afternoon which should have taken a whole day. He didn't expect her back until dinner time. Should she take advantage of the time to escape? She looked in the mirror again and adjusted it with trembling fingers.

Running had never been worth the punishment after he'd caught her, but she couldn't endure much more from him. She shuddered. Best not to be caught.

She pressed the button to lower her window and let the crisp, clean air energize her. October leaves painted the mountains scarlet and orange as they lined the Tennessee country road. She sighed at the canopy of glorious maple trees.

Megan Jane checked once more behind her before pulling onto an abandoned dirt trail. She shut off the motor and tugged the keys slightly out of the ignition to stop the alarm from ringing. She'd gone through her escape plan over and over in her mind, but so much could go wrong.

Licking her lips, she fumbled with her seatbelt, but it wouldn't unlatch. She took several deep breaths to calm herself and willed her fingers to stop shaking. The belt clicked open, and she stepped out of the spotless Mercedes. She turned away from the road and headed to a field.

Leaves crunched under her feet as she went to a cluster of bushes. She stopped in front of a little pile of white stones, crouched, and moved them aside. After sweeping the leaves away with her fingers, she brushed a thin layer of dirt off the site. No one had disturbed her hiding place. She exhaled and lifted a giant plastic bag out of the natural crevice. Then she stretched the sack open and tugged out a battered suitcase.

A bush rustled. Her shaking hands released the lid of the suitcase. Had he found her already? Her pulse jerked. She broke out in a sweat, slowly stood, and turned around. Her gaze swept the meadow. A rabbit scurried around a tree, and the air swooshed out of her lungs. She twisted back to the old piece of luggage and squatted in front of it. Pain shot through her ribs and she winced.

She raised the cover of the case again and lifted out a brown backpack. She transferred several changes of clothes, a dark wig, and a pair of reading glasses from the baggage to the items already in the pack. It had taken months to hide them, one at a time.

It had taken longer to fill the thick envelope she pulled out of the inner pocket. She confirmed that her new passport and five, one-hundred dollar bills were there. She gulped in air to calm herself.

After closing the empty piece of luggage, she slid it back into the plastic bag and buried it. If something went wrong, she had her hiding place. She brushed a thin covering of dirt over the site so it looked undisturbed and arranged the stones in the heaped circle the way she always kept them. Her mind ran through every detail again to avoid the mistakes of the last time. Or the time before. Or the time before that.

She adjusted the strap of the backpack on her stiff shoulder and ran back to the Mercedes. The GPS would reveal the location and lead one of her husband's detectives to her hiding place, so she pulled onto the road and drove a mile before turning onto another dirt trail. A ragged sigh escaped her throat as she shut off the engine and tossed the keys to the floor mat.

Lord, help me trust you.

The overgrown bushes on both sides of the car concealed it, so the vehicle wouldn't be seen from the road. Stepping out of the Mercedes, she drew a deep breath. The sharp breeze lifted her hair. She tasted freedom. Wasting time was dangerous, so she quickly removed the cash and credit cards from her billfold and stuffed them into her backpack. She tossed the empty wallet to the ground.

Scott often went through her dresser drawers searching for items she shouldn't have, but he'd never examined each undergarment.

Stretching open a bra, she exposed the slit in one of the pads that uplifted and added the folded bills to the money already stashed there.

Her gaze flitted over the car. Had she forgotten anything? Her mind once more raced through her plan. She yanked her bracelet off and hurled it. As she ripped off her purple blouse, she was satisfied the buttons popped and flew in different directions. She tossed the garment to the ground. Then she lowered her skirt and undergarments, and she let them fall to the dirt. She slipped into new panties and another padded bra. She breathed harder, trying to catch her breath as she squeezed her size four hips into size two jeans. With unsteady fingers, she put on a brown shirt and buttoned it. Then she combed her hair into a loose bun and slipped on the wig. Peering in the side-view mirror, she adjusted the black hair so it looked more natural.

She popped the trunk and leaned as far inside as possible to tug loose a corner of the carpet. Seeing the thick envelope, she rolled her eyes heavenward and sighed.

Thank God Scott hadn't found the thousand dollars when he searched her car. If he had, he'd have punished her. She shivered at his last discipline. She folded the currency and slid it to the bottom of her backpack. Maybe she'd saved too much. No, during her last escape, he'd found her because she didn't have money to travel any farther.

She flipped her purse upside down to scatter the contents on the front floorboard. She left them where they landed and tossed the bag to the ground. Then she reached for the stilettos she'd abandoned in the car and put them on. After stomping her left foot in the ground to break off the heel, she hobbled forward a few steps and stumbled out of the shoes.

A pebble cut her foot when she stepped on the blacktop. She hopped and cried out in pain. Looking around, she hoped no one had heard, but no one had ever heard her screams. She ducked behind some hedges to put on her socks and tennis shoes.

What should she do with her rings? If he ever found her without them, he'd kill her. She decided to hold on to them to pawn later if she ran out of funds. Too bad, she hadn't thought of that the last time she left. The rings had cost ten thousand dollars. Burying them was a waste of money. She slid them off and stuffed each one deep inside a folded cuff of her socks since she couldn't think of a better hiding place.

She darted behind more bushes, picked up a stick, and dug a hole. She filled it with her credit cards and covered them with dirt and leaves. The police would assume her credentials had been stolen.

She hiked down the road to the four-way stop and waited for the trucker. The driver rolled through at the same time of day during apple harvest, but she might be placing herself in greater danger by relying on a stranger. Her choices were limited.

Megan Jane breathed deeply to halt a sob of relief as the semi-truck drew closer. It slowed. Gray puffs of smoke blew out of the two chimneys. Red apples were painted on the side with 'Horrigan Fruit Company,' written above the bushel of fruit.

When the truck stopped, Megan Jane strolled to the driver. "Hello. Can you give me a lift?"

"I'm headed to Nashville."

"That's where I'm going."

"Climb aboard."

She ran around to the passenger side and extended both her hands to pull open the heavy door. She'd be safe once inside the steel transport. Clutching the metal rails, she lifted a foot and climbed three high steps. After clamoring onto the torn seat, she set her backpack between her legs on the floor.

The driver reached toward her, and she jerked away wondering if she should hop out while she had the chance.

"I wasn't going to hurt you. The metal clasp of the seatbelt sticks in the holder. I was trying to loosen it for you."

"Sorry. I guess I'm a little jumpy today."

After handing it to her, he fiddled with the rows of controls and switches in front of him.

The semi bounced over the country road. The movements jolted her even with her seatbelt fastened. "I appreciate the ride."

"I own the truck, so I can pick up people if I want." He shouted over the rumbling diesel engine. "The vehicle's forty years old, which is why it's noisy."

She cringed when he yelled, but it was the only way to hear above the thundering roar of the motor. Checking her disguise in the side-view mirror was a challenge, with the seat bumping her up and down. It was out of character for her to hitchhike and accept a lift in a semi. Her husband would never start his search with the truck.

Thank God the driver hadn't recognized her.

Her face had been on national television every week for the last ten years.

CHAPTER TWO

Megan Jane winced with every jolt of the truck. The longer she sat on the lumpy cushion, the more the bouncing jarred her injured ribs. She glimpsed the speedometer out of the corner of her eye. The decrepit vehicle probably couldn't go faster than forty miles an hour.

A male screamed, and she lurched forward. Who was that?

The driver patted the microphone. "Relax. It's only my radio, and the report isn't for me." He applied the brakes.

Was he stopping because he wanted her to get out? Had he received a signal from her husband?

She wiped her sweaty palms on her jeans when the rig came to a halt with a noisy swish. "Is something wrong?"

"It's a four-way stop. The air brakes take a long time to stop this rig." He pressed pedals and shoved levers. "I hate this ancient truck but driving it pays the bills."

She tapped her fingers against her lap. Then she clasped them together to stop their quivering. As the old semi plugged down the twisting road, her gaze flitted to the radio.

"By the way, my name's Tony."

"I'm aaah … Jane."

When would her old nickname come out naturally? She repeated *Jane* silently over and over again to fix it in her mind.

He pushed the clutch and downshifted. "What are you going to do in Nashville?"

"I'm looking for a new job."

"Do you go to church?" He patted the Bible next to him.

"Yes, I do." Over the years she had spent more time at church than she had at home.

"What one do you attend?" He slowed and veered to the left.

Lying was foolish. She'd told so many lies, it was hard to keep track of them. She always had to think of a new one to cover the last untruth.

"The Worship Center."

She went there every day of the week. She attended ladies' Bible study on Mondays and visitation with her husband on Tuesday nights. Scott and she were present at Wednesday services and for choir practice on Thursday nights. They hosted the Friday evening potluck fellowships, and filmed the weekly broadcast on Saturday.

Tony glanced in the rearview mirror. "I attend a small church. I don't care for a megachurch."

It wasn't her choice either.

A verse popped into her head. *Trust in the Lord with all your heart. Lean not to your own understanding.* She wished she'd taken her grandmother's Bible, but if it were missing, Scott would know she'd run again. It was best if people thought she'd been kidnapped.

When they arrived in Nashville, he slowed the vehicle. "Where do you want to go?"

Local buses and taxis stopped at malls. "Are you driving past Cool Springs Galleria?"

He clutched and downshifted. "Yes, I can let you out there."

A few minutes later, he stopped at the main intersection in front of the shopping center.

"Thanks for the lift."

"You're welcome. I hope you find a good job and a wonderful church."

"I will. Thanks." Her first spontaneous grin in fifteen years felt good.

She jumped out at the traffic light and jogged across the street. Then she walked briskly to the main entrance to check for bus routes, but there weren't any, so she stepped inside.

She asked a woman coming out of the closest store, "Excuse me, where is the schedule for local buses?"

"They no longer stop here."

"That's too bad," she sighed in disappointment. "Thank you."

Now what? Jane looked left and right before entering the food court where an elderly couple ate in the dining area. It appeared safe enough to sit for a few minutes.

She caught an enticing whiff of tomato, oregano, and pepperoni. Her stomach growled and reminded her how hungry she was. After buying a slice of pizza with extra cheese, she sat facing the door and kept her eyes on the entrance. She ate her piece slowly and wanted another but hesitated. It would be best not to buy any more in case she had to leave.

A young woman in hospital scrubs came through the main door. She pushed an elderly lady in a wheelchair to a table about two yards away from Jane's.

The nursing assistant's nametag read, 'CNA Morgan Platt.' She applied the brakes and turned to the white-haired lady. "Mrs. Sully, I'm going to the restroom. Then I'll bring your dinner." She left.

As Mrs. Sully opened her black purse, it slipped out of her hands and overturned. The contents scattered on the floor.

Jane jumped up and collected a wallet, lipstick, and cough drops. Three bottles of prescription pills rolled to her, so she grabbed them and handed each item to the elderly woman.

Mrs. Sully smiled. "Thank you, dear. You sure are fast. I could use a quick-thinking girl like you."

Jane's heart swelled with confidence. "Why do you need a quick-thinking girl?"

"I have some workers that help me several times a week. My son stays with me at night, but he'd like to hire a live-in caregiver. There are plenty, but they cost more than I can afford."

"I used to work in a nursing home with seniors, but my license expired."

The assistant returned with a steaming plate of food, which she set in front of Mrs. Sully. "After you eat, we'll buy that present for your son."

Jane smiled at Morgan. "Hello, I'm Jane." She had to keep thinking, *Jane*.

Mrs. Sully lifted a fork of macaroni and cheese. "I spilled the stuff from my purse and this nice lady picked up everything for me. Jane used to be a nurse and knows how to care for older folks."

Morgan set her cold drink on the table. "I need to cut my hours and work only two days a week. I have three children and am going back to school to finish my RN degree. We've been looking for someone to help me care for Mrs. Sully."

The white-haired lady smiled at Jane. "You seem nice. Are you looking for a job?"

"Well, I ... yes." She'd planned to go to Chicago and lose herself in the crowd, but the woman offered her a job, and she'd never been able to secure employment the other times she'd run away. Since local busses no longer left the mall, accepting a position might be the answer to her prayer. But Nashville wasn't far away from her husband.

"Would you be able to live in and take care of me on the days Morgan is off duty?"

"Yes." It was the type of job Jane had hoped to find up north.

"Give me your number, and I'll have my son call you."

"I don't have a phone."

"Can you come home with us now? My son will stop after work this evening and check out your credentials." Mrs. Sully put a bite of meatloaf in her mouth.

"Yes, I can. Thank you."

After the older woman finished her meal, Morgan tossed the trash in a nearby bin. "Let's buy that gift." She turned to Jane. "Do you want to wait here and then follow us home in your car?"

"I don't have a car."

"Do you drive?"

"Yes, but," she hesitated, "my husband and I are separated. I had to leave the car with him."

"I know what that's like. My husband took everything, too. Come with us, so we can leave together when we're finished."

After Mrs. Sully completed her shopping, Jane helped the older woman into the vehicle. As Jane climbed into the seat next to Mrs. Sully, she glanced behind and froze.

Her husband had found her.

CHAPTER THREE

Jane bit her lip as the car backed out of its parking space and pulled in behind Mrs. Sully's van. Jane fidgeted when the vehicle followed them out of the mall and onto the road. She couldn't see through the tinted glass to distinguish Scott or one of his spies driving the black Mercedes. When the car turned right at the first light, she slumped in her seat and let out a ragged breath.

Never knowing when or where Scott would catch her, terrified her as much as waiting for him to execute one of his punishments. He had made up the rules as he went along, so she never fully understood that it would be impossible to do everything right. She almost wished Scott would jump out and snatch her so her punishment would be over with.

Jane memorized the roads and paid attention to the scenery as Morgan drove. Thirty minutes later, she turned into a high-class neighborhood. Mowed lawns and clipped hedges surrounded the brick homes with attached garages. Morgan drove to the end of the last road and into a wide driveway in front of a ranch-style house. The nursing assistant pressed the garage door opener.

After the vehicle was inside, Morgan and Jane stepped out. Jane held Mrs. Sully's arm and led the hobbling woman into the house. Jane looked over the pleasant kitchen, decorated with lime-green cushions on the chairs and an olive-colored tablecloth with matching curtains. After assisting Mrs. Sully to her chair, Jane returned to the van to help Morgan carry the sacks from the van.

When all the purchases were in the house, Morgan hung the key chain on a peg by the back door. "Mrs. Sully, I'll bring your medicine."

"And then, please show Jane around the house."

Mrs. Sully's son arrived as Morgan finished the tour with Jane. Morgan introduced them. "We met Jane at the mall today. She helped your mother."

"You can call me Peter." He shook Jane's hand. "It's nice to meet you."

"Your mother mentioned that you were looking for a live-in caregiver. I'm interested in the position."

"Do you have references?"

"Excuse me." Morgan grabbed her purse. "The sitter is waiting for me, so I need to go."

"Thanks, Morgan." Peter turned back to Jane.

Without references she had never been able to secure employment the other times she'd escaped.

Lord, please let someone give me a chance.

"I'm sorry I don't have any." Jane took a breath to calm her racing heart.

Peter leaned forward and shook his head. "I'm sorry. I can't hire you without them."

Tears filled her eyes. As she bent over to reach for a tissue in her backpack, her blouse shifted. She tugged it back to cover her shoulder and glanced at Peter. His mouth had fallen open.

If Jane's husband had seen the blue contusion, he would never have let her out of the house that day. She pulled out the Kleenex.

"How much experience have you had?" The compassion in Peter's voice stung her eyes.

"Three years working in a nursing home before I married. My husband didn't want me employed and told me to let my nursing license expire, so I did."

"Wouldn't it have been better to keep it up?"

"I wish it had been possible. It would have been of use to me now that we've separated." Her stomach fluttered. "My husband told me if I worked, it made him look like he didn't provide well."

Scott had wanted her by his side while he climbed the church ladder. He prepared a long list of responsibilities for her as pastor's wife, so she didn't have any free time.

"I'd like to give you a chance. Can I see your driver's license?"

Her hand rummaged around in her backpack. With trembling fingers she gave the license to him. Too bad she hadn't paid someone to make her a fake license. Why had she been so gullible to think no one would ever ask to see it?

What if Peter wanted her to sign government forms with her social security number? That was the law, but many people who hired home help either didn't know the law or didn't care. Maybe he was one of them. If not, she'd find a reason to leave.

Peter jotted some notes and then handed the license back to her. "Excuse me while I speak to Mom."

After he left, Jane looked over the room. A worn leather lounger sat in the corner. Several tall lamps stood behind cushioned chairs. The brown and cream plaid furniture had been popular back in the fifties. The dark colors didn't appeal to her. Thick beige carpeting matched the curtains. Pictures that looked like family lined the mantle and covered the walls.

Peter was laughing when he came back in the room. "Mom likes you. She's old-fashioned and trusts you because you don't have tattoos or rings in your nose. She insists we give you a try."

Jane took a moment to thank God for her grandmother's strict values. Scott asked her out because she looked like the all-American girl. Her wholesome appearance appealed to older folks. According to Scott, that's where the money was.

"Thank you." Jane smiled again.

"Would you agree to a probationary period of two weeks and see how everything goes?"

"Yes. That sounds good." Relief flowed through her.

"When Dad died, Mom's income was cut in half, but she had the same bills. Would a thousand dollars a month plus room be acceptable?"

"Yes. That's generous of you." She hadn't forced her smile and again it felt good.

"You're the first person we've hired as a live-in, so I could be forgetting something important." Peter handed her a set of keys. "These are to the house and car. You'll need to drive mother to her doctor's appointments and run errands."

"I look forward to caring for her." She clutched the keys.

"Mom can't live alone. I didn't mind staying here every night, but it will be good to sleep in my own bed. I've always enjoyed Mom's company." He closed the blinds. "There's a phone and a television with cable in the bedroom at the end of the hall. You can use that room. I'm a fill-in pastor and haven't been able to take any evening services since I started spending the nights here. I'd love for you to meet my pastor."

The blood pulsed in her ears. Hearing the word pastor, she thought of her husband. Had she fallen into the hands of another domineering minister? Rubbing her forearms, she tried to get rid of the goose bumps. Maybe she should run, not accept the job.

"Call me this evening after you and Mom are settled, so I won't worry. I'll phone again in the morning to see how everything went." He handed her his card and walked to the door. "Good night."

After he left, Jane slid the chains in place on the front and back doors. She was safe for the moment. Peter looked to be in his late fifties. Maybe he wasn't like her husband, but his age didn't guarantee he wouldn't hurt her.

When Morgan had given Jane the tour earlier, the nursing assistant pointed out the schedule and list of medications for Mrs. Sully on the kitchen door. After memorizing them, Jane went to the elderly woman, who was yawning.

Jane smiled. "I believe it is bedtime. Where are your night clothes?"

"Under my pillow." She dozed off again. Then her eyes opened. "I've had a long day."

After Mrs. Sully was ready, Jane tucked the older woman in bed. Jane poured water into a glass and set it on the bedside table with the bell to ring if Mrs. Sully needed help. Leaving the night light on, Jane headed to her room.

She stepped into her bathroom and twisted on the hot water tap. Under the warm flow of water her muscles relaxed. She dried off and slipped into her nightgown. Crawling into bed, she thanked God for a place to live. The Lord had worked everything out and given her a job. If her plan succeeded, people would think she'd been abducted.

The house, rent, water, and lights were in Mrs. Sully's name so Jane would have no public records or accounts in her name. No one would ever find her, but she wasn't that far away from Memphis and Scott.

Mrs. Sully had liked Jane, and Peter believed her. So she shouldn't have been surprised at how easy it had been to secure the job. Some Christians were too trusting. Jane used to trust everyone, too. Even worse, she'd believed everything a man told her.

The job was an answer to her prayer and a gift from God. Unless Peter's pastor knew Scott, and the job was a trap to catch her? Would Scott come to the door tomorrow and drag her back?

CHAPTER FOUR

Like other mornings, Jane stopped in Mrs. Sully's bedroom to check on her before going to the kitchen.

The older woman had thrown back the covers, so Jane approached the bed. "It's my first Sunday here and I'm not familiar with Nashville. I can drive you to church if you showed me the way."

"I'm not feeling up to it. You go. Before you leave will you bring my navy-blue pants and flowered blouse and help me to dress?"

Jane tugged the pants off the hanger and dropped to her knees to lift the older woman's legs into the trousers. "I don't want to leave you alone, so I'll stay home."

"I like to watch Rev. Scott Collins on Sunday mornings."

Jane flinched. Bile rose in her throat and her stomach heaved. She turned away from Mrs. Sully and choked down her nausea.

After the woman was dressed, Jane asked, "Can you use your walker to go to the living room?"

"Yes." Mrs. Sully stood and leaned on the walker.

After Jane settled the older woman in her lounger, Jane picked up the remote. She pasted a pleasant expression on her face, sat on the couch, and clicked on the television. Her hand trembled as she flipped to the station for the Worship Center. Images of her husband flashed on the screen before the camera moved in for a close-up of him. Jane dropped the remote and gripped the arms of her chair.

A wide grin spread across Mrs. Sully's face. "You sat up straighter so you must like Rev. Collins, too."

Jane tried not to hate him. She let out a deep sigh to calm herself. "I've heard lots of his sermons." As she clutched the arms of the chair her fingers throbbed. Scott had clenched her hands so tightly that pain shot through them. She released her hands and spread her palms flat on her lap hoping the agony would leave.

She had managed over time to control her pain and keep her fake smile in place in front of the camera. As she watched the rerun, her mind flashed back to that day the station filmed it. She shivered.

Jane thanked God Mrs. Sully fell asleep, so Jane could turn off Scott's voice. She scowled at her broken fingernails and chipped polish. Scott would be angry with her for not taking care of her hands.

She picked up the huge Bible on the coffee table and read the verses her husband had preached about. What did they mean? She never thought they meant what Scott told her.

Mrs. Sully woke and asked, "Can you find my reading glasses?" The older woman patted Jane's hand.

Jane brought them and sat down.

Mrs. Sully put her glasses on and glanced around the room. "Be a dear and bring me my address book."

A moment later, the older woman sighed. "I need a pen. There's one in the drawer by my bed. Will you bring it?"

Jane didn't mind the chores and was used to jumping up and down when ordered to do so. She giggled. Life with Mrs. Sully was happier and easier than it had ever been with Scott.

"Now sit down." Mrs. Sully leaned back in her recliner. "You can stop running around."

Jane swallowed a chuckle. "May I borrow your sewing basket so I can hem my skirts?"

"Yes, dear, the container is in the hall closet."

Jane left and returned with the sewing basket and several skirts she'd bought at the thrift store. She selected the appropriate needle and threaded it.

"Not many your age know the difference between needles and stiches."

"My grandmother was a professional seamstress, so I learned early."

"You need to go out and make friends on your day off, instead of staying in your room and reading books."

Jane was too terrified. She looked over her shoulder whenever she picked up the milk or Mrs. Sully's prescriptions. She should have gone to Chicago like she'd planned. Had she made the right decision by staying in Nashville?

Could she trust Peter Sully? He'd promised to bring his pastor to meet her one day, but Jane didn't want to talk to the minister. Peter's pastor could be Scott's friend, who waited for the right moment to hand her over to her husband. The needle slipped out of her hand.

"Don't worry about me." Jane picked up the threaded needle.

"I'm concerned. Your complexion is so fair for your black hair. It looks lighter when you don't wear make-up, which proves you need some sunshine."

Jane snipped the thread and shoved the needle in the pin cushion. "You've guessed my secret. My hair hasn't always been this color. It was brown before I married."

"Morgan suggested you wore a wig, but I think it's your hair."

Relief washed over Jane. "It's mine." She had bought dye the first day she ran errands for Mrs. Sully and colored her hair the same shade as the wig.

Mrs. Sully clicked on the television. "My hair was lighter when I got married, too. By the way, do you mind taking me places?"

At first Jane didn't like being out in public and driving Mrs. Sully, but she was getting used to it. "I enjoy taking you to your doctors' appointments and to visit your sister."

It took only a few minutes to help the older woman out of the car and into where she was going. Jane wasn't out in the open long enough to be scared. During the long waits, she read books.

Jane picked up a large needle and another skirt to hem. The doorbell rang, and the sewing slid out of her fingers. Chimes echoed through the house. Her hands shook. Who could that be on a Sunday afternoon?

"You sure are nervous." Mrs. Sully reached over and patted Jane's arm. "It's only my son. I know he already stopped by this week but wanted to come again after church today."

Jane peered out the window before unlocking the door for Peter. He stepped inside. "Good afternoon. How's Mom? How are you doing?"

"We're fine, thank you."

Peter walked around the kitchen as if he were an inspector. "Mother adores you." He leaned his hip against the counter and smiled. "I'm impressed. The house hasn't been this clean in years."

Jane looked down at her reddened hands. At least this time her wounds were self-inflicted.

*****

Without expenses, Jane saved her salary each month. Terrified Scott could track her, she didn't set up a bank account. She divided her funds into bundles and sewed a false bottom in her backpack where she hid the money.

Time flew by and soon six months had passed, the longest stretch she'd ever been free of her husband. She studied nursing at the library on her days off and stopped taking precautions, except to keep her hair dyed black.

On her way home one day, she stopped at the pharmacy to collect Mrs. Sully's medications. After picking up the prescriptions, she strolled out of the building. Basking in the brilliant sunshine, she hummed "Amazing Grace, how sweet the sound that saved a wretch like me." Her heart burst with happiness. *Thank you, Lord, for helping me get away from him.* She had much to be grateful for including a comfortable place to live and employment with a sweet lady. 'Thro' many dangers, toils, and snares, I have already come,' The Lord had brought her through much. 'Tis grace hath brought me safe thus far, and grace will lead me home.' God was good and she loved Him. She was free at last.

Approaching the car door, she took out the keys. An eerie sensation crept up her spine. She slowly turned her head left and right. She caught a glimpse of a camera, as a man put it in the front seat of an old Honda. Fear clawed at her heart. Icy terror sent shivers down her spine.

Run, Jane, run.

CHAPTER FIVE

Rev. Scott Collins sat behind the massive rosewood desk with inlaid panels. He leaned forward from his leather chair and took the photo from his best private investigator, Ben Grant.

Scott glared at the picture of the dark-haired woman wearing glasses. "Yes, this is my wife."

"I snapped it in front of the pharmacy." Ben handed Scott more photos.

"I've told my members she's taking care of her grandmother. You've done a great job for me. Give me the address."

"I need to check out a few more details, first." Ben stood.

Scott steepled his fingers to control his annoyance. He'd been impressed with Benjamin Grant's impeccable recommendations, but why did the private investigator have to do everything by the book? Scott stared at the photos again and recognized the Nashville neighborhood. One of the pictures showed a house number. It would be easy to track down the location on his own. He leaned back in his chair. He had what he wanted and swallowed his anger with the detective.

Too bad he had church that evening, otherwise he'd pick up Megan. Tomorrow was the annual board meeting and he needed to give a presentation. A few more days shouldn't matter. If his wife had stayed in the same place for six months, she'd be there when he arrived.

He reached in his jacket pocket and handed a wad of cash to Ben. "Your work is finished. I appreciate the great job you've done."

"Since she's run away before, how are you going to keep her here? You can't handcuff her to the bed." Ben chuckled as he pocketed the money.

Scott's heart pounded. Had Ben learned what Scott had done to her? "Don't worry about my wife. I know how to control her."

"I'll call tomorrow night with a positive address." Ben shook Scott's hand. "I appreciate the job. I hope all goes well with your ministry. My mother loves your television program."

After Ben left, Scott picked up the pictures the investigator had left on his desk. Scott stared at each one taking in the details. Scott's excuses for Megan's absences were getting old. He taught his church members how to have a solid marriage. If they or his television viewers figured out that his wife had left him, he'd be ruined. Scott hurled the heavy paper weight against the wall.

He had worked hard to shape Megan into the perfect wife. It had been a challenge and taken persistence. He clenched his fist and pounded his palm. Too bad he had to punish her again, but she had to know her place. He had liked Megan when he first met her. She quickly learned to smile and jump when and where he told her, but after the first time she'd left him, it had been harder to control her. Scott had never understood why she ran away when he had given her everything any woman wanted.

*****

Jane decided to tell Peter Sully why she had to leave. Running off without an explanation would be irresponsible and make Mrs. Sully and her son worry.

"I left my husband because he hurt me. I tried to leave him other times, but he always caught me."

"Why didn't you report him to the police?" Peter asked.

Over the last few months, Jane came to trust Peter and thought of him as a sweet uncle. No, that wasn't true. He didn't behave like her two uncles, who both had tried to molest her. Thank God her grandmother had intervened and sent them away.

"My grandma raised me. Scott threatened to hurt her if I didn't do what he told me to do." She drew in a quivering breath. "Half the police officers believe Scott is a saint and would never beat anyone. No one suspects a pastor of hurting his wife."

Peter opened and closed his mouth. After fumbling for words, he leaned closer to her. "Stay here. If you go, it will place you in greater danger."

"I can't. It would be more dangerous." Jane rubbed her temple. She had no other option but to run and get away from her husband. "Scott told me he didn't enjoy disciplining me and always apologized. If I hadn't made him so angry, he'd never have lost his temper." Her heart beat faster as she wiped tears off her cheeks.

Peter whispered, "But he kept hurting you again and again."

"Yes." Jane mumbled.

Peter nodded heavily. "Where are you going?"

She sniffed. "I don't know."

"I can drop you someplace downtown in the morning, if you like."

"Thank you." She bit her lip.

She'd go to the bus station and then walk to the train stop. She planned to jump on whatever train departed in any direction to confuse the man with the camera who had followed her. Maybe she'd be better off going to Canada, England, or Australia, but if she used her passport now when her husband was close, he might find her. Leaving the States would be her last resort.

*****

Early the next morning, after Peter arrived, Jane hugged Mrs. Sully. "Sorry I need to go. I'll miss you."

The older woman sniffed. "Come back as soon as you can."

Jane smiled, "I will."

During the drive, Peter handed Jane a letter of recommendation and an extra five hundred dollars, which she stuffed in her bag.

"When my wife was dying of cancer, I suffered with her. No man who loves his wife hurts her like your husband did." He brushed a tear off his cheek.

"I'm sorry for your loss."

"Change your mind and stay with Mom so I can help you."

"It's too dangerous. Your mother isn't strong. If my husband found me in your home, he might hurt both of you."

"I appreciate your consideration for her, but I want to help."

"You already have. This extra money and letter will help me to start over again." She patted her bag.

Peter stopped in front of the bus station, lifted a card out of his pocket, and wrote on it. "Call me when you can come back or if you need help."

"Thank you for your kindness. Your mother is a sweet lady. I wish I could stay and take care of her." Jane grabbed her backpack and stepped out of the car. "My husband can afford a hundred private investigators. That's how he found me the last time. Please be careful."

After waving to him, she stepped inside the station and headed to the ladies room. She washed off the dark makeup and blended a lighter shade on her face before applying pink lipstick. She slipped into Capri pants and a green tank top. Then she tugged on a short, red wig before leaving the stall.

Lord, help me get away with this new disguise.

She glanced in the mirror and straightened her hair. Then she walked through the waiting area and left by the back door.

After buying a ticket, she climbed on the first train that halted in front of her. Jane changed trains all day. No one followed her. She waited only a few minutes between departures.

The speaker announced that a train for Pittsburgh departed from gate 10, so she purchased a ticket. No one in the depot looked like a detective Scott might have hired. The one man who might be, wasn't paying any attention to her, and he had no camera. She climbed the steps, entered the train, and found an empty seat in the passenger car.

Then out of the corner of her eye, she saw a flash.

She scrunched lower in the seat. Not again. Her hands shook as she replaced the reading glasses with sunglasses. She lifted her head to where the flash had been and breathed in deeply as a young woman snapped pictures of an older gentleman.

Jane pulled out the reference from Peter Sully and read. "To whom it may concern. Jane White has been a live-in caregiver for my elderly mother for six months. Jane was a reliable and efficient worker who faithfully cared for my mother and managed her home. Mother thrived with Jane's care and devotion. She cooked, cleaned, and maintained the accounts. She is hardworking, thoughtful and honest. I highly recommend her. It is with regret that she, out of necessity, has had to leave our employ. We trust you, too, will find her a reliable worker. Sincerely, Peter Sully."

She closed her eyes and thanked God for the recommendation. Peter had been decent and had given her a chance to prove herself. Her heart swelled with peace. She refolded the paper and slid the letter into the envelope which should make securing employment easier.

Hours later after the sun set, Jane left the train in a little town called Hickory, thirty miles from Pittsburgh. She slung her backpack over her shoulder and stuffed her cold hands into her pockets. Marching down Main Street, she passed a hardware store, several dress shops, and a small post office. She spotted an open Laundromat with a bulletin board full of notices, so she stopped to read them.

There were no job postings, but someone was selling a bicycle. Should she buy it to have transportation? Riding a bike in the snow would attract attention, so she passed up the sale.

She shivered. The temperature had dropped to below freezing the previous night. Her light-weight jacket didn't keep her warm from the cold March winds. Too bad she hadn't purchased a heavy coat while she'd worked for Mrs. Sully, but she'd kept putting it off.

Jane asked a woman washing clothes, "Are there any motels in this town? I'm traveling through and want to rest."

"There aren't any here." The woman shook her head. "There's a lady at the end of Main Street who has a sign in her front yard that reads, 'Rooms for rent.' Maybe she'll give you a place for the night."

"Thank you. I'll check it out."

"Do you have a car?"

"No." Jane clamped her mouth shut before blurting out she'd left the train.

"It's at least a mile. If you wait until my clothes are finished, I can give you a ride there."

"I appreciate that, but I've been sitting and need some exercise." Jane didn't like conversations with strangers. Most people asked too many questions, making it hard to keep up her charade.

She stepped out on the long sidewalk that stretched before her and shuddered. The second time she ran away, her husband had caught her walking down a street in Memphis. He'd pulled up next to her, grabbed her, and tossed her in the back seat. Shivers ran up and down her spine as she recalled that punishment.

She picked up her pace and blinked several times to ward away the tears. Her eyes scanned the road for moving vehicles coming toward her, but there weren't any. The small town of Hickory made it easier for one of Scott's detectives to spot her. So she hurried down the sidewalk. Her heart pounded. If he caught her, he might lose all his control.

The sound of a car engine startled her. An uncontrollable quiver ran from her shoulders to her legs. She dared not look back.

A verse in her grandmother's Bible came to her. *Oh Lord my God I take refuge in you. Save and deliver me from all those who pursue me. For they will tear me like a lion and rip me to pieces with no one to rescue me.* Too bad she had to leave the Bible behind for it had given her much comfort. The older woman had underlined many verses that gave Jane hope over the years.

She forced one trembling leg in front of the other. She better not get caught because his wrath heightened each time he'd found her. The car engine behind her grew louder. Was it Scott? If so, this time he would kill her. Looking down the road, she searched for a hiding place, but she saw none.

Run, Jane, run.

No. Walk. If she started running, he'd spot her. Any sprint on Main Street would draw more attention to herself. Keep calm. Stroll like you don't have a care in the world.

She saw an alley a few yards ahead. Ducking into it, she backed up against the wall of the closest building and held her breath. Sweat drops beaded on her forehead in spite of the cold. Her limbs trembled. She willed herself to peek into the road. Under the street light, she spotted a gray-haired man driving an old-model car.

After it passed, she breathed easier and glanced down the road again. There were no other vehicles. That had been close. No, it hadn't. Her paranoia had taken over.

She walked to the end of the street and found the sign advertising rooms. She marched up the rock path and knocked on the door.

A white-haired lady opened it. "Can I help you?"

"I'm looking for a place to stay. Someone told me you rent out rooms."

"That's true, but only to those I know. Who are you? Do you have any credentials?"

Jane handed her Peter Sully's reference letter.

The older woman unfolded it and read silently. "This is nice." She gave it back to Jane. "But I don't know Peter Sully, either."

"I'd be a good renter and will pay you a week in advance. How much is it?"

"A hundred dollars."

"Peter Sully gave me a five hundred dollar bonus. Will you accept cash?"

Jane immediately regretted her words. She should never have announced that she had that amount of money on her. Why did she have to be so trusting? That's what often got her into trouble.

The woman reached for the hundred dollar bill. "I'll show you to your room. There's a small television, but no cable."

Jane followed the landlady down the hall. She opened the door for Jane, who went into the bedroom. A flowered quilt covered the double bed. Blue drapes hung in front of the window.

"Thank you." Jane set her bag on the dresser. "What about the bathroom?"

"It's at the end of the hall. You'll share it with the other residents. You have the bottom shelf in the refrigerator. You can use the kitchen from eight to ten in the morning, one to three, and six to eight for supper. Here's the key to the front door."

Inside her room, Jane sank onto the bed. That had been easy. Was God helping her escape? Or was she fooling herself?

It wasn't prudent to stay in a little town where folks knew all the neighbors, but hiding a few days inside the house would keep her off the streets.

She needed to buy groceries, find a heavy coat, and figure out another disguise. It all required her to go out in public, but she'd have to risk it in the morning.

Maybe the guy with the camera had given up.

CHAPTER SIX

The sun descended as Scott parked his car on the curb next to the well-manicured lawn. Hopefully, someone besides Megan would see him coming. If she saw him from inside the house, she might run. He climbed the three steps and frowned at the peephole in the solid oak door. He pressed the white button, and the ding-dong chimed.

Heavy footfalls sounded and the door opened. "Hello, may I help you?"

Scott shook the older man's hand. "I'm Reverend Scott Collins."

"I'm Peter Sully. Are you visiting the community to encourage folks to go to church?"

"No." Scott held out a photo. "I'm looking for my wife. This is a recent picture of her."

"Is she lost?"

"Yes."

"Come in and have a seat so I can see the picture under the light." Peter pointed toward a worn couch.

After Scott was seated, he handed the photo to Peter, who carried it to a desk lamp and switched on the light. "Who is this?"

"My wife. She ran away because she was ill and confused."

"Why do you think she's here?" Peter ran his fingers through his graying hair.

"A private investigator tracked her to this address."

"This picture bears a slight resemblance to the woman who worked for me and cared for my mother."

"Where is she?" Scott rubbed his palms together in slow motion.

"She left and didn't tell me where she was going."

Scott leaped to his feet. "Left? When? Where?" He wanted to punch the man but controlled his rage by crossing his arms.

"A few days ago."

"Was it her vacation?" Scott asked, as he sat back down.

"She had urgent business. She didn't tell me when she'd return. Maybe you can check back then." Peter handed the photo to Scott. "Since she left, I've had to move in with Mom."

Scott could get a search warrant from a judge, a friend of his, but Megan couldn't be in the house. Through the doorway to the kitchen, Scott noted the open briefcase on the table, the half-filled pot of coffee, and stack of dirty dishes. The son had to be staying with his mother.

"May I speak to your mother? She might know this woman's plans."

"Mom is resting. Besides, she tells me everything."

"My wife suffers with mental illness. She needs medication and must be committed to a psychiatric hospital."

"That proves it." Peter chuckled. "The lady who worked here couldn't have been your wife. She was as sane as you and me. She cared for Mom and managed my mother's home, finances, medications, and appointments."

Scott slowly unbuttoned his jacket and reached in his pocket. Clutching an envelope, he opened it and handed Peter a stack of wedding pictures. "Here are some photos of what she looked like when we were married."

"These don't resemble the woman who worked for me. I'm sorry you drove here for nothing." Peter stood. "I'll see you out."

When the door closed behind him, Scott glanced around the deserted street. Reaching his car, he brought his fist up, smashed the doorframe, and shouted. "Megan, Megan, when I have my hands on you, you'll wish you were dead."

*****

Jane thanked God for the icy snowstorm which kept the women inside the boarding house on Sunday morning. She went to the kitchen, toasted some bread, and poured a cup of coffee. Then she sat at the table with a couple of the residents.

Someone sighed. "We can't go to church."

"I'll turn the television on to Rev. Scott Collins's service." The landlady stood in the doorway.

The others followed the older woman. Jane swallowed and went with them. It surprised Jane that so many people tuned into her husband's program. Seeing her husband again on the screen before her, she breathed deeply to slow her racing heart.

He wept. "My church board agrees with me that my precious wife has been mentally unstable for a long time."

Slowly Jane turned her head to the left and then to the right. Seeing the mesmerized expressions of the other residents, she shuddered. Scott, the man of God, convinced the world Jane was crazy. Sweat broke out on her forehead.

She wished she had her grandmother's Bible, but she remembered the verse. *Those who know your name, Lord, will trust in you. For you Lord have never forsaken those who seek you.*

She lifted her head to the television again.

"My wife needs psychiatric help immediately. Here is a picture of what she last looked like." He held up a photo of her with black hair. "Please be on the lookout for Megan and help me find her."

Jane thanked God that she had colored her hair red and curled it. She looked heavier in lighter makeup and loose, gypsy-like clothes. She wore scarlet and orange bead necklaces and colorful bracelets to draw attention away from her features.

Thank God she didn't look anything like the photo.

"The police report indicated foul play." The interviewer asked, "What makes you think she ran away?"

"I want to apologize to all my viewers. Megan had been acting strangely for the last couple of years. I tried to conceal her unusual behavior, but my wife needs help if she is to be treated. I'm taking donations on her behalf to hire more investigators to find her."

Jane remembered the shopping bags of cash she'd seen by Scott's desk each week. Her breath quickened. After every service, a number of people had always come forward and handed money to Scott and asked for prayer for a loved one. Had Scott ever prayed for anyone?

The correspondent looked at the camera. "If you have seen her, call the number on the screen."

Scott lifted his signature handkerchief out of his pocket and wiped his teary eyes. "We have a court order for my wife to be committed to a mental hospital for a psych evaluation."

The blood pulsed in Jane's temples. Her breath came out in ragged gasps. A psychiatric evaluation would prove her sanity, but Scott would make sure she received the 'correct' diagnosis. Over the years he'd contributed to the mental hospital and had written it off on his taxes as a charitable donation.

"I'm begging you." Scott looked into the camera as tears streamed down his face. "If you have seen my dear wife, tell me. This is what she last looked like."

Her photo filled the screen. Taking in a deep gulp of air, Jane squeezed the arms of the chair. If the police posted her picture in every station, she'd never get away from him.

When the program ended, a resident at the boarding house turned to Jane. "She's a lucky woman. My husband never cared if I lived or died. He didn't take care of me when I was sick."

Another young boarder sighed. "I'm going to pray that Megan Collins saw this program and will run home to that loving husband of hers. Her life with that handsome man of God must have been perfect."

Jane shivered. If they only knew the truth. She pressed her fists deep in the folds of her skirt. She couldn't stay in Hickory, but maybe she should. None of the boarders or the landlady had recognized her.

"I've always loved Pastor Scott. He's a genuine man of God. Look how much he adores his wife." The landlady asked, "Would any other husband go to all that trouble to protect and search for his mentally unstable wife?"

"Probably not," Jane mumbled.

"By the way, Jane, I noticed you don't have a coat. That little jacket of yours can't be warm enough. I have an older one that I wore when I was your size. It's a bit out of style, but it will keep you warm with this blizzard that's come our way. You can have it if you want." The elderly woman stood. "Here in Pennsylvania, it sometimes stays cold until May."

"That's kind of you. Thank you."

The Lord had always taken care of Jane and would do it over and over again. She should never have doubted God's provision.
Help me keep trusting you, Lord.

CHAPTER SEVEN

Jane scanned the want-ad section of the local newspaper and found a position for a live-in caregiver north of Pittsburgh. She telephoned and talked a half an hour with Sharon, who needed someone to look after her mother. Jane arranged for an interview the next day.

Expecting to secure the job, she packed and left the boarding house by taxi. No trains traveled to Maple Hurst, so she took three buses and walked the last few blocks. She wore the warm coat the landlady gave her and carried her backpack stuffed with essentials.

She searched for the address among the brick and stone houses that lined the street. After locating the numbered mailbox, Jane walked up the drive that wove through the snow-covered lawn. She climbed the steps of the porch and pressed the doorbell.

A middle-aged woman opened it. "Hello, you must be Jane. I'm Sharon. Please come in to the living room." She led the way and nodded toward the older man by the window. "This is my brother, Timothy Gaffney."

He shook hands with her. "Please have a seat." He pointed toward a green brocade chair.

Before sitting down, Jane handed him the reference letter from Peter Sully.

Tim joined his sister on the cushioned couch. Leaning forward, he read the letter aloud. "This is an excellent recommendation."

"Thank you. I have a four year degree in nursing, but unfortunately, I let my registered nursing license expire."

"We planned to hire a nursing assistant. We can't pay you nurse's wages without a license." Sharon glanced at her brother.

Tim shrugged. "She trained as a nurse and would be familiar with the medications that Mom is taking and their side effects."

"Yes, and I used much of my knowledge taking care of Mrs. Sully. May I meet your mother?"

Sharon stood. "Come this way."

Jane followed Sharon to the opposite end of the ground floor. They went into a large sitting room with a couch, two stuffed chairs, and a recliner, where a gray-haired woman sat and watched television.

"This is Jane White." Sharon patted the older woman's hand. "She's the lady we talked about yesterday."

"It's nice to meet you, Mrs. Gaffney." Jane stepped closer. "What are you watching?"

"Clark Gable. Don't you think he's handsome?"

"Yes, he's very good-looking." Jane smiled.

Jane noticed the walker next to the lounger. A portable commode sat between the double bed and a small table with a folded wheelchair next to it. Jane glanced in the bathroom and found it standard for the handicapped with lots of rails and a step-in bath with a bench.

"I hate interrupting Clark Gable." Sharon grinned at her mother. "So we're going back into the living room."

After they were seated, Sharon turned to Jane. "Based on our lengthy phone conversation yesterday and meeting you in person, we decided that if you want this position, we'd like to give you a two-week probation period before we take you on permanently."

"Thank you."

"Mom is eighty and in good health for someone her age. She had a heart attack several years ago and is on numerous medications. Here's a typed sheet of her pills and daily schedule."

Taking the papers, Jane scanned the medications and then read the schedule of meals, bath, doctors' appointments, hairdressers, and visits to her friends.

"Would you ladies excuse me?" Tim stood and turned to Jane. "Sharon takes care of the details regarding hired help. I have an appointment and need to leave. I'm sure you and Mom will get along well."

The front door closed. Sharon glanced out the window. "Let me show you around the house."

Sharon pointed out the closets with supplies, the laundry room, food pantry, and bathrooms. Then she stopped in front of a large bedroom with a private bath. "This is your room."

After explaining how to lock up and set the security codes, Sharon picked up her purse. "Keep a ring of keys with you, so you'll never be locked out. It's late and I need to go. I'll call tomorrow and check on you and mother."

"I'm sure we'll get along well." Jane followed Sharon to the door and locked it after she left. Jane glanced at the empty kitchen trashcan and caught a whiff of bleach that left an orderly, clean impression. The countertops sparkled and the curtains were clean and pressed. She peeked out the side door as she double-bolted it. An older vehicle was parked in the two-car enclosed garage. A shelf with key rings on pegs was mounted next to the door with each set clearly labeled. She reached for the spare set for the house and the car.

On the way to her bedroom, she checked on Mrs. Gaffney, who still slept. Jane left the television on in case the woman woke.

In her room Jane put the keys in her backpack. She opened the door of the walk-in closet, where she hung her coat, two skirts, and a couple blouses. She unpacked the rest of her bag, but left her stash of funds hidden in the bottom of her backpack. All the drawers in the two dressers were empty so she put her underwear and nightgown in the top one.

It surprised her that Tim and Sharon hadn't asked to see any identification, but believers were more trusting than unbelievers. During the phone conversation, Sharon mentioned how active she was in her church, so the job had been worth checking out.

"Sharon, you out there?" Mrs. Gaffney called.

Jane went to the woman's room. "Hello, did you have a nice nap?"

"Who are you?"

"I'm Jane and will be staying here to look after you."

The woman's eyes widened. "Where's Sharon? I want to talk to my daughter."

"Okay," Jane picked up the old-fashioned telephone receiver. "I'll dial her number for you."

After giving the phone to Mrs. Gaffney, Jane left the room but stayed in the hall in case her new charge needed her.

A couple of minutes later, the elderly woman laughed and called, "Jane, come here." She handed the phone to Jane. "Talk to my daughter."

Jane put the receiver to her ear.

"Mom woke up a bit confused after her nap." Sharon giggled. "That's normal. Is there anything you thought of since I left?"

"According to the schedule your mother has an appointment with Dr. Pelzer, the heart specialist at ten in the morning. Can you give me directions?"

"You'll need to leave at nine. Mom knows the way, but if she falls asleep in the car, there's a GPS with all the necessary addresses."

"Thanks. I'll talk to you tomorrow. Goodbye."

Jane turned back to Mrs. Gaffney. "What time would you like to wake tomorrow to get ready for the doctor?"

"Seven should give us time for breakfast and a bath in the morning."

"Yes, ma'am." Jane glanced at the clock. "I'll start supper."

Jane went to the kitchen and opened the refrigerator. She reached for the baked chicken, while thanking God for giving her another job. How could she stop Scott from coming after her? Thinking of his vicious rage, she shuddered and almost dropped the platter. Having a temper wasn't against the law.

As she put the meat in the microwave, she considered the minor allegations regarding donations over the years. Many people handed Scott cash or sent it to him through the mail. He called it his pocket change, but some months he bragged it was over fifty thousand dollars.

She bit her lip as she warmed up the creamed corn. She doubted those monetary gifts had ever been documented and put in the church accounts for she'd often seen him counting the cash. So she had never risked grabbing some of it and running.

After she heated the chicken, she put the potatoes in the microwave. Scott's pocket money might have totaled half a million a year. Where had all of it gone? She opened the microwave to test whether the potatoes were hot. If she could prove that he had misappropriated funds, maybe he'd be arrested for embezzlement.

How could she do that? She could scarcely keep a step ahead of him.

*****

Over the weeks, Jane settled in and enjoyed her job caring for Mrs. Gaffney. A cleaning lady came twice a week to do the housework, and a nursing assistant relieved Jane two afternoons. When Mrs. Gaffney was awake, Jane labeled old photos with the woman and sorted through yarn and scraps of cloth for the sewing circle.

After working four months, Jane started going to the library on her day off.

The first time she went, she stopped at the reference desk. "Where can I find information on embezzlement, income taxes, and church deductions?"

The librarian wrote out some websites and gave the list to Jane. "You can check these sites out."

"I don't know how. Can you show me?"

"Let's sign you in to one of the guest computers and set up an innocuous e-mail address in case one of these sites requires that." The librarian pointed out some reference books on the way to the computer.

After showing Jane the basics of the internet, the librarian left.

Jane prayed for wisdom. Her heart lurched and fingers shook as she touched the keyboard. How much could she learn without giving her name and address?

Scott had never allowed her to have her own bank account, nor was her name on any of his. She opened an internet search to access her husband's records, but without his passwords, it was futile.

She missed church, so while on the computer, she found three Wesleyan churches. Scott had criticized the denomination and claimed he'd never set foot in one of their sanctuaries, so Jane should be safe attending the largest one, where she could lose herself in the crowd and hide if she needed. She wrote down the name, address, and times of services before logging out.

That afternoon when she arrived home, she called Sharon. "I'd like to go to church. Could I trade one of my days off for Sunday morning?"

"I'm sorry, Jane. I've never been able to find anyone to work on Sunday. Before you arrived, different family members stayed with Mom on Sundays. I go to an early service but would be glad to come by for an hour so you could attend a later service."

"I'd appreciate that."

Her hand shook as she put the receiver back. She had second thoughts. Her stomach churned. Would someone recognize her at church?

CHAPTER EIGHT

Jane buttoned up her blouse from the thrift store and tucked it in her flowered skirt. She checked the hem line in the full-length mirror. She'd only paid a few dollars for the outfit, but it was nice enough to wear to church. Would anyone recognize her with short red hair, loose-fitting clothes, and tinted glasses?

News people had flashed photos of her on television with black hair and wearing tight pants. She felt reasonably safe leaving the house, but walking into the church, she had second thoughts. She scanned the heavy oak pews. Families, couples, and young adults crowded into the sanctuary.

An older woman appeared to be alone in the last seat, so Jane sat next to her and smiled. "Good morning."

"Morning. I'm Minnie Jones. Is this your first time visiting us?"

"Yes, it is. I'm Jane."

Minnie leaned closer. "My daughter is about your age, but she's working in the nursery this morning. I'd love for you to meet her. Can you wait a minute after church?"

"I'm sorry, not today." Jane glanced at the pulpit, crossed her arms, and rubbed her goose bumps. "I have only an hour off to attend the service and need to go back to work."

"My daughter is in charge of follow-up with church visitors. She is always looking for new friends." The older woman gave Jane a card. "Write your number on this, so my daughter can call you this week."

Jane took a deep breath as she accepted it. After jotting Mrs. Gaffney's number, she handed the card back to Mrs. Jones.

Then Jane shivered. Giving a stranger Mrs. Gaffney's home number would make it easier for Scott to track her there. She resisted the impulse to snatch the card out of the older woman's hand.

*****

Early the next morning, Jane answered the phone. "Hello."

"Is this Jane?"

The phone shook in her hand. One of her husband's hired investigators found her. She should hang up. No, the person would phone right back. Or the caller might be suspicious.

She hesitated so long the person on the other end started talking again. "This is Cindy Jones. You met my mother, Minnie Jones, in church yesterday."

Jane's voice wobbled, "Yes."

"I'm in charge of following-up on visitors that come to church. I'd like to meet you. Would you like to join me for coffee this week?"

Jane's heart pounded. Did people still meet for coffee? But the woman sounded nice.

"Hello… Hello… Jane, are you still there?"

Jane spent long days with Mrs. Gaffney but had grown a bit tired of just the older woman's company. Jane wanted to talk to someone closer to her age.

She gripped the phone tighter. "I … I … have Tuesday afternoon off."

Jane shouldn't have given information to a stranger. One of Scott's investigators might be waiting outside the house to grab her. She stepped behind the kitchen curtain and peeked out the window. Why had she been so naïve and given the number to a complete stranger at church? Scott could have hired Cindy to lure her someplace, but what did Cindy have to gain by tricking Jane? Money. Her husband offered a reward for her return. Most people would do anything for money, and Jane's husband was proof of that.

"Jane… Jane…?"

"Yes, I could meet you at the diner, downtown Main Street at two."

"Sounds good. I'll see you then."

After Jane hung up, her hands kept shaking. Why had she agreed to meet Cindy? It was so unlike Jane, but at least in a restaurant, she could run away easier.

*****

On Tuesday afternoon, Jane went inside the diner and sat in a booth facing the door. She spotted the back exit, kitchen, and restroom. She was a few minutes early, so she picked up the menu.

A tall woman around Jane's age and about thirty pounds heavier came into the restaurant and walked up to Jane. "Hello, I'm Cindy Jones."

"I'm Jane White."

How did that slip out? She never intended to give her maiden name. She should be more careful.

"I'm sorry I missed you at church. How do you like taking care of Mrs. Gaffney?"

Jane's mouth fell open as the blood pounded in her ears. "How do you know where I work?"

"Mrs. Gaffney has had the same phone number for years and everyone in town knows her. She used to work on town committees with my mother. Mrs. Gaffney doesn't get around much anymore."

If Mrs. Gaffney was that well-known, Jane could easily be found.

Taking a gulp of air, Jane looked at the menu. "I like working for her."

"I've already had lunch, so I'm only having dessert." Cindy put the menu down. "The coconut cream is marvelous. I'm trying to lose weight, but I also like to enjoy the freedom the good Lord gives me."

They both ordered the coconut pie and coffee. After the server poured the hot drink, Cindy picked up the cup. "My mother thought you might need help. She recognized the signs."

A sudden coldness swept through Jane. Her hands shook and coffee spilled as she set the cup back on the table.

Cindy reached out and put her hand on top of Jane's. "I understand. I've been there."

Jane hesitated. "What are you talking about?"

"My mother told me that you looked around as if someone was after you. You stiffened and started sweating, but the air conditioner was set too low on Sunday. You sat in the back in an aisle seat in case you needed to leave."

Jane blinked several times. Had she been that obvious?

"Your secret is safe with us. I know what you might be going through. I had to escape from my husband. Over the years he drove me to the hospital with cracked ribs, a fractured wrist, and a broken jaw. I always gave some excuse like I slipped or fell down the stairs."

"Did they believe you?" Jane's eyes went to the front door.

"It didn't matter for I never pressed charges." Cindy shrugged. "I couldn't take him to court. He'd have beaten me to an inch of my life or hurt one of the children."

Cindy sounded as if she had gotten away from her husband and no longer hid from him. Jane needed help to escape from Scott and sensed a kindred spirit in Cindy.

Jane's tremors slowed, and she picked up her coffee again. "My husband seemed to be the perfect man when I met him, but three months after the wedding, he changed. The least provocation, a spoon on the counter or a towel improperly folded, threw him into a rage. I learned to keep clothes, linens, and dishes exactly the way he liked, and I had better not forget. He told me I wasn't submissive, so he needed to teach me how to be a good Christian wife."

The two women stopped talking when the waitress delivered their slices of pie.

After the server left, Cindy picked up her fork and stuffed a small morsel into her mouth. "It's delicious."

Jane took a forkful and gulped. "My husband kept me isolated and dependent on him."

Cindy sighed. "It started like that for me, too. The last time my husband drove me to the hospital, a nurse escorted him to the desk to complete forms. A woman from a local shelter slipped into my room. I was afraid to take her business card. What if my husband found it?"

"He'd hurt you again."

"I memorized her phone number and called her one day when I was alone. She warned me I needed to run if my life or those of my children were in danger. She suggested I save money to buy gas, food for the children, and a motel room, to get away."

Jane nodded. "I saved money for three years. My husband expected me to buy expensive cosmetics. He checked them out to make sure they corresponded with the receipts."

She paused while the waitress refilled their cups. When they were alone again, Jane continued. "One day after I finished a jar of expensive cosmetics, I realized he'd never know if I filled the bottles with imitations. So I kept buying the brands he expected but returned them for cash, which I saved. Walmart was near a coffee shop with his favorite blend, so I parked there and walked to Walmart to purchase cheap imitations to replace the expensive cosmetics."

"That's ingenious." Cindy sipped her coffee.

"I'm not too smart, or I'd have thought of it ten years ago."

"What about the car? These tyrants always take the keys."

"Scott wanted me to have an expensive car to keep up his image. He was too busy to run his own errands so gave me a list but tracked all my stops on the GPS." Jane described the steps she'd taken to leave her husband.

"You're clever and could help other victims." Cindy finished her pie. "The woman at the shelter advised me to hide a spare car key where only I could find it in a hurry. I made two extra sets and hid them in my children's backpacks."

"Great idea. You'd never leave without your children, and they wouldn't leave their backpacks."

"The counselor instructed me to keep everything I wanted to take in one area so I could grab it fast. Never pack ahead of time."

"I learned that the hard way. When Scott found my stuffed suitcase the first time, he handcuffed me to the bed and gave me a chamber pot." Jane crossed her arms and rubbed them to get rid of the goose bumps. "How old are your children?"

"My son is fourteen and my daughter is twelve. Bradly needs a positive role model. Several men in church with sons of their own have taken an interest in him. They've invited him to games, gone camping with him, and taken him out for pizza."

Jane took a sip of water. "What happened that made you finally leave your husband?"

"At first he only hurt me, but when Dwayne punched my son, I realized my husband's outbursts were becoming worse. He raised his fist again and I stepped between him and my son. I yelled 'I'm calling the police' and Dwayne stormed out of the house. I phoned the woman from the shelter. She gave me an address and told me to get in the car with my children and come." Cindy swallowed. "Two hours later, I went to a safe house with my children, my driver's license, and the little cash I had."

"Did you ever go back?"

"No. I heard about women who returned for money, pictures, documents, or clothes, and that's when they were caught."

Jane shook her head. "Why are we such idiots?"

"We forget our priorities. There's nothing on earth worth jeopardizing our children's well-being and our lives." Cindy shrugged. "After I escaped, I needed counseling."

"Is it always necessary?" Jane glanced at her shaking hands and gripped the coffee cup tighter.

"It isn't required, but a good advisor can help you start over again with the right attitude and support. It's important for healing, but no one can make you do it."

Jane's gaze wandered to the exit door, but no one had come into the restaurant.

"There's a support group of doctors, counselors, and lawyers who are committed to us. They secured loans for me to finish college."

Jane lifted a trembling hand to brush a tear off her face. "What happened to your husband?"

"He took up with another woman and stopped looking for me. He later divorced me. A counselor suggested that my children and I move across the country. My mother lived here and wanted to care for my son and daughter so I could attend school. If you settle down far away from a bully, he'll think twice before coming after you."

"There's no evidence against my husband to prove he hurt me, but he may be embezzling church funds. He forbade me from using the computer and never put my name on any of the accounts."

"There's a lawyer who works pro-bono for us. Would you mind if I discussed this with her?"

"If you think it would help, please tell her."

"Your husband sounds charismatic and well-liked by his members. His popularity makes it easier to steal from his followers. If he's an embezzler, Eileen may be able to collect enough evidence to take the case to court." Cindy took a deep breath. "Why don't you divorce him?"

"He thinks he owns me. If he can't have me, no one can. He threatened to kill me if I left him or tried to divorce him. I've been uneasy the last few days, as if someone's following me."

Cindy reached for Jane's hand. "Come with me right now to a safe house."

"No, I couldn't leave Mrs. Gaffney without giving notice. She'd worry herself sick if I disappeared. As long as I'm inside her house, I'll be safe enough."

"I'd never try to force you or any other woman to do something. I'll trust you to the Lord's care and say a prayer for you. I know you'll be careful. When you're ready, I'll be here." Cindy slid a business card across the table.

Jane couldn't run forever. She needed help, but who could she trust? "It's hard for me to trust someone."

"You can rely on me and the others in our group." Cindy glanced at her phone.

Jane knocked her cup over. Grabbing napkins, she asked, "What's happening?"

"I received a text and need to go. Would you like me to take you someplace?"

"No thanks. I have Mrs. Gaffney's car."

If everyone in town knew Mrs. Gaffney, someone could tell her husband where she was. Maybe someone already had informed Scott.

CHAPTER NINE

Benjamin Grant sipped on the coffee the pastor's secretary brought him. The cup and saucer looked like expensive antique china. He took note of the rosewood furniture with inlaid panels decorated with crosses. How much money did the pastor of a megachurch make, and what did he do with it?

"It's been four months since she left the Sully's. I thought one of the other investigators would pick up Megan's trail from Nashville, but no one has." Reverend Collins leaned forward. "I want to re-hire you to find her again for me."

"I'd be glad to search for her."

Reverend Collins's smooth-talking answers troubled Ben, who had initially disliked the famous pastor. That had been reason enough for him to turn down the job when it was first offered. He didn't care for the minister's blown-dry hair. Was he as fake as his capped teeth? Ben suppressed a shudder at the hard glint behind the pastor's blue eyes. Ben had faced and fought foreign enemies, but the expression on Scott's face sent a tremor of fear down Ben's backbone.

"I've been trying to protect my wife from people who might take advantage of her." He pulled a handkerchief from his breast pocket. "She's out there alone and helpless, so someone could hurt her."

If that was true, Ben needed to give his full attention to locate Megan Jane Collins.

The reverend wiped his eyes. "She might hurt herself."

"Why do you think she'll harm herself?"

"She's unable to have children, is depressed, and suicidal."

Some of the pastor's statements didn't make sense. If she had wanted to kill herself, why had she found a job and worked for six months? Ben wished he hadn't taken the case, but his mother's two surgeries drained his account. He put his cup on the saucer a little too hard.

"I hoped to have Megan safe with me before anyone learned of her unstable emotional status." Rev. Scott leaned back in his cushioned chair. "I had to watch over her night and day. I never let her out of my sight unless I knew where she was going."

"Your church members mentioned you were inseparable."

"We've been devoted to each other." Scott stuffed the handkerchief in his pocket.

"You've done everything you can to find her. You announced on your Sunday program your wife was missing, so I'm sure if one of your million viewers sees her, he'll tell you."

"I've almost given up hope." Scott's chin quivered.

Ben wasn't falling for the pastor's ploys. "I'll keep looking."

"I don't understand how my wife was able to leave without money."

"Why didn't Megan share a bank account or credit card with you?"

"She never had a head for figures and insisted I take charge of the funds. I didn't want to worry her, so I gave her everything she needed."

Ben didn't like the way Scott spoke of his wife in the past tense. "Since she worked at Mrs. Sully's for months, she's capable of keeping employment. She may have secured another job."

"Something was strange about that situation." Scott's brow creased. "You need to go back there and find out why she was there and what she did. I've a gut feeling she and Peter were involved."

"Peter must be twenty years older than she is. Are you suggesting your wife was unfaithful?"

"No. No." Scott glared at Ben. "I'm upset. Forget it."

"Do you have any hidden resources she could tap into so she can survive?"

"No, and speaking of money, here are some funds to start again." Scott opened his drawer, reached for a thick envelope, and handed it to Ben.

"Thank you." Ben nodded toward the treadmill in a corner of the room. "Do you work out often?"

"Yes, every day. I must keep in shape to appear before millions of fans."

The word "fans" sounded strange coming from a pastor.

"Our body is the temple of God, and we are commanded to take care of it." Scott put on his television smile.

"I stopped working out last year when my knee acted up again." Ben glanced down at his stomach. "I need to get back in shape and lose about twenty pounds."

"Exercise is hard work but necessary."

"May I see the original photos that were taken on the day she disappeared? I'd like to start over and figure out her plan." Ben took the envelope of photos from Scott. "To understand your wife better I'd like to go through her belongings."

"I didn't allow that when I hired you, and I can't let you invade my wife's privacy now."

"If I could check out what she read, how she arranged her clothes, or set up her kitchen, it would help me understand how she thinks. I might have a handle on where she went."

"Take my word for it. Her closet looks like every other wife's wardrobe. Everything is in place."

"If nothing is out of order, there's no harm in my looking around. I apologize if I've upset you, but I need to understand her. Is she tidy? Messy? Forgetful? Does she pay attention to detail?"

When Scott finally agreed, he drove Ben to his house. Scott led the way upstairs to the huge master bedroom, which looked like a luxury hotel between guests. There were no feminine touches to show which side of the room belonged to Megan.

"Where did your wife keep her clothes and shoes?"

"That side of the room is hers." Scott pointed.

Ben opened the closet. Each hanger was one inch from the next as if she had measured the distance. She organized clothes according to color and size and arranged each pair of shoes toe to heel in the original boxes. Leaving the closet, Ben went to the chest of drawers. He didn't want to upset Scott by disturbing his wife's belongings, so Ben used a pen to carefully lift underwear, sweaters, and socks to look under and behind them. "Is your wife always this neat and orderly? It looks like she folds everything as if she was in boot camp. Do you tell her to keep things this way?"

Scott snarled, "Are you implying I forced Megan to be tidy?"

"If she does this to please you, then maybe it's her nature to be disorderly."

"She was the perfect wife and did everything the way I liked it."

Ben could believe that, but Scott was speaking in the past tense again. Ben suppressed a shudder. There wasn't a hint of Megan's personality anywhere in the room. When he opened the bedside table drawer, he found a well-worn Bible.

He flipped through the pages. "May I take this?"

"Why?"

"Why didn't she take it with her?"

"It's her grandmother's. Megan didn't have her own Bible."

"Wouldn't a pastor's wife need one?"

"I instructed my wife on the correct interpretation of Scriptures." Scott reached for the book and glanced at several underlined passages. Then he handed it back to Ben. "Take it if you think it will help you find her."

After Ben put it in his briefcase, he turned around and almost bumped into his client. Scott hadn't left Ben's side since they entered the room, and his closeness irritated Ben, but he had a job to do. Kneeling down, he looked under the bed.

He pulled out a ceramic container. "Is this what I think it is?"

"Yes, it's an antique chamber pot."

"Most people display these."

Lifting the cover, Ben caught a whiff of bleach as if it had been used. An uneasy feeling crept over him. Why would Megan need a chamber pot when the bathroom was only five yards away?

As he slid the container back under the bed, he glanced up and noticed a worn circle around the bedpost. His heart clenched. He'd seen that only once before as a police consultant. A father had handcuffed his teenage daughter to the bed so she wouldn't run away.

Ben's ex-fiancé had been unfaithful to him. But not even her actions would justify handcuffing her indefinitely to a bed and giving her a chamber pot. Taking another moment, he studied the indentations around the bedpost. A tremor ran down his backbone. He needed to find Megan before Scott did.

*****

After leaving Rev. Collins's house, Ben phoned Peter Sully and arranged to meet him. Ben drove straight to Nashville and arrived around the time most people sat down for their evening meal. He rang the bell set in the wood trim of the brick home, anyway.

When the door opened, Ben introduced himself and showed his credentials.

"I'm Peter Sully." The heavy-set man shook Ben's hand. "Mom and I were about to eat supper."

"Go ahead and take care of her. I know what it's like. I keep an eye on my own mother. I'll wait in my car until you're finished."

"Come with me and I'll introduce you to her. Then you can wait in the living room."

Ben followed Peter into a kitchen where an older woman sat at the table.

"Mom, this is Benjamin Grant. He stopped by to visit me."

"Sit down and eat with us. I enjoy meeting Peter's friends."

Peter shrugged and pointed to an empty chair. He turned to the cupboard and collected another dinner plate, silverware, and a napkin for the table. After filling a glass with iced tea, he put it next to the setting.

"You have a nice home." Ben would respect Peter's wishes and not say anything to worry Mrs. Sully. "Thank you for inviting me to eat." He looked at the checkered tablecloth and the hot pads hanging above the stove. It was a comfortable kitchen.

Mrs. Sully asked, "Will you pray, Peter?"

Afterwards, Peter served his mom meatloaf, mashed potatoes, and beans. Then he passed the platters and bowls to Ben. "Help yourself."

His mother put a forkful into her mouth. "Son, your meatloaf is good, but not as delicious as Jane's. That girl cooked so well and I miss her. She was the best caregiver I ever had."

"I liked her too, Mom."

As Mrs. Sully sipped on her iced tea, she scrunched up her face. "You didn't add enough sugar. Jane always mixed it the way I like it. She did everything to please me."

Ben buttered his roll. "She sounds lovely. I'd like to meet her."

Mrs. Sully handed the glass to her son. "She had a pleasant personality, too."

Peter stirred in more sugar and gave the drink back to his mother. "Yes, she did and worked hard. She kept the house in good shape."

After supper, Peter started a pot of coffee. "I'll be back after I take Mom to her room so she can watch her program."

When he returned, he asked. "Would you like some coffee, or I have soft drinks?"

"Coffee, please. Black."

Peter poured two cups. He handed one to Ben and sat across from him. "It surprised me how quickly you got here."

"I'm worried about Megan Jane." Ben lifted the cup. "She trusted you, didn't she? I've a feeling you know more than you're saying."

"You're working for her husband to find her, right?"

"Yes, but I'd never do anything to put her in danger."

Peter's hand shook. "I think her husband hurt her. I saw the bruises."

"What bruises?"

"When she came to apply for the job, I noticed black and blue splotches on her shoulders. My heart went out to her when she tried to hide them."

Ben leaned forward. "She worked here six months and must have felt safe. What did she use for identification?"

"Her driver's license. To be honest, I never checked it out. I glanced at her name and saw Megan Jane, so I assumed she used Jane as her first name, which some people do. Mom has a keen sense of good and evil in a person. She liked Jane right away, so I hired her." Peter finished his coffee. "If that man hadn't caught up with her and taken her photo, she'd still be here. Mom and I hated to see her leave. I wrote her a letter of recommendation she deserved and kept a copy for myself. Would you like to see it?"

Ben nodded.

Peter opened the desk drawer and picked up a file. He handed the investigator a paper from it.

Reading it, Ben frowned. "This makes no sense. Her husband announced on television she needs to be committed to a mental hospital."

"There's nothing wrong with Jane. I'd never have allowed her to stay here alone with Mom if I thought she had mental problems."

"Did you help her leave?"

Peter turned away slightly. "I won't break her confidence."

"I understand. You're an honest man." Ben pulled out his business card and handed it to Peter. "I need to find her before she falls into the wrong hands."

"I drove her to the bus station downtown."

Ben stood and shook Peter's hand. "Thanks. Say a prayer for her safety."

"I will. I'm a praying man."

"So am I." After leaving the Sully's home, Ben called a colleague, who secured the video surveillance tapes from the bus station. Ben collected them and checked into a motel room. As he watched the film, he spotted Jane.

Thank you, Lord.

Fifteen minutes later, he recognized her again leaving the restroom in a red wig with paler foundation and pink lipstick.

He made several photos of her and then drove to the bus station. Ben went inside and approached the ticket seller. After showing his credentials, he handed one of the pictures to him. "Have you seen this woman?"

"Yes, but she didn't get on the bus. She went out the back door."

As Ben headed to his car, a sharp pain in his knee halted his steps. Leaning down, he rubbed the throbbing joint. Why did his knee have to act up now? How could he ever find Megan when he could barely walk? He opened the glove compartment and removed a bottle of Tylenol. He shook out three and swallowed them with some leftover coffee.

Taking deep breaths, Ben fought through the pain as he went to the train station. When he arrived, he started his search all over again.

How could one little gal escape fifty investigators and hundreds of police officers?

She was either smart or determined to never be found. Or both. She might even have someone helping her.

He collected more surveillance tapes from the train station. Ben could scarcely keep his eyes open, but he went back to his hotel room to watch them. He spotted her entering a train going to Pittsburgh, when he dozed off.

After a good night's sleep, he limped to his car and drove to the Pittsburgh local library to check the want ads in the newspapers from the day Megan left Sully's house. He called everyone who advertised for a caregiver, but all the ads led to dead ends.

Where had Megan gone?

CHAPTER TEN

Jane stopped to pick up Mrs. Gaffney's prescriptions at the pharmacy, located in an older section of town and bordering the slum. Jane didn't like going there, but Mrs. Gaffney explained that the pharmacist's son had grown up with her son. The older woman wanted to support the floundering business.

After parking in a place next to the front entrance, Jane looked around. Mrs. Gaffney's car stood alone, so Jane locked the door before going into the pharmacy.

When she came out twenty minutes later, a police officer approached her. "Good afternoon. May I see your identification?"

Her heart stuttered.

"Is … is … is there a problem, officer?"

"Please show me your driver's license."

She fumbled with the zipper to open her purse. When she reached for the license, it fell out of her hand and landed on the asphalt. She squatted to pick it up. Giving it to him, she kept looking at her shoes and hoped he wouldn't recognize her.

The officer studied the card and cocked an eyebrow. "Are you Megan Jane Collins?"

Her throat tightened. She opened and closed her mouth several times, but nothing came out of it.

"You don't look like Megan Collins. Why do you have her license?"

Fear held her in its grip. She clutched her throat and whispered. "I'm try… try…"

"Wait here while I check this license out." He studied the license as he walked to the corner of the parking lot and climbed into his car.

Run, Jane, run.

She stuffed the car keys in one pocket and Mrs. Gaffney's pills in another one. Then she dropped her purse and kicked it under Mrs. Gaffney's car. She sprinted across the large field next to the pharmacy. Her mind flashed back to high school when she'd taken up cross-country running. Her coach called her Jane since there were several other runners named Megan on the team.

She could still hear her coach's voice. "Run, Jane, run."

Her eyes swept over the vacant lot, and she increased her pace. Seeing the giant sewage pipes, she searched for one in which to hide. She was half the size of the officer, so if she crawled into one that fit her dimensions, the officer couldn't come after her. She hesitated only a moment as she looked for the smallest cylinder.

"Stop!" The officer yelled. "I told you to wait."

Jane picked up speed. The thumps of his heavy boots pounded behind her. She ran faster. Would he shoot her, if she didn't halt?

Seeing the perfect-sized tube, she dropped to the ground and squeezed inside. After she had wiggled into it, she breathed deeply to calm her throbbing heart.

A hand grabbed her ankle. She kicked with her other foot and broke free, and then she crept farther inside the pipe. Moving slowly down the length of the culvert, she shuddered. How long would it be before they caught her?

She crept along the dark space, quiet as possible. Then she touched what felt like a human foot and choked on her scream. In her terror, she must have imagined it. She didn't want to touch it again, but she did. Her fingers shook as she patted the sole of a foot. She took in a ragged breath and willed her heart to slow down. If it kept pounding, she might die of a heart attack in the sewer pipe.

Backing out wasn't an option. She'd go right into the waiting arms of the police, but she didn't want to be stuck in an iron cylinder with a dead person. She held her breath and lifted a shaking hand to check the foot again. The bare toes were small and warm. No, no, not a dead child. Her mind played tricks on her.

"Hello. Hello," she whispered. "Can you hear me? Are you playing hide and seek or running away?"

No response.

Lord, help.

With a gentle touch she pressed on the top of the small foot, searching for a pulse. She found a weak, thumping beat. If only she had a flashlight. In the tight space she slid her hand up the child's leg and patted a stomach, arms and chest. "Hello. What's your name? I want to help you. Please answer me." She choked back another scream. What if the child was unconscious or worse?

Hoping the little one wasn't comatose or bleeding to death from a wound Jane couldn't see, she kept speaking. "Let's go outside. This place is too dark and dirty. I'll help you find your mommy."

If something blocked the opposite end, or the child's head and shoulders were caught, Jane needed to go out the culvert with the child the same way Jane entered it. She ran her fingers gently over a small face, head, braids, and an earring in a pierced ear.

Nothing seemed to restrain the little girl, but something might be. If only she had a flashlight. Without knowing the child's injury, Jane shouldn't risk pushing her, but neither could she leave a helpless child in a sewage pipe to die. Jane had no choice but to pull the girl toward her and back all the way out.

What would she do if she had the child out and the officers grabbed her? She'd turn herself in and plead guilty, but she was only guilty of being Megan Jane Collins, unless her husband had trumped up some charge against her. She shivered.

Prison couldn't be any worse than what she'd already endured.

Jane couldn't tell how serious the girl's injury was, so Jane lifted and dragged the child a little at a time before stopping to rest. Jane ran her hands up and down the girl's pants again to check for bleeding. Even if the child's legs were hurt, Jane had to risk moving the little one. Taking a deep breath, she focused to slow her racing heart. Freeing the child might mean the difference between her life and death. Jane clutched the child's calves and pulled gently toward her.

Maybe it was a blessing her husband often confined her in close quarters. Her heart pounded as she slid the child a few inches at a time inside the dark smelly pipe. After a few minutes, she stopped and wiped the sweat from her brow with her fingertips. "My name is Jane. I'm going to help you find your mommy."

Speaking to an unconscious patient helped the injured wake up, so Jane talked. "Did you crawl in here? If you came in on hands and knees, did you come by yourself? Did you get tired and decide to take a nap?"

Jane panted and fought to maneuver the child closer and closer to the light. Jane had learned how to survive in confined, dark places. So the Lord must have sent her to rescue the little girl.

"I didn't pay attention to the length of the pipe, but it's taking me a long time to move you out. What time did you crawl in here?"

No one larger than Jane could have placed the child in there. What if the girl wasn't hiding? Someone could have hurt her and shoved her into the culvert with a long tool and left her for dead. Jane shivered at the possibilities. She stopped again to catch her breath. Hopefully the girl had been playing a game and crept inside of her own free will, but why hadn't she come out on her own?

When Jane's legs hit the earth behind her, her heart thumped so hard, she stopped to take another gulp of air before sliding out and getting to her knees. The sunlight had faded. She braced herself for a gunshot or the feel of handcuffs. She scanned the vacant lot and let out a huge sigh. Relieved to be alone, she blinked several times to focus before pulling the girl all the way out of the pipe.

After lifting the child out, Jane ran her fingers lightly over several long gashes and dried blood that covered the girl's forehead. "Open your eyes and tell me what happened to you? I'm checking your pulse again. Thank God. It's stronger. Can you hear me now?"

Where were the police? Maybe they were needed elsewhere, or the Lord had sent them away. She would rather be caught and tortured than abandon an injured child in a sewage pipe. She could never face her Maker with that on her conscience.

She ran her hands along the filthy pants and the torn blouse the little girl wore but saw no other injuries. Dirt covered her dark skin and kinky black braids, which looked like a good disguise. So Jane smeared more dirt all over her own face, neck, and shoulders.

Glancing toward the parking lot of the drug store, she sighed in relief. No police officers. She cradled the girl in her arms. As she picked her up, she gasped. "You're heavier than you look, but I'm glad your mommy is feeding you well."

As she carried the child, she stumbled back to the pharmacy. She kept her head lowered to avoid the video cameras as she walked inside and toward the cashier. She yelled, "Help. Help." She laid the little girl on the counter.

Several employees ran to her. Jane yelled, "Call 911! I found this child in a culvert over there in the empty field."

Jane backed away as they approached. She dashed out of the store before anyone could question her why she had crawled into a sewage pipe. She hurried to Mrs. Gaffney's car and reached underneath for her purse. Fumbling with the keys, she dropped them and bent to pick them up. She stayed crouched by the driver's door while she unlocked it.

She slid into the seat and clutched the steering wheel. After catching her breath, she pulled into traffic and headed to Mrs. Gaffney's house.

A police car with wailing sirens and flashing blue lights zoomed past her. An ambulance followed. The emergency vehicles headed toward the drug store. That had been a close call. She had almost been caught. The officer couldn't have known that she had driven Mrs. Gaffney's car. That should buy her some time to return the vehicle and think about her next move.

Jane prayed for the child. How long had she been in the culvert? Was anyone looking for the little girl?

Lord, please let her be all right.

The officer had taken her driver's license, which proved she'd been in the drug store parking lot. Without a license, she'd need to be extra careful. Follow all the speed limits. Stop at every four-way stop and red light. She'd drive in the slower lane and keep watch in the mirror for police. Now she had another reason to look over her shoulder.

If the police stopped her without a license, would she be arrested? She had no idea what happened to people who couldn't present a driver's license during a traffic stop. She hated being so naïve, but Scott had kept her in the dark in so many ways.

Should she carry her passport around with her to hand to an officer in case she was stopped?

Jane peered in the rearview mirror. Grime covered her and she smelled like the sewer pipe she'd been in. She held no resemblance to

Megan Jane Collins. Thank God no one would recognize her in her revolting disguise.

Trust in the Lord.

Once again she wished she had her grandmother's Bible. It had given her so much comfort and encouragement.

By the time she drove into the garage and closed the door behind her, Jane's hands shook so much she dropped Mrs. Gaffney's prescription. After picking it up, she tiptoed into the house. She crept past the living room and glanced at Mrs. Gaffney, sound asleep in her recliner. The nursing assistant, who had come to relieve Jane for her afternoon off, also slept.

Jane went into the bathroom and twisted on the hot water. She stripped and stepped under the flow. Thank God she had a place to clean up.

Five minutes later, she wrapped her wet hair in a towel and dressed in a fresh outfit. After stuffing her dirty clothes in the washing machine, she checked on Mrs. Gaffney, who still slept next to the snoring assistant.

The worker opened her eyes and whispered. "I didn't hear you come in."

"I tried to be quiet. I'm settled in for the night. I'll see you on Thursday afternoon."

After the nursing assistant left, Mrs. Gaffney woke up. Jane brought a fresh pitcher of water and poured a glass so the older woman could take her medication. "I collected your prescription."

"Thank you, dear."

"I'll start dinner." Jane smothered a yawn. "What would you like? There's roast beef or baked chicken."

"Baked chicken with potato salad and coleslaw."

Who had betrayed her? Jane had liked Cindy but what if she had turned Jane into that police officer? No, not Cindy, but if she needed funds, it would be easy. Jane didn't believe that Cindy had betrayed her, even though Scott had offered bribes and rewards to everyone for Jane's return. Anyone could deceive her for the money.

Should she run or stay with Mrs. Gaffney?

CHAPTER ELEVEN

Jane's husband never came to Mrs. Gaffney's house to drag Jane home, and no police officer arrived. No one with a camera spied on her. So Jane stayed and cared for the older woman.

After errands, a week later, Jane pulled in front of the garage and pressed the remote to open the door. Her head jerked at a glimmer of metal behind the hedges. Jane's heart pounded as she drove the car forward and closed the garage door. She slid out of the front seat and crouched under the window in the garage, and then she stood and peeked outside.

She stared at the row of shrubs where she'd seen the camera and caught a glimpse of a tall, well-built man in jeans and a black shirt. He limped behind a bush. For a fleeting moment, she took pity on him, but her husband would never hire someone unfit. An investigator would have watched from a long distance with a telephoto lens, so maybe he was a reporter. But why would a photographer be interested in her? Unless he recognized her, and if so, she needed to run again.

The door to the house opened. Mrs. Gaffney's daughter came into the garage. "What's happening?"

"Someone's creeping around outside."

The doorbell rang. Jane lurched to the side. Her hands shook, and she dropped her bag.

"You sure are tense today. That's just my son at the door. He's been visiting a friend down the road. I called him to come to his grandma's house." Sharon went inside.

Jane opened the car door to collect the groceries she'd bought. Going into the kitchen, she put the milk and yogurt in the refrigerator. Then she headed to the living room to speak with Mrs. Gaffney and her daughter.

Sitting across from them, Jane put her purse on her lap. "Something important has come up and I need to go out of town for a few weeks to take care of it."

"You are supposed to give us notice."

"I know, but this was unexpected." Jane shivered.

"If you must leave, I can give you a ride. Where do you want to go, the airport or the bus station?"

"The bus station." Jane stood. "Can you wait a few minutes while I pack my bag?"

Sharon nodded

In her bedroom, Jane went to the chest of drawers and stuffed her clothes in her backpack with a new disguise on top of everything. The doorbell rang, and she turned to the chime. Her stomach clenched. Taking in a ragged breath, she tiptoed to her doorway and peeked down the hall.

She couldn't hear the person Sharon spoke to. What if it was Scott? She froze. The front door banged shut. Her heart thudded faster.

Jane zipped her bag and picked it up. She squared her shoulders, stepped into the hall, and went straight to the living room.

Scott would never hurt her in front of witnesses. So it would be best to face her husband with others in the room. He had too much at stake, but if he was angry enough he might do anything.

"I thought I heard the doorbell." Jane looked at Mrs. Gaffney, her daughter, and grandson.

"It was the little boy down the street selling tickets to a raffle at his school." Sharon stood. "Are you ready to leave?"

Jane hugged Mrs. Gaffney. "I apologize for this inconvenience. I wish I didn't have to go away so suddenly."

"You've been a wonderful caregiver. I'm sorry to see you leave."

Jane held Mrs. Gaffney's hand. "I'll be back as soon as I can."

"I'll stay with mother until I can secure someone from the temporary agency. She'll be fine while I drop you at the bus station and take my son home."

After they were in the car, Sharon backed out of the garage. "I'm sorry to see you go. Mother will miss you so much."

"I've enjoyed caring for her and will miss her."

A few minutes later, Sharon pulled into the bus station parking lot. "Is there anything I can do that will persuade you to stay?"

"No, thank you. You've been kind. I'll call as soon as I know when I'm coming back."

Jane went into the ladies room and put on a brown wig, burgundy lipstick, and darker foundation. Then she changed into jeans and a clingy sweater.

When she came out, she read the roster of departures. A bus scheduled to leave for New York City in five minutes pulled into the station. Her husband would never find her there. She bought a ticket and waited. After the last passenger entered the bus, Jane ran to it and climbed inside.

She thanked God when the door closed behind her. She walked down the aisle to have a clear view outside the back window. The man with the camera from Nashville was standing next to a navy-blue Honda. Jane put her sunglasses on and looked at him to memorize his features before sitting down in an empty seat near the back. When the vehicle was rolling down the highway, Jane turned around to see out the rear window. The man in the Honda trailed the bus. Her heart lurched. If he was one of Scott's investigators, he'd follow her all the way to New York. She crossed her arms and rubbed them to calm the shakes.

Lord, please help me.

For two hours, the Honda stayed behind the bus. Bile rose in her throat. She shuddered at the guy's persistence which reminded her of her husband's determination.

The bus driver announced. "We're stopping to refuel and clean the vehicle. Everyone must step off."

Jane slid between two large men descending the bus, and headed to the smoking section in back of the station. She stopped, turned, and peeked at the man who had followed her in his Honda. He was parking his vehicle. She ran around a corner and searched for a side street. Seeing one not far ahead, she jogged toward it.

Help me to trust you, Lord.
Do not let my enemies triumph over me.
Guard my life and rescue me, Lord.
For I trust you, Lord.
But where could she hide?
Nowhere.
Run, Jane, run.

She spotted a public library not far down the road and hurried inside. She went into the restroom. If the man with the camera didn't see her get back on the bus, he'd know she'd stayed behind.

She rummaged around in her backpack for a new disguise but had only a few options. She shook out the wrinkles in her one dress before changing into it. Tugging off her wig, she stuffed it in her bag to discard later. She pulled her hair into an old-fashioned bun and applied her makeup. Peering into the mirror, Jane looked like she was on her way to church.

Where was she? She'd been so worried about the guy in the Honda she'd failed to notice the name of the town. Leaving the restroom, she went to the newspaper section and found the most recent copy of the Warwick, Pennsylvania news. She carried it upstairs to a private study room. After moving a chair so her back faced the window in the door, she buried her head in the paper.

Jane glanced at her watch. She'd wait one hour and leave. She closed her eyes and pictured the man following her. He appeared about forty, six feet tall, and maybe two hundred pounds. He was average-looking with a crooked nose. His hair needed a trim and a comb, proving he'd been in a hurry. His clothes blended in well, but she'd recognize him again.

Unless he had given up searching for her.

*****

Ben wouldn't stop looking for her. His eyes scanned the area around the bus station. How could she disappear right in front of him? He'd had no trouble as an officer in Special Forces locating the enemy and bringing him in. So why was it so hard finding a pastor's wife? Megan wasn't an average minister's wife. If she'd been held captive for fifteen years, she would be determined to stay hidden from her husband. Ben rubbed his chin. Where would she go?

He suspected Scott might hurt her and wanted to warn her. Where were all the other private investigators that Scott had hired? Had one of them snatched her and taken her back to Scott? Ben's heart plummeted as he stared at the bus pulling away without her on board. No other vehicles had departed the station, so she must be in town, but he hadn't seen any taxis. That meant she'd left on foot or hid someplace nearby.

If she had seen him in there, she might have left the bus only to get away from him. He could scarcely limp with his bad knee and couldn't run after her.

He went into the station and spotted a rack of brochures. He picked the one that listed motels, hotels, and bed and breakfast establishments. Ben phoned all eight places, but no one had seen a single woman. He decided to try again later.

Maybe there were other lodgings in the area that didn't have pamphlets. He checked a few listings on his phone. Nothing. So he headed to the library to look at the local want-ads.

Grateful for the elevator, he stepped inside and pressed the button. When the door opened, he glanced at the rows of books and walked past the study rooms. The last one was occupied by an older woman with brown hair in a bun. She sat with her back to the door. Not unusual for people who wished to avoid distractions. The set of her shoulders and different clothes told him it wasn't Megan Jane. Besides, she was too smart to stop in a library while on the run.

But he'd check the room again before he left.

*****

Jane heaved a sigh as she finished reading the want-ads. A couple of the positions sounded good, but she couldn't stay in Warwick. She discreetly looked over her shoulder, but there was no one on the other side of the study door.

Her stomach fluttered. She dreaded leaving the library. Scott had always caught her out there on the road. She lifted shaking fingers to check if her hair was still neatly arranged.

She closed her eyes and saw her grandmother's Bible. *Lord, come quickly to my rescue. Be my rock of refuge, a strong fortress to save me. Lead and guide me.*

Give me courage, Lord. Show me.

Jane glanced at her watch. She couldn't put off leaving any longer. A church flyer had fallen out of the newspaper, so she picked it up. "Spring luncheon and tea at Community Church. Everyone welcome."

It would be easy to lose herself in a church crowd. Women always cooked extra food for those events hoping to reach the community, so Jane wouldn't be taking a meal from the hungry. It would give her another hour to decide where to go next.

She flung her backpack over her shoulder and headed toward the front desk. "Can you give me directions to Community Church?"

"It's outside of town near the interstate. Do you have a car?" The librarian asked.

"No."

"It's about ten miles from here. Would you like me to call a cab for you?"

"Yes, please."

Jane waited in the foyer until a taxi stopped in front. She ran out, slid into the back seat, and asked the driver to take her to the church.

He turned onto the highway and a few minutes later pulled up in front of the building. Jane paid him and got out. Seeing the full parking lot, she breathed easier. She went inside and mingled with the people, and then she moved to the buffet serving line. She helped herself to cheese and crackers, grapes, and a tuna salad sandwich. When her plate was full, she picked up a glass of punch.

As she bit into the sandwich, she noticed a white-haired man stop next to her. He clutched his chest and dropped to the floor. She set her plate down and knelt next to him. She yelled, "Call 911!"

Others knelt around the man while Jane checked his pulse and respirations before starting CPR. Several chest compressions later, she stopped and found a faint pulse.

He blinked and seemed to focus. "Who are you?"

"I'm helping you. Where does it hurt?"

The man closed his eyes. "My chest."

She held his hand. "Stay still until the ambulance arrives."

In the distance, sirens wailed.

When the paramedics raced into the church and approached the patient, Jane slowly slid back a little at a time so she wouldn't draw attention to herself. Once she was through the crowd, she went outside. Seeing a taxi drop off people, she silently thanked God for a way of escape. She ran to it and leaped into the back seat.

"What's the name of the town about ten miles north of here?"

"It's called Belton."

"Can you take me there?"

"Be glad to." The driver turned on the meter.

"Is there a motel in Belton?"

"No, but there's a boarding house. Would you like to go there?"

"Sounds good, thanks."

Jane took a calming gulp of air and relaxed as the taxi drove out of Warwick and onto a country lane. When it arrived in Belton, the driver went down several long suburban streets. Jane sat up straighter as they passed a mission thrift store with its lights on and cars parked in front. A pharmacy sat in the middle of the next block, so she asked, "Would you stop here please?"

The driver parked. "The boarding house is two more blocks down the road."

"Thank you. I can walk the rest of the way." Jane paid the fare and waited for the taxi to leave. Then she turned back the way she had come.

Jane walked to the thrift store and went inside to look around. Too bad the mission shop didn't have any wigs. Sometimes they did. She'd make do with scarves. She picked up several sets of clothes, a giant purse, and a yellow backpack that must have been a teenager's. After purchasing them, she went into the ladies room and locked the door. She dressed in jeans and a blue sweater. She left the clothes and wigs she'd worn recently inside the old backpack but removed her personal effects and money. She stuffed these and her purchases in the new bag.

On the way to the boarding house, she stopped at the pharmacy and bought black hair color. She tossed her old bag into a dumpster as she left the drug store. She went down the street and found the rooming house. With a shaking finger, she rang the bell.

An elderly woman opened the door. "May I help you?"

"I'd like to rent a room for a few days. I've been on a bus to New York City."

"I'm Mrs. Morley, the landlady. It's a hundred dollars in advance for a week."

Jane handed her the money wondering why the older woman didn't ask any questions. If the landlady accepted anyone into her home, it might not be safe, but Jane had no other place to go. Grateful for a roof over her head, she thanked God.

"Follow me." Mrs. Morley led the way upstairs and unlocked a door. She handed Jane a key. "This is yours. The bathroom is at the end of the hall."

Turning the knob, Jane started to go in.

"Would you like some supper?" The landlady asked. "I have some leftover spaghetti and lemon pie."

Jane hadn't eaten much at the church and was hungry. "Yes, I would. Thanks." She put her bag in her room, locked the door, and went with the woman to the kitchen. After joining the landlady at the table, Jane ate. She yawned and feigned fatigue as the reason for not answering the woman's questions.

After supper, she helped the older woman fill the dish washer. Then Jane went to her room. She would need to wear a scarf until she could color her hair. She organized her new purchases into disguises and repacked them for a quick escape.

She locked her door and turned on the little television to an old black and white movie. The actors' voices took her mind off her near capture. She lay on the bed and closed her eyes. When she woke up, she peeked into the hall. Seeing no one, she headed to the bathroom. The quiet house felt safe.

Thank you, Lord, for helping me escape again and keeping me ahead of Scott's investigators. Maybe this time she had lost the man following her.

CHAPTER TWELVE

Ben, a well-trained soldier, recognized the importance of staying focused. Men in combat learned to eat and sleep when given the chance, so he stopped at a restaurant for a meal. His concern for Megan had dampened his hunger, but when the waitress set a bowl of beef stew in front of him, he thanked the server and picked up the spoon. In battle-mode, he focused on eating and finding Megan.

He prayed to reach her before her husband did. Ben had gone back upstairs to double-check the study room, but the female in different clothes with the bun had left. No woman could change her appearance that quickly, especially a pastor's wife.

After the waitress collected his empty plates and re-filled his coffee cup, Ben called a couple of lodgings advertised in the local news. No one had seen anyone like Megan, who probably waited until dark to check in for the night. There were few places to hide in the small town of Warwick.

He drove to the closest motel and got a room. After propping his painful leg up on several pillows, he swallowed a couple tablets of prescription medication the doctor gave him. He'd been shot in the knee as a Special Forces Officer and lost all prospects of becoming a US Marshal. He had had surgery at the time to remove the damaged cartilage, but recently bone scraped on bone, which hindered his job performance as an investigator. The doctor recommended a total knee replacement, but in Ben's mind, only senior citizens, like his mother's friends had them. So at forty-two, Ben wasn't ready for it.

Ben called each lodging one more time. No Megan. He slumped against the pillows. Where could she be? How had she disappeared? He clicked on the television to watch the news and weather.

"Now for the local news. An unidentified female attending an event at Community Church saved a man's life. She started CPR on a gentleman having a heart attack. Many of the guests caught it on film, so let's take a look."

Ben's heart clenched as he stared at Megan Jane, the lady with the brown bun. He had underestimated her abilities. If the news aired in Memphis, Scott Collins would see it. Megan was in greater danger, but where had she gone? Ben broke out in a sweat.

The interviewer held the microphone in front of a white-haired man in an emergency room. "What do you think of the Good Samaritan?"

"I thank God she came when she did, or I'd be dead."

The announcer turned to the screen. "Who is this angel who disappeared in the commotion? Where did she go?"

And what kind of woman would stop and give CPR to a stranger at the risk of being caught?

Ben phoned the news station. "Did anyone talk to the woman who saved the gentleman having the heart attack?"

"Someone saw her jump into a taxi."

Ending the call, Ben phoned the only cab service in Warwick and located the driver who had taken Megan.

The man chuckled. "She sure is a popular lady. You're the fifth guy who's called about her."

Ben's heart lurched and fell to the pit of his stomach. Before hanging up, he had the address of where the taxi had dropped Megan. If the driver had given that location to all the others who asked about her, it was too late to save her. One of Rev. Collins's private investigators had already located her, or the reporters had found her.

He punched in Rev. Scott Collins's number and waited. When Scott answered, Ben gulped. "This is Benjamin Grant. I apologize for calling so late. An urgent, personal situation has come to my attention. I need to take myself off the case. I'd be glad to return the last installment you gave me."

"No, keep it. You did more than any other investigator. Could you recommend another guy to lead the search?"

"I'd have to check my contacts."

"Do you know Daniel Fuller? He had excellent recommendations, but he was working on another assignment when I interviewed investigators."

"No, sir. I've never met him." Ben hesitated. "If he has good references, he should be fine. After I finish my business, I'll get back to you."

Ben hung up and searched Daniel Fuller online. It brought up lots of information suspecting the former police officer of killing his wife. Ben scrolled down the page and found a newspaper article with the headline. "Police officer accused in wife's death."

Ben's heart pounded faster. Dan might be responsible for his wife's death, and if that was true, he'd hurt Megan or worse when he located her.

"Annabelle Fuller, wife of Sergeant Daniel Fuller, was found dead of an overdose. She had been institutionalized several times for depression and suicidal tendencies over the years."

The article quoted her husband. "I worried about her and managed her medications for her safety. I gave her the tablets each morning and evening. Perhaps she saved them over time and swallowed them all at once."

Daniel could have killed her. No autopsy was performed. Over their ten years of marriage, Mrs. Fuller had been admitted to the hospital for injuries on four separate occasions.

In a later article, the coroner had ruled that Mrs. Fuller's death was a suicide. No charges were ever filed against her husband. Ben couldn't shake the eerie sensation that came over him. Dan sounded like a man who mistreated women.

Ben called a friend at the police station and learned the name of a nurse who worked in the emergency room where Mrs. Fuller was treated. He filed the name and number away to call in the morning. Ben needed to reach Megan before one of Scott's hired men did. He prayed that Dan wouldn't find her. The pain medication increased his drowsiness. The more he prayed, the harder it was to keep his eyes open. If he hadn't been up for the last twenty-four hours, he might have driven to the boarding house in Belton. Too bad it had an unlisted number, or he'd call. But that meant no one else could phone. It was midnight and there was nothing else he could do but pray.

So he prayed falling asleep.

*****

Jane woke to the aroma of fresh coffee. She'd slept well but needed to stretch her stiff muscles. Glancing around the small room, she tried to remember where she was. She had been running away from the tall, well-built man with the camera and ended up at a boarding house in Belton, Pennsylvania.

She needed a cup of strong caffeine but didn't have a robe, so she dressed in a red and orange flowing skirt with a maroon blouse and followed the scent to the kitchen.

A girl stood in front of the counter. "Would you like some coffee? Mrs. Morley lets us have as much as we want."

Jane accepted the mug. "Thanks. I'm Jane."

"Emily Roper." Her cell phone rang. She answered it and pointed to the refrigerator.

Jane opened it, found French vanilla creamer, and poured a generous amount into her cup.

When Emily finished her call, she sat at the table. "I'd love to show you around, but I'm in a hurry to get to the library for research on a paper in my criminology class."

"Where is the library? I need to do some work."

"Come with me if you want. I'll leave in half an hour."

"Thanks. I'll get ready." Jane carried her cup to her room.

Walking past the bathroom, she saw it was in use. Jane asked another girl in the hall. "Is this the only shower for boarders?"

The girl nodded and left. As Jane headed to her room, Mrs. Morley motioned her over. "I overheard your conversation. You seem a bit more mature than my other boarders. You can use my bath if you leave it tidy afterwards."

Jane used the same low tone. "Thanks. Give me a moment to collect my soap and towel."

She picked them up and followed the landlady. Jane never talked to strangers but sometimes necessity forced her to.

When she first left Scott, she had tried to avoid most people for she wasn't sure whom she could trust. She hadn't been used to the freedom of talking to strangers without her husband hovering over her. As the months passed, the memories of his mistreatment had begun to fade, so she spoke more to people she didn't know.

Jane met Emily in the hall. They went outside to an old Toyota. Emily slid into the driver's seat and Jane went to the passenger side. The girl started the engine and drove to the library. After they were inside the building, she showed Jane where the computers, study rooms, and newspaper racks were. Jane selected a computer that faced the door to watch people who came and went.

Several hours later, Emily approached Jane at the workstation. "I need to go to class. Would you like to come back to Mrs. Morley's house with me?"

"No thanks." Jane smiled. "I've more research to do. I'll find my way there. I need to stop at the store."

"I'm glad you mentioned it. You need groceries. Our time to cook in the kitchen is after six. If the other boarders don't have work or class, we sometimes eat together and all go to church on Sundays. You can come with us, if you want."

"I'd love to go to church, but I'm only passing through on my way to New York City."

"What will you do there?"

"I'm an experienced caregiver. The pay in New York is much better than Tennessee."

How did that slip out of her mouth? Now Emily knew where she had come from. Jane needed to be more careful but talking to the young girl had been easy.

Jane had no desire to go to New York. She closed her eyes and imagined gunshot wounds, knife fight victims, and beaten-up prostitutes in the emergency room. She shuddered.

New York was the last place she wanted to go, but it might be the safest city to get lost in.

*****

Ben prayed he wasn't too late as he drove to the boarding house in Belton. Seeing no other cars in the drive or around the house, he sighed in relief. The owner must park in the garage, so he walked to the door.

An older woman opened it. "Hello."

"Hello." He smiled. "I'm looking for Jane. Is she in?"

"I don't allow any of my ladies to have gentleman callers."

If that were true, Megan would be quite safe in the house.

Her eyes ran up and down his large build. "I don't permit any men in my house. There are fewer problems that way." The old woman put her hands on her hips. "Are you a boyfriend?"

"No, ma'am, nothing like that. I have an urgent message for her."

"Why don't you call her?"

"She doesn't have a phone."

"Every young person has one."

"If she has, I don't know the number. Can you give it to me? I'd prefer calling her."

"I'll give her a message if you like."

Taking out a pad and pen, he wrote. "I must talk to you before Scott does. I'll be back later. Benjamin Grant." He tore off the page and folded it. Then he handed it to the older woman. "Thank you, ma'am. I'll come back later for an answer. Maybe Jane will let me take her to supper tonight."

She nodded. "I'll hand this to her myself."

Ben hobbled to his car and parked on the side street to watch both the front and rear doors. He doubted Jane would agree to talk to him, but if she was inside and decided to run, he could go after her, but not too fast.

He hoped she hadn't already left, or he'd be sitting there indefinitely.

*****

Scott closed the men's prayer breakfast with a loud "Amen." When he returned to his office, he called Dan Fuller's number. "This is Rev. Scott Collins. If you're finished with your assignment, I'd like you to find my wife."

"I can meet you in your office in an hour."

By the time Dan arrived, Scott had lined up the photos of Megan on his desk. Dan picked up several pictures in his massive hands. His huge size would intimidate any female. Dan seemed capable of keeping everyone in line.

"I'm glad you called because I've had lots of experience finding wives and re-uniting them with their husbands."

"My wife was at my side for fifteen years. She sat in front of me during each service and with me every week for our television program." He hesitated. "As a Christian husband and the head of my wife, it is my duty to protect her and tell her what's best."

Dan took out a notepad. "I agree."

"If you're going to work for me, I'd like to know about your wife's death. I read she committed suicide. Why did it happen?"

"My wife was accident-prone and always tripping on the stairs, falling down, or walking into doors. She developed a low self-esteem from all her mishaps, and that depressed her. We went to therapy, but it didn't help."

"I've counseled many couples. Unfortunately not all end happily ever after."

"I did everything for my wife." Dan pounded the desk with his fist. "I made great sacrifices so she could have a life of ease and comfort. She paid me back by swallowing a bottle of sleeping pills."

"Women," Scott sighed. "We do everything for them, but it's never enough."

"I told my wife what to do for her own good."

"Yes. That sounds like mine. She had to be told exactly what to do."

Scott could hardly wait to get her back. He'd missed her.

CHAPTER THIRTEEN

Jane left the library and seeing a Pizza Hut, went into it. She ordered a personal-size pepperoni pizza to celebrate slipping past her husband's hired man. When the meal arrived, her mouth watered at the oregano and garlic. After eating, she headed back to the boarding house but stopped at the grocery store and pharmacy.

As she reached the front door, the sun had already set. She inserted her key in the lock, but it stuck, so she shifted her bags to one hand to jiggle the mechanism. A sack broke. Apples and oranges rolled down the sidewalk. She dropped the other bags and ran after the fruit. When she lifted her head, her throat tightened at the blue Honda. Then her heart stopped.

How had he found her?

In slow motion she backed up a few steps. She gasped, unable to breathe. Maybe he hadn't seen her. She abandoned the fruit on the cement and ran to the front door. After the lock turned, she flung the door open and raced inside. She bolted it behind her, but that wouldn't stop one of her husband's hired men from coming inside. Slumping to the floor, she tried to catch her ragged breath.

The man's relentlessness terrified her. It reminded her of Scott's persistence. An eerie silence filled the house. She stood and tiptoed to the kitchen and peeked in it. No Scott. She crept past the living room, but it, too, was empty. She rushed down the hall. Where were the boarders? Had she walked into a trap? Maybe Scott would jump out from a closet and snatch her. The thought of him sneaking up behind her and grabbing her propelled her into her room. She slammed and locked the door, and collapsed on the bed. Sobs racked her body as tears streamed down her face.

Words from her grandmother's Bible came to her. *Do not fret because of evil men. For like the grass they will soon wither. Trust in the Lord and do good. Commit your way to the Lord. Trust in Him. Be still before the Lord and wait patiently for him.*

The Lord would help her. With a clever disguise, she could walk right past the car so the man never recognized her. She picked up the box of hair color called 'soft black.' Tears blurred the instructions. She blinked them away and closed her eyes. After cutting off her hair below her ears, she colored her hair and eyebrows.

She went to collect the black marker the boarders used to leave notes. After picking it up from the kitchen counter, she pulled back the curtains and peeked out the window. Her heart thudded as the same man who had followed her limped to his car. He was handicapped. She could run fast and certainly outrun him.

Jane returned to her room to finish her new appearance. Using the Sharpie, she painted tattoos of arrows and flowers on her exposed neck and arms. Then she stuffed her legs and hips into her tightest jeans and put on a low-cut sweater. Her new disguise so shocked her, she jumped back from the mirror.

The doorbell rang. Jane dropped the red lipstick and turned to the closed door of her room. Chimes echoed on and on throughout the house. She gripped the dresser and waited.

Lord, send him away.

She released her hold on the drawer and exhaled. The expected crash of the front door never came. She eased her bedroom door open and went to the kitchen to look out the window. The stranger was climbing back into his Honda. She breathed easier.

Why didn't she run out the back door when he rang the bell at the front door? Maybe Scott had been right. She wasn't too smart.

In her room, she stuffed her belongings into her backpack with her cash equally distributed in the pockets. She laid out three more disguises and packed them to grab a new outfit if needed. She checked in the closet and under the bed making certain she didn't leave any traces behind. She had paid up for a week, so she could disappear any time after dark.

Hearing the back door open, Jane's heart beat faster. Her eyes scanned her room for a weapon. Anything. Nothing. She backed up behind her bedroom door to be out of sight when it banged open. Changing her mind, she unlocked the door and pulled it toward her and hid behind it. The man would see the empty room and pass on by.

"Jane?" Mrs. Morley called. "I have a message for you."

Hearing the older woman, Jane stepped out from behind her hiding place.

Mrs. Morley stopped in the doorway. Her eyes flew wide. She blinked and gasped. "Is that you, Jane? What did you do to yourself?"

Her lips quivered. "I wanted one of those makeovers."

"Why did you cut off your beautiful hair? What will that well-mannered gentleman say when he sees you?"

Well-mannered gentleman described her husband in public. So who was the man in the Honda? The pulse in her temples throbbed.

"Your visitor told me to give this to you."

Jane reached for the note.

The older woman glanced into the room and looked around as if searching for someone. "I told him I don't allow any of my girls to have male callers in their rooms. It's nearly suppertime, so he should be back in a few minutes." The woman turned and walked toward the kitchen. She glanced back at Jane once more and shook her head.

Jane opened the wrinkled note and read it. It wasn't her husband's writing, and she didn't recognize the name. She stuffed the paper into her pocket and tiptoed into the living room to look out the window again. She stared outside at the man waiting in his car, if only it were dark so she could leave. She remembered her apples and oranges on the sidewalk and went to the opposite window. Her fruit was gone. She returned to her room and paced, waiting for it to get dark.

A short time later the front doorbell rang. Jane ran to the back door and stepped outside but forgot her backpack. If only it was dark. Then she would have run even without the bag.

She peeked around the corner and waited for the man to get back in his Honda. Then she slipped back in her room.

Lord, please let it be dark soon.

Someone knocked. She leaped off the bed and grabbed her backpack. Her heart stuttered. She turned to the door. With a shaking hand, she twisted the knob.

"Jane?" Emily cocked an eyebrow as she stared at the disguise. "Is it you?"

Jane breathed easier. "Yes, it's me. I'm leaving this evening. I wanted to have a different look when I go to New York."

"You succeeded. If this wasn't your room, I wouldn't have known you." Emily's cell phone rang. She glanced at the screen, pressed a key and put the phone away. "A gentleman was looking for you. He left this note."

Jane took the paper wondering what more he could say. "Thanks. Can I use your phone if I pay for the call?"

"My parents bought me unlimited time, so you don't need to pay." Emily handed Jane the phone.

"It will take me a few minutes to dig out the number. After I use it, should I take it to your room?"

"Bring it to the kitchen and you can join me for supper."

"Thanks, but I've already eaten."

After Emily left, Jane opened the note. "You might be in danger. Please come to the door when I ring again so I can give you the details."

She had spent the last fifteen years in danger, so what was one more threat? She stuffed the note in her pocket and found Cindy's number. "This is Jane."

Cindy asked, "Are you okay?"

"Some private investigator is waiting for me outside. I'm not sure I can leave without him catching me and hauling me back to my husband."

"Stay there and I'll send someone to get you."

"I can't risk it. I don't want anyone else hurt. I'll try to sneak away. Did you keep all the notes of our conversation?"

"Yes."

"If I disappear and am never heard from again, I'd like your lawyer to start an investigation. I can't let my husband get away with this."

"Jane, if you can wait there until tomorrow, I'll come myself."

"If I get free of this guy, I'll e-mail you."

"Use an innocuous one."

"It is Z3NG75@yahoo."

After saying goodbye, Jane went to the kitchen and returned the phone to Emily. Glancing out the window, Jane stared at the man waiting in his car. Her breath came out in ragged gasps.

She returned to her room and paced until all the lights were turned out and it was pitch dark. Then she tiptoed to the back door, slid open the bolt, and turned the knob. She slipped into the darkness.

A man yelled, "Megan, stop!"

Run Jane, run.

*****

When the back door slowly opened. Ben hobbled toward it as fast as he could on his bad leg. As Megan ran by, he reached for her. His hand closed around a strap of a backpack. She wrenched away. His leg twisted. He lost his balance and fell.

Unbearable pain exploded in his knee. Fire jolted through every nerve in his leg. Rolling on the ground, he writhed in agony.

Watching her run away, he shouted, "Megan, please stop. I won't betray you to your husband." He frowned at the backpack in his hand. Did he have her only means of staying safe and escaping from Scott?

The outside lights clicked on. Mrs. Morley opened the door. "Jane, are you out there?"

"It's me, Benjamin Grant. I came earlier and left a note for Jane."

"I'm calling the police." She raised a baseball bat. "How dare you try to come into the house to see Jane at this hour?"

"Yes, please, call the police."

She stepped back. "You want me to phone them?"

"Yes," He groaned. "Maybe they can help."

"Why don't you stand up?"

"I'm injured."

"Did Jane hurt you?"

Ben gagged on a chuckle. Jane couldn't hurt anyone. If she did, he would have welcomed it. "No, I've a bad knee and fell."

Mrs. Morley lowered the bat and approached him slowly. "I heard the commotion and checked her room, but Jane isn't there."

"I wasn't trying to come in. I've been waiting for her to come out tonight."

The old woman gasped, "Were you meeting Jane right here in my back yard? I told her I don't allow any hanky-panky."

"No, ma'am. I had a feeling Jane was trying to leave tonight. I had to speak with her. It's urgent."

"Where was Jane going at this hour?"

"I don't know. May I talk to you sitting up?" He clutched his knee with both hands. "Can you bring a chair?"

The woman nodded and went back inside the house. A few minutes later, Mrs. Morley and three young ladies came out with a kitchen chair. Ben put his hands on the seat, and keeping his weight on his good leg, pulled himself to stand. Breathing hard, he hopped around and sat down. "Thank you."

Emily placed her hands on her hips. "Jane is not the type of girl to meet men in the middle of the night. She told me she wanted to go to church with us."

Ben reached into his pants pocket and took out his key ring. The indescribable pain, more agony than the torture during the war, swept over him. He couldn't go to his car without his cane.

"Would one of you bring my cane from the back seat of my car? This key will open a dark-blue Honda at the side of your house."

"I'll go." One girl reached for the keys.

Another resident moved closer. "I'll go with you."

"After I have my walking stick, I'll be on my way."

"Not without an explanation. Where did Jane go?" Mrs. Morley asked. "Is she coming back?"

"Jane is running away from someone. I'm a private investigator and need to reach her before she is hurt." He handed a copy of his license to Mrs. Morley.

The girls came back with the cane and gave it to him.

He stood and leaned on it. Taking his license back from the elderly woman, he gave her a business card. "If Jane contacts you, please call me right away."

Emily asked. "Did Jane run down that alley?"

"Yes." Ben groaned as another pain shot through his knee.

"I have an idea where she went."

"Can you show me? I'd be glad to pay you for your time."

"There's no need for that. I like Jane. Let me help you to your car."

Ben leaned on the girl as they hobbled to the street. He opened the passenger door for her. "What's your name?"

"Emily." She got in and fastened her seatbelt.

Supporting himself against the car, Ben worked his way around to the driver's side and slid into the seat. "Which direction?"

"That alley goes to Main Street. I use it as a short cut to the all-night store. Go right and right again and I'll show you where it comes out." She pointed. "The large convenience store is at the end, so we'll look there."

He followed her instructions. Was God about to answer Ben's prayer? Or was Emily distracting him so Jane could get away?

CHAPTER FOURTEEN

Jane stopped running to catch her breath. She went into the small grocery store, where she'd bought her fruit that afternoon. She thanked God she'd stuffed an emergency stash of money in her pants pocket while she had paced in her room. With a couple thousand dollars she could go far without her backpack.

She stepped up to the cashier. "Are there any buses leaving tonight?"

"The town's too small to support a bus station, but I've seen some pulling out of the convenience store at the end of the road. A couple of them stop about this time."

"Thanks."

Jane walked quickly to the store and into the restroom to check her disguise. Then she squared her shoulders, opened the door, and went to the clerk.

"What time do the buses leave?"

"I'm new here and don't know the specific times. Around midnight a bus goes north, another drives south and one goes east." The woman pointed to the other side of the store. "You can wait at one of the deli tables. When a bus arrives, you'll have to ask the driver."

If Jane sat in the well-lit area anyone might spot her, but if she went outside and hid in a dark corner, someone might grab her. She'd be in greater danger out in the dark, since she might have three hours to wait. She went to the farthest booth in the back corner and sat down facing the door.

Seeing Emily run into the store and look around, Jane turned to the side and lowered her head. She took a couple of deep breaths. Had the college girl seen her? Without her backpack, Jane had no way to change her appearance. If Emily was in a hurry to pick up something and leave, she might not look in Jane's direction. No. She walked straight to Jane and sat across from her in the booth.

Emily shrugged and looked around. "What are you doing here? It looks like you're waiting for someone."

"I'm taking a bus."

"A private investigator is looking for you. He wants to warn you about some bad guys."

"Did he leave?"

"No, I brought him here."

"You … you … brought him! How could you do that to me? Why?"

Emily threw her hands up. "He's a nice man. Mrs. Morley and the girls believe him."

How could so many women trust a man because he acted nice the first time they met him? Jane had done it and the man turned out to be a monster.

"He reminds me of my dad." Emily put her hands on the table. "He's thoughtful and kind."

That's what everyone told her about Scott. She shivered.

Emily pleaded. "He's trying to save your life."

Of all the ploys Scott had used to trick her, that had been the worst one. Her husband had hired a pleasant man everyone would trust. Jane flinched as the seat shifted. The investigator sat, blocking her in the booth.

She turned. "You! How could you deceive this nice girl?"

"I didn't trick anyone." He handed her the backpack. "I brought you this."

"You tried to take it away from me."

"No, I wanted to talk to you."

Taking her bag, she gasped, "It's heavier." Her brows narrowed as she peeked inside. "You picked up my apples and oranges? Did you hide a GPS in there, too?"

"I wouldn't do that to you." He extended his hands outward with his palms open.

Her suspicions took over. He might have put a tracker in her bag and then pretend not to follow her. Later, he could snatch her when she was alone.

"Scott would and did." She glared at him. "Why were you waiting in your car?"

"I wanted to speak to you alone, but every time you see me, you run."

"I can't trust you." She looked wildly around before slumping in her seat. Trapped, she mumbled. "It's all over."

Emily scooted to the edge of the seat. "Do you want me to leave?"

Jane didn't want to cry, but tears filled her eyes and streamed down her face. She reached across the table and grabbed Emily's hands in both of hers. "Please stay. I'm in danger."

Emily's eyes widened as she looked behind her and then down the aisles.

"No." Jane nodded toward the man next to her. "From him."

"We got off on the wrong foot, or leg," he rubbed his knee. "Mine is killing me. I don't want to run after you anymore."

"Well then, don't. Go away and leave me alone. Tell my husband you couldn't find me."

"I no longer work for your husband. I'm not telling him anything but trying to help you."

"Who are you?"

"Benjamin Grant, a private investigator, originally hired by your husband to find you. I asked to be excused from the case."

"Why?"

"I don't trust him." Ben leaned forward. "Tell me what your husband did to make you run away."

Jane pulled a paper napkin from the holder to wipe her eyes. "My husband hurt me every day either physically or emotionally. I ran away several times, but he always found me and punished me."

Emily sniffed. "What a horrible man."

"Why didn't you report this?"

"He threatened to hurt my grandmother. He's paying for her nursing home care."

"Didn't anyone see what your husband did to you? He is the pastor of one of the largest churches in Tennessee. Someone should have witnessed his behavior."

"No one ever suspected."

"I believe you. Walking through your bedroom, I saw the worn bed post."

Her shoulders shook as she lowered her head.

"What does that mean?" Emily asked.

"Every time I left, or he suspected me of leaving, or he went someplace where he couldn't take me, he handcuffed me to the bed."

Emily gasped. "He sounds awful."

"I want to help you. After taking myself off the case, your husband hired Daniel Fuller, an ex-police officer. His wife died under mysterious circumstances." Ben pulled out a business card and added several numbers to it. "Call me anytime you need help. I'll say nothing to your husband."

Emily reached for Jane's hand. "Let this man help you. I trust him."

"I trusted my husband and look what I got for it. I like you, Emily, but you never lived with a beast who tormented you almost every day and wouldn't allow you to leave. Now he's out there hunting me down to take me back to him." Jane scowled at Ben. "Let me out, Mr. Grant. I want to leave."

Ben slid out of the booth. "Daniel Fuller is neither a nice man nor a Christian."

"Are you suggesting you are?"

"Yes."

"What church do you attend?" Jane cocked an eyebrow.

"Wesleyan."

"That doesn't mean I can trust you. Look at my husband, a well-known pastor."

Ben grimaced. "Just because a man is a minister doesn't mean he is a Christian."

Jane kept looking toward the front door, expecting Scott to burst through it. He'd yank her out of the booth and break one of her arms doing it. No, he wouldn't. Not in front of witnesses. He'd convince them she was ill, and they'd let him take her home. That would be worse.

Ben leaned on his cane. He smiled at her as if he was one of the good guys.

But she knew better. What if he pretended to be hurt to gain her sympathy? He grimaced when he moved, which suggested a real injury. He'd probably hold her responsible for it, just like Scott who blamed her for everything that went wrong.

He reached out for her hand.

She shrank away. "Tell me why I should trust you. You've been employed by my husband. How do I know you won't take me back to him?"

Were those tears in his eyes? She almost felt sorry for him, but her husband always hired men she'd feel sorry for to get her to go with them.

Ben shifted his weight on his cane and moved away from the booth. "I guess you can't trust anyone. I wish you'd try to trust me. With Dan Fuller and your husband both after you, I don't know how you can escape them by yourself. Dan is ruthless. I want to help, but if you won't let me, at least I'll pray for you. Call me if you need my help."

She mumbled. "Sure, as if you'll help me."

Emily whispered, "You could try to trust him, and if he betrayed you, then punch him where it hurts. Besides, he's old and injured. He can't run after you too fast."

Even with his injury, he appeared stronger than her husband. He could have overpowered her or found an excuse to get rid of Emily, but he didn't.

She glanced at the wall clock, eleven. A passenger bus pulled up in front of the store. How could she get rid of Emily and Ben? She adjusted the weight in her backpack and took a few steps, but Ben and Emily came with her.

Ben asked Emily. "Can you get home by yourself?"

"Sure. What are you going to do?"

He looked at Jane. "If you get on the bus, I'm following you in my car."

"If you're not going to turn me in to Scott, why come after me?"

"You're in danger. I'm trying to keep you safe."

Why would a strange man offer to protect her? What did he want from her?

Jane gave up. No point in running. Ben had found her several times already, and this time he wouldn't take his eyes off her.

Maybe he wasn't like her husband, but all men were. No, some men were worse than others. She shuddered.

"I believe you'll be safe at Mrs. Morley's boarding house, so I'd like to drive you back there. Tomorrow morning I'll come and take you both out to breakfast so we can formulate a plan on where you can hide."

Emily shook her head. "I have to go to work in the morning."

Jane shivered as she walked with them to the Honda. She didn't trust him. He sounded too nice to be for real. He acted like Scott did at first. He even unlocked the door and opened it for them as if he had manners like her husband, who pretended to be the perfect gentleman in public but not in private. Tremors ran up and down her spine as she stared down the deserted road. If she started jogging, maybe she could escape.

Run Jane, run.

CHAPTER FIFTEEN

Ben stood still and waited for Megan who turned away and stared at the convenience store and the buildings down the road.

He whispered to her, "Please don't run. You'll be safer if you stay here and let me help you in the morning. Daniel is cruel, and you won't escape from him."

Ben breathed easier when at last she entered his car. He hobbled around to the driver's side. "Does Mrs. Morley have a home phone, so I can call if I have news for you?"

"Our landlady goes to bed early. Let's not bother her." Emily jotted something and handed the slip to Ben. "Here's my number. Call me, and I'll give Jane the message."

Ben dropped them off at the boarding house. "I'll pick you up tomorrow morning at nine and take you out to breakfast. Then we'll work on a plan."

"Good night." Jane walked with Emily into the house.

Would Jane try to run? He couldn't stay awake any longer and his leg hurt worse. He should call his assistant, but by the time George arrived, it would be too late.

Lord, I can't watch her. I put her in your care.

He drove down the road to a motel and checked into a room. Then he phoned Emily. "This is Benjamin Grant. Sorry to trouble you this late, but would you mind checking on Jane and see if she's okay."

"Hold on while I look."

Emily came back a couple minutes later. "Jane's in the bathroom taking a shower."

"Thanks." He bathed and dressed in fresh clothes. Then he swallowed his prescription pain meds. Stretching out on the bed, he nodded off.

*****

Jane waited until Ben had driven away from the boarding house and Emily went into her room. Then Jane stepped into the bathroom and closed the door. She turned on the cold water in the shower. Five minutes later, carrying her bag, she crept to the back door and inched it open. Slipping into the yard, she sprinted down the alley.

She spotted the tail lights of a bus next to the convenience store and ran to the vehicle. The driver had already closed the door, so she pounded on the metal until he opened it.

"We're going to Orlando, is that where you want to go?"

"Yes."

She didn't want to go to Florida, but she could. Her pursuers would conclude that she had got on the New York bus.

The driver wrote on his clip board. "I'm running late, so I'll collect your ticket money at the next stop about an hour from here."

"Thanks. What town is that?"

"Springfield, Pennsylvania."

Grateful for the shadowy interior, she walked down the aisle past several sleeping passengers and found a seat as far from them as possible. Had Ben told her the truth? Was Scott's hired guy, Dan Fuller, ruthless? She shivered.

Could she trust Ben? Then she gasped and turned her bag upside down on the empty seat next to her. One by one she picked up each item and examined it. No GPS. Ben had told her the truth.

At one in the morning, the driver announced, "Springfield."

She stepped off the bus and paid him. She searched for a hiding place. The dark station was locked and the parking lot was darker. The bus pulled away. Too late to climb back on it.

Looking down the street, she noticed a well-lit but rundown motel. She headed toward it. In her foggy exhaustion, she didn't pay attention to her surroundings.

Four grungy-looking fellows came out of an alley and surrounded her. One demanded, "Hand over your bag, and we won't hurt you."

She gripped her backpack tighter but pretended to lower it. "I've got a hundred dollar bill my employer gave me. You can have it."

Jane started to open her bag as one drunken assailant turned to argue with another ruffian. The third one bent over and vomited. She circled around them. The fourth thug grabbed her arm. She twisted and swung her heavy bag at him. He reached for it but staggered. She ran down the street as if a legion of demons chased her.

Her heart raced in her throat. She'd taken first place in cross-country running in high school. God had blessed her with speed. Getting away from the drunken men had been easy, or God had taken care of her again. She ducked between two buildings to catch her breath. A moment later, she peeked out, but no one followed her.

Trust in the Lord. Please help me, God.

By the time she reached the motel lobby, she had a stitch in her side. She tapped on the desk bell several times to rouse someone. A white-haired man stepped into the foyer. He yawned. "What do you want?"

"Do you have a room?"

"Seventy dollars in advance."

Jane still clutched the hundred dollar bill she nearly gave to the assailants.

He mumbled, "I don't have change."

She closed her bag. "If you give me a receipt for this, tomorrow morning we'll settle it."

He handed the slip to her along with the key. She found the room, unlocked the door, and stepped inside. After locking up, she collapsed on the bed.

Lord, I can't go on much longer like this.

Should she have trusted Ben? No, he would have hauled her back to her husband.

*****

Ben answered his phone. "Yes, Emily. Is Jane there?"

"Jane's not here. I can't find her anywhere in the house. Her room's empty. Earlier this evening she used my cell to make a call."

"Who did she call?"

"I don't know."

"Can I look at your phone to see?"

"Sure. Anything to help Jane."

"On second thought, I wouldn't know which calls were yours and which were hers. Could you look through the recent ones and write down the numbers of any you didn't make?"

"Of course."

"It's too late to do anything tonight. I'll phone in the morning for the information."

After ending the call, he prayed.

Lord, help Megan trust someone someday before it's too late.

CHAPTER SIXTEEN

Scott ushered Dan into his home office and sat down. Scott sighed. "I hope your news is important to call me out of bed at this hour."

"I found your wife. Your former investigator has betrayed you." Dan opened his coat pocket and removed an envelope. "Look at these photos."

Taking the pictures, Scott studied each one carefully until he came to one of Ben helping Megan and another woman into a car. Crushing the photo, he screamed, "How dare that man resign from my employ and go after Megan for himself."

"I've seen that happen in my work, so I told my men to follow Ben and Megan."

Scott slammed his fist into the coffee table. "I trusted him and even let him go through Megan's things."

Dan stood. "I'll bring them to you."

"I'm coming with you. Where are we going?"

"Pennsylvania." Dan gathered the pictures and put them in a neat stack. Then he slid them into his pocket. "We might need these to show people when we get there. Don't you have your television broadcast today?"

"Yes, but bringing my wife back and taking care of Ben are more important." Scott opened his desk drawer and picked up a key. "I need to collect a few supplies Megan will need, so make yourself at home."

Scott left the room and headed to the far end of his house. He unlocked a door, moved aside some wood, and unlocked a couple more doors. He ran down the stairs. In the basement, he picked up a pair of handcuffs, a roll of duct tape, some rope, and a small Taser. Grabbing an old briefcase, he opened it and tossed in his provisions.

He picked up a box and took out a larger Taser. He silently thanked his law-enforcement buddies for the police-issued model. As a pastor he could never have marched into a store and bought it.

Laughing, he remembered how he'd purchased the smaller one. He claimed it was for his wife. The salesman assumed it was for her self-defense. What a joke that had been.

"I can hardly wait to punish you this time, Megan." He raced up the stairs and went outside with his new investigator.

Dan slid behind the steering wheel of his old Chevy, while Scott slipped into the passenger side. After they were on the interstate, they headed to Pennsylvania.

Scott grinned. *Soon you'll be all mine again, Megan.*

*****

Early that morning, Ben called Emily. She gave him the number Jane had dialed when she had borrowed the phone. He pressed it in, but his call went to voice mail, so he left a message.

He drove to the convenience store and spoke to the clerk, who recognized Jane's photo.

The worker sighed. "She boarded a bus for Orlando."

Ben wrote the name and number of the bus driver. Then Ben called and described Megan.

The driver answered. "I remember her. She got off at Springfield, Pennsylvania."

"Are you certain?"

"Yes. I was worried about her."

Ben drove to Springfield and parked where the bus would have stopped. He searched the area. Megan had been staying in boarding houses, but at that time of night she might try a hotel. Spotting a cheap one in walking distance, he began his search there.

He pulled in near the office and headed to the lobby. A woman screamed. The shout came from the first section of rooms. Number 102 was the only one with a vehicle in front of it, but Megan didn't have a car.

His heart lurched. They'd found her. As he limped toward the room, stabbing pains in his leg slowed him down. Another shriek pierced the air. Shivers ran through his spine. He worked through the agony to hobble faster and reach her.

Taking out his gun, he tried the door. Surprised to find it unlocked, he pushed it open and stepped inside. Ben spotted Megan with blood on her face as she crawled away from Scott. Splinters from a broken mirror covered the dresser and fallen lamp.

Dan reached for his weapon.

"Don't do it," Ben yelled. "Put your hands behind your heads."

Ben aimed at the two men. "Keep one hand behind your head and use the other to throw your guns on the far side of the bed. Both of you."

Dan did as he was ordered.

"You too, Scott."

"I'm a man of God. I don't have any weapons."

"Dan, toss the weapon that's fastened to your ankle, too."

Scott glared at Ben and stepped toward Megan. "You have no right. She's my wife."

"Stop! Stop right there." Ben didn't waver. "Keep your hands behind your heads."

The men stood at the foot of the bed, the only open space in the small room. Ben needed that area to confine them, but first he had to get Megan out of there.

"Megan, can you come to me?"

Nodding, she pushed herself off the floor and shuffled to Ben.

His leg cramped up on him, forcing him to breathe harder. He should have called in his assistant, but it was too late now. Sweat broke out on Ben's face as he held his position and fought off the pain.

He'd lost a client several years ago by not admitting how bad his wounds were. Pride. By not asking for help that woman had died. He'd refused to admit he needed assistance to keep her safe. Back then, he'd allowed his arrogance to take over and failed to protect a helpless female in his charge. He wouldn't let that happen again.

Keeping his weapon aimed at the men, he reached into his pants pocket and removed his car keys.

Scott growled. "Mr. Grant, you had no right to interfere. You removed yourself from the investigation so you could have my wife for yourself. I'll see that you lose your license for this. I'll make certain that you never have a job in any type of law enforcement ever again."

Ben kept his eyes and gun on her attackers. "Megan, do you want to go back to your husband?"

"Never." She lifted trembling fingers to her cut lip.

"Scott, you need help. Find a good counselor."

"Not me. Megan's the one with the problems. I have a court order to take my wife to a mental hospital for a psych evaluation. She's been depressed and suicidal. She's a danger to herself and others." Scott lowered his hands a little.

Ben yelled, "Keep your hands behind your head."

Scott put his hands back.

"Megan, go to the car and wait for me." Ben handed her the keys.

She reached for them and left.

Scott screamed, "You'll pay for this. I'll come after you and every member of your family."

Ben spotted the handcuffs and the duct tape on the bed. Keeping his weapon aimed on the two men, he picked up the cuffs. "Where are the keys to these?"

Dan glared. Scott smirked. They kept silent.

"Scott, sit down on the floor and lean against the back end of the bed." Ben tossed the handcuffs to Dan. "Let me see your hands while you cuff Scott to the iron leg of the bed."

After Scott was cuffed, Ben ordered. "Dan, get down on the floor." Ben tossed the duct tape to Dan. "Tape your ankles together."

Ben limped behind Dan. Ben put his gun in his chest holster and taped Dan's hands behind his head.

"I'll bet you've never tried to keep a wife in line." Scott glared. "Your woman probably walks all over you."

"Seek professional help before you do something you'll regret." Ben covered Scott's mouth with a piece of tape. Then he slapped tape over Dan's mouth.

Ben took the handcuff key and the two Tasers out of Scott's open briefcase. He picked up Megan's backpack from a chair and tossed it over his shoulder. Leaving the room, he locked the door behind him.

Intolerable throbs burst through his leg as he stumbled to the car. When he reached it, Megan unlocked the door from inside. He slid into the driver's seat.

Her lip was bleeding and a hand print marred the top of her cheek. The red area around her eye started to swell.

Megan burst into tears. "If you hadn't come when you did, I might be dead."

"I thank God, I found you." Ben never understood how any man could hit a woman. Scott was twice Megan's size and strength but so was Ben, and he'd never struck a female.

Ben opened the glove compartment and reached for a package of tissues, which he handed to her. He suppressed the urge to grab his pain medication. He shouldn't take it in front of her for that would make him look weak. "I'm driving you to the hospital down the road. It's not far."

With her hand, she shielded the sun from her eyes. Ben leaned toward her and lowered her windshield visor and then handed her his sunglasses.

"Thank you." She reached for them with a shaking hand.

A few minutes later, they arrived at the hospital. The police photos and reports would take a long time. He didn't want to take up space near the door, so he parked in the visitor's parking lot.

After pocketing the car keys, he turned to Megan. Her lip had stopped bleeding, but nasty bruises were forming on her neck and arms. The seam at the shoulder of her blouse was ripped and a couple of buttons were missing.

He was sorry he'd slept last night. If not, he might have reached her before her husband had. But would she have believed he was trying to help her?

Did she trust him now?

CHAPTER SEVENTEEN

Megan stepped out of the car before Ben could reach her side and help her out. She spotted the emergency room door, a distance away.

She turned to Ben. "Didn't you have a cane with you at the convenience store?" She could use the walking stick to threaten Scott and Dan, if they had freed themselves, but maybe Ben's gun would frighten them away.

He scowled, "Thanks for reminding me." Ben opened the car door and picked up the cane.

Megan shuddered because he sounded annoyed. She angled two steps away from him as they walked down the row of parked vehicles.

Someone screamed. Megan glanced to the left. A woman with three children ran toward them. Megan stopped and looked at the boy, who had cuts on his knees and hands. The two younger girls appeared to be twins. One girl clutched a dirty arm. Blood ran out of the other girl's nose.

"Help." The woman yelled, "My child is bleeding to death."

They had all stopped in the parking lot.

Megan pulled out several tissues from the package Ben had given her. After folding them to make the wad thicker, she went closer to the little girl with the bleeding nose. "Can I stop the bleeding?"

The child nodded. The mother mumbled, "Yes, please."

Megan squeezed the bridge of the nose and covered the youngster's nostrils with the thick tissues. She smiled at the other girl. "What's your name?"

"Megan."

"My name is Megan, too. What's your sister's name?"

"Morgan." The little girl stared at Megan's face. "Were you in an accident, too?"

"Just a little one, but how did you girls hurt yourselves?"

"We were riding our bicycles. Tommy bragged that he was faster and could beat both of us to the end of the road."

The mother put her arms around Morgan. "You aren't allowed to go on that street because it's gravel."

Megan asked, "What happened?"

"We crashed into each other before we got to the finish line. Mommy said if we didn't obey we'd be in lots of trouble."

Megan had disobeyed and got punished for it, too. She lifted her head and searched for Ben. Why had he left? Her heart beat faster. Why would Ben rescue her and then disappear? She had started to trust him, but he'd taken her backpack with all her money. She glanced around the parking lot. People came and went, but not Ben.

A moment later, he limped toward her, accompanied by a nurse. The gloved medical worker carried several wet washcloths.

She spoke to Megan. "Ma'am, you look as bloody and beaten as this little girl. I'll take over so you and your friend can go into the emergency room."

Moving away, Megan turned back to the child and watched the nurse. When she removed the tissue, the bleeding had stopped, so she put a fresh cloth over the child's nose. The nurse washed off the girl's face with a corner of the wet rag.

When Megan was free of Scott, she'd go into pediatric nursing. After she married, he wouldn't let her work in the hospital. When she mentioned it, he punched her and told her to never speak of it again. Six weeks later her bruises were gone along with her hope.

Megan went with Ben into the emergency room and walked up to the desk.

The receptionist handed her a pen and a clipboard with forms to complete.

"Let's sit over there in the corner facing the door." Ben hobbled toward the bench.

After they were seated, she looked down at the papers. With tears in her eyes, she lifted her head. "Scott hit me hard. I'm having trouble reading this. I don't know anything about insurance. He handled it."

"Fill out the papers as well as you can."

Thirty minutes later a nurse called, "Megan Jane Collins."

Megan stood.

"I'll wait for you here." Ben looked toward the main door and then handed her the backpack.

"I'd feel better if you went with me to the examination room." She glanced at Ben's gun which had stopped Scott.

Nodding, he lifted his cane and stood.

They followed the nurse into a small cubical.

"Take a seat on the end of the bed." The nurse read the forms on the clipboard.

Ben sat in the chair next to the bed and rubbed his knee while Megan explained what had happened.

The nurse wrapped the blood pressure cuff around Megan's arm. "Your vital signs are good. Your form says you have no health problems."

The doctor came in and read through the papers. Then he pulled the curtain around her. He and the nurse examined her. "Your ribs don't appear to be fractured but I'll order some x-rays to be sure. I'll prescribe pain medication for you."

After the physician left, a nurse wheeled her to x-ray.

When Megan returned, the doctor came back. "No broken bones, and no signs of a concussion, so we don't need to keep you."

A female police officer arrived. She glared at Ben. "Are you a family member?"

Megan turned to Ben. "Mr. Grant saved me from my husband who did this. I'd like Ben to stay."

He introduced himself and showed his credentials.

The officer wrote down Megan's statement and photographed her face. "I see more bruises forming on your arms."

"I'll step out so you can take the rest of the photos." Ben limped out of the cubicle.

A few minutes later, the officer poked her head into the hall. "You can come back in now."

The officer wrote pages of notes. "Are you willing to file an assault charge against your husband?"

Megan started crying. "That will anger him more, so he will hurt me again. Or he'll be so outraged he'll kill me when he gets his hands on me."

The policewoman patted Megan's folded hands. "I can't guarantee that won't happen, but if he isn't stopped, he may end up killing you anyway."

Megan shivered. She'd lose either way. "Yes. I'll file and sign the charge."

"Good. Then we can start the process of your husband's arrest."

After Megan signed the police report and was released to go, Ben asked. "Are you hungry?"

"Just a little. I haven't had anything to eat since yesterday."

The police officer smiled. "After eating, come to the station so we can set you up with help from social services."

Ben nodded. "I'd be glad to bring her, but maybe we need that prescription filled first."

After collecting the medicines, Megan whispered. "We can eat now."

In the parking lot, she walked close to him as they returned to his car. With her backpack dangling from his shoulder, he opened the door for her.

Ben turned to Megan. "Can you eat a hamburger or French fries?"

"A milkshake?" She whispered.

He pulled into the street and drove a few miles. "Would you like to go inside or through the drive-thru?"

"Will my face frighten anyone?"

"No. The icepack they gave you in the ER reduced the swelling. The cut on your lip is hardly noticeable. There's some black around your eye but it's not too bad. You can wear the sunglasses."

She glanced at his gun. "Let's go inside."

After parking near the door of Hardees, he accompanied her to a booth. "Is this seat okay?"

She sat facing the door and had a clear view of the check-out, too.

"I'll get the food. What kind of milkshake would you like?"

"Vanilla, and some ice water, please."

He limped to the counter. After a few minutes, he turned away from the register with a tray in his hand. His cane clattered to the floor. As he bent toward the walking stick, a drink slid off the tray. He scrunched up his face and twisted away from her. Then he crouched. Wobbling, he lost his balance and nearly tumbled to the floor.

She ran to him and reached for the tray. After setting it back on the counter, she picked up his cane, handed it to him, and turned to the cashier. "I'm sorry we spilled a drink on the floor. Can you bring a mop and give us another cup of ice water, please?"

After setting the new drink on the tray, she led the way to the table. "Thank you for buying this."

The rage that flashed across his face sent shivers down her spine. She wanted to run from his pinched expression and narrowed eyes.

Megan set the food and drinks on the table. Her hands shook as she slid the tray in the rack behind her. "I'll be going now. Thanks for your help."

She had been right. Ben was like her husband. Ben had only pretended to be a nice guy.

Run Jane, run.

*****

Ben tried not to appear angry but mortification consumed him. The woman he'd promised to protect had helped him as if he were an invalid. He hated feeling weak and couldn't rid himself of the shame of being helpless. His stomach clenched. Annoyance had taken over his face.

He lifted a hand in supplication and stepped forward to persuade her not to leave. She jumped away from him as if he would strike her. His heart lurched. He'd broken the fragile trust she'd had in him.

His pride had reigned again. Why had he let his irritation with his injury show? Pain shot through his leg. He could scarcely stand but had to stop her from leaving the restaurant by herself, or Scott would catch her. Humiliating himself again in front of her might be the only way to convince her to stay.

Ben wiped the anger off his face with his hand. He relaxed the muscles around his eyes and lips, and let them settle into a pleasant expression. God told him to give up his pride. Maybe the only way to keep Megan there would be to tell her why he was upset, but a real man didn't admit his pain or weaknesses to a woman, especially not one he'd promised God to protect. Would she trust him again?

Her eyes moved from the floor to the door as if she was ready to bolt.

Ben sent up a silent prayer for help. He'd seen her compassion toward a sick person and an injured child. If he humbled himself and told her the problem, she'd stay. It might be the only way to keep her there and safe. Ben had no idea how many hired men watched the motel or how soon Scott and Dan would escape the restraints.

He hesitated so long she eyed the door again and took a step toward it. He was desperate to keep her there, so she'd be safe. If admitting his flaw stopped her from running off alone and being caught by Scott, he'd do it. That humiliation would be more painful than his knee injury.

Tears formed in his eyes. "Please forgive me." Ben ran a hand through his hair. "I was angry at myself, but not at you. I'm annoyed at my limitations because of this wretched knee injury."

Her eyes moved again from his face to the cane and to his knee. She stared for a long moment. Then she nodded and sat down in the booth. Ben breathed easier when she slid farther in on the seat and picked up her ice water.

Thank you, Lord.

But that had been too easy. Did she fall for every sob story? If he had been one of the bad guys who told her a tale of misery to persuade her to stay, would she have believed that, too? Maybe that's how she had fallen for Scott. She'd been too gullible.

She asked, "Does it hurt badly?"

"Yes." Ben mumbled as he pulled out his handkerchief and wiped his face. Now what? She'd ask about his injury, and he didn't want to talk about it. But if telling the story kept her there, he'd bite the bullet. How ironic. A bullet in the knee had started all the trouble.

"I'm sorry for your pain." She sipped on her ice water.

He smiled at her. "Would you mind if I prayed?"

Without agreeing, she closed her eyes and bowed her head.

He prayed. "Lord, I thank you I found Megan in time and we were able to have her treated at the hospital. Touch her. Heal her. Give her peace. Forgive me for being so proud and not willing to admit when

I'm weak and can't do something. Thank you for this food. Show us what to do next in Jesus name. Amen."

He opened his hamburger, sprinkled salt on it, and closed it. After swallowing a bite, he asked, "Where were you headed when your husband and Dan found you?"

"I don't know. I was trying to get away from you."

His heart tightened. "I'm not working for your husband and will never turn you over to him."

"He always hired nice guys like you to come after me, but seeing you point a gun at my husband makes me want to believe you. "

"There's an Underground Railroad for women who want to leave their tormenters. Have you thought about that?" Ben finished his hamburger.

"I have."

"Your husband and Dan will never give up looking for you." Ben sipped his coke. "If you don't accept some help, your husband might catch you again and throw you in that mental hospital."

CHAPTER EIGHTEEN

Scott grimaced at the torn upholstery in Dan's old Chevy. The seats had been re-stuffed and were comfortable, but Scott loathed their shabbiness.

Dan raised the binoculars. "My car blends in well and is perfect for surveillance."

"You have a point." Scott leaned his head out the open passenger window. "They'll never spot us in this clunker." His eyes moved left and stopped at the old Honda.

Scott pounded his fist into his hand when Megan and Ben had stepped out of the vehicle. "He'll pay for taking my wife for himself." He snapped pictures of Ben holding the door of Hardees open for Megan. "These photos will come in handy to prove Megan's unfaithfulness, but I hope it won't go that far." Scott put the camera down. "Thank God for sending an angel to help us get free so I could see this with my own eyes."

"That was no angel. She was the cleaning lady." Dan tapped the steering wheel. "I'm glad I keep a spare set of cuffs and keys in my glove compartment." He laughed. "You taught Megan a good lesson. Aren't you grateful I sent away all my men when we arrived at the motel, except that one guy as a lookout across the highway?"

Were it not for Dan's hired man, they'd never have caught up with Megan and Ben so quickly. Scott didn't trust most people and wondered how trustworthy Dan's associates were. Scott couldn't take the risk of being threatened or bribed by someone who had seen something he shouldn't have.

"Your wife was alone in the room, so we could handle her." Dan tapped the steering column as if he were nervous. "I tried to find dirt on Ben but only discovered one incident. A woman got shot and killed in Iraq while Ben escorted her as a witness against a terrorist group."

"Could we use that against him?"

"I don't think so. An investigation cleared Ben, but an incident like that might make people question his character."

"As a pastor, I can't divorce Megan. Having her committed would be the best solution, but it looks like she is winning friends who could testify for her. I'll never be able to control Megan again, especially if Ben has been influencing her."

"There's always a way to regain power over your wife." Dan pulled out his wallet and opened it to a photo. "Look at my wife. She was beautiful."

Scott stared at the picture. "I'll bet you had to keep the men away from her."

"That's what I've been trying to tell you. Once Megan is out there in the world, it'll be difficult to keep her away from other men. But you can always get her back and turn the situation in your favor."

"How?"

"You'll have to be stricter and need to hurt her grandma, not permanently, just enough to make the old woman suffer. Then Megan will do everything you say. Too bad you don't have children. You can always use the kids to make their mother mind."

Scott frowned. "Dad was a preacher and kept Mom in line by whacking her a few times so she never misbehaved. A Christian husband forces his wife to obey for her own good."

His mother had never run away like Megan had, but his mom obeyed much better than Megan did. His mother practically bowed before their father whenever they were in public. Too bad some folks misinterpreted her submission.

Scott turned to Dan. "If a man doesn't take charge of his wife, she'll be tempted to stray. Her eternal soul could be in danger."

"I had no idea we were responsible for their souls."

"Hebrews 13:17 says we must give an account to God on how we care for their souls. If Megan is having an affair with that private investigator, I need to stop it and convince her to ask forgiveness so she'll be saved from eternal damnation." Scott kept his eyes on the windows of the restaurant.

Dan asked, "Did anyone in your church ever accuse you of being too strict with Megan?"

"No. I'm the perfect husband according to my members."

Dan hit the steering wheel. "Once I hit my wife too hard. A broken rib punctured her lungs. I had to take her to the hospital, which was hard to explain."

"One of my deacons was trained in torture to obtain information from hostiles during the war. He taught me some tricks to keep Megan under my control without leaving noticeable marks." Scott removed a business card from his jacket pocket and handed it to Dan.

He glanced at the card. "That sounds like something handy to know."

"A few times I lost my temper and failed to follow the correct technique."

"What happened?"

"I had to keep Megan hidden until the bruises disappeared." Scott looked out the window again. "Tell me everything you learned about Benjamin Grant."

"He was a Special Forces Captain and the best shot in his company. He can take out two guys bigger than he with a few blows." Dan exhaled loudly. "Now he's too religious, but I don't know how that can work to our advantage."

"What are you talking about? He's not a pastor."

"He lives his religion by working in a soup kitchen, helping the homeless, and teaching Sunday school. He's in charge of something like the Christian boy scouts and even done missionary work."

Scott clenched his jaws. No Christian man could ever be that saintly. Ben Grant had to be a hypocrite. Grabbing the binoculars, Scott peered more closely at Megan and Ben. "They're getting up. Let's see if they leave together."

*****

Ben suppressed a shudder. No one deserved what Megan had suffered, no matter what she'd done. Dating and long engagements should be mandatory to understand each other before the wedding. He had learned that lesson the hard way while overseas. His fiancée, Charlotte, had slept with half the men in his unit before they shipped out. His friends told him about her indiscretions. When she broke off the engagement, he was relieved but also bitter and wanted nothing to do with any female.

But then he repented and gave his heart and life to Christ. God took away his resentment. Ben hadn't trusted any woman for over a decade until he met Megan.

He hobbled along next to her. After opening the door of his Honda, he waited for her to get inside. Using the car as a crutch, he limped around to the driver's seat. His leg throbbed, but he didn't want to take pills in front of Megan.

Pride had won again. No, he wouldn't let it. He had to purge himself of his disgusting pride so Megan would trust him.

He swallowed his pride and opened his mouth. "Can you take that bottle of pain tablets out of the glove compartment and hand me two, please?"

She gave him the tablets with a bottle of water. The smile she sent him turned his humiliation into a victory.

"Here's my phone. Call Cindy and ask her to meet you. Maybe we can hide you until everything is settled."

She took the cell phone. After leaving a message, she returned the device to him.

Ben pulled out of the parking lot and into the street. He adjusted the rearview mirror and glanced out the side one. Changing lanes, he looked out the mirrors again.

Megan asked, "What's wrong?"

"It's nothing."

"I know when something's troubling a man." She whispered, "I walked on eggshells for fifteen years. So tell me."

"It looks like Dan and your husband are behind us. I never thought they'd follow us after you signed that report."

"Nothing will ever stop Scott."

"Couldn't God stop him?"

"Yes, but God doesn't go against a man's free will. Scott chooses to mistreat others. God can change Scott's heart, but he has to want to change."

Ben handed her the phone again. "Phone that police officer who gave us her number. Then call Cindy again."

"The female officer didn't answer, but I left a message." After Megan had hung up, she pressed in Cindy's number and explained her husband was following her. Megan listened and then ended the call. "She and her group must be pros. They have a covert contact in the local police station. We should park in front of the building, go inside, and ask for Helen Chalk. She'll drive me to a safe house. Then a couple of uniformed officers will escort you to your car to protect you from Scott and his hired man."

He could take down a preacher and a flabby private investigator, but he kept his mouth closed. He'd let the police escort him, if it would help Megan to keep trusting him.

CHAPTER NINETEEN

Scott gripped the door handle of the car and stared ahead. "Move closer to them. Maybe we can force him to stop, so I can take Megan."

"They might see us and call the police."

"Get as near as you think you can." Scott leaned forward.

"They had to leave together because there was only one car left in the parking lot."

A few minutes later, Ben parked behind the police station.

Dan pulled into an adjacent lot facing Ben's Honda. "What do you want me to do now?"

Scott cursed. "What the …?"

Ben escorted Megan into the building.

Then two uniformed officers accompanied Ben outside to his car.

Scott growled, "Where's Megan? Did you see where she went?"

Dan picked up the binoculars and scanned the area. "She didn't come out of any of the other exits."

"What's she doing in there?"

"Maybe she's filing that police report. The motel is in this town. We're in their jurisdiction." Dan dropped the binoculars.

"Megan would never sign a police report. She knows I'd thrash her for that." He growled, "What are those police officers talking to Ben about?"

"Something's wrong. I don't like this. We're leaving." Dan started the car. "I'll follow Ben."

"Good idea. When I get home, I'll call my police contacts in Memphis. They owe me and will tell me what happened to Megan in this station."

Two officers marched to Dan's vehicle.

One glared at Rev. Scott Collins, "We have some questions for you."

The officers escorted Scott into the station.

*****

As soon as Megan went into the police station, a female officer with a nametag that read, 'Helen Chalk,' whisked Megan into a broom closet and locked the door.

"Sorry for the hurried welcome, but the ladies restroom isn't safe." Helen switched on the light.

Megan whispered, "Cindy assured me I could trust you to take me to a shelter."

"I've read your file. I'm taking you to a transit home."

"My husband followed us here."

"He's a fool and won't get away with this. A couple of officers will bring him into the station for questioning."

Helen handed her what looked like a police uniform. "Put this on."

"Isn't it illegal to wear this?"

"It's not an official uniform. It's a costume used for parties."

Megan shuddered. With trembling fingers, she reached for the trousers and stepped into them. Then she slipped into the jacket and buttoned it.

Helen lifted an old suitcase off a shelf and stuffed Megan's backpack in it. "We picked this up at the thrift store and keep it on hand to transport belongings of victims." Helen snapped the luggage shut and turned off the light. Then she opened the door and picked up the suitcase. "Follow me to the side exit." She stopped in front of the door and turned to Megan. "Wait here until I bring my vehicle to this exit. Then step outside and hop in. After we start moving, take off your hat and slide to the floor."

Megan watched for the vehicle. Seeing it stop, she went outside and climbed inside. When the locks clicked, her heart thudded faster. She couldn't catch her breath. A few minutes later, she peeked out the window. She shuddered as they drove past the motel in Springfield, Pennsylvania, where her husband had beaten her. She slumped to the floor, removing her cap.

The van stopped a short while later.

Helen announced, "We're here." She opened the side door. "No one followed us. You're safe for now."

Safe? Would Megan ever be safe again? On trembling legs she stepped out of the van at the curb in front of the last house in the cul-de-sac. She wiped sweat off her face, looking around the middle-class subdivision. Single-storied wood and brick homes with mowed lawns and mailboxes lined the streets.

Helen took Megan's arm and guided her up the driveway, past an older car, and to the back of the brick home.

A middle-aged woman opened the door. "Hello. I'm Sylvia. Please come in."

Sylvia and Helen looked like they could be related. Both ran their fingers through their short, bleached-blond hair. They had brown eyes and were a few pounds overweight.

Megan followed Helen into a yellow-tiled kitchen, past a round table with chairs and a china buffet. They went down a short hall and into a living room with wall-to-wall tweed carpeting.

"Please sit down." Sylvia smiled. "I'm pleased to meet you, Megan Jane. Or what would you like me to call you?"

"You can call me Megan." She sat on the couch.

Helen sat next to her. "I'm a volunteer with the support group, but I'm also a police officer. Whenever a victim needs immediate transport to a safe house, I take some time off. Cindy called and filled me in. You'll need to keep out of sight for a couple of weeks until your face heals. I'll have to take the costume back with me when I go."

Sylvia sat in a recliner. "Half the men in this town are the bad guys."

Megan shivered and started crying.

Helen put her arm around Megan. "There are surveillance cameras around this building and the perimeter of the yard for your protection. Do not go outside for any reason. Don't worry. The house is safe."

Megan's mouth dropped open. That was hard to believe. She'd never been able to hide from Scott. No place had ever been secure. He'd always found her.

"Some years ago, they caught the police chief beating his wife. He learned the address and security code for the shelter, where his wife hid. He broke in and almost killed her. Her brother rescued her in time. The chief had given the code and number to other men who tortured women. One of them murdered his wife. All of those guys still live in this town, so our organization disbanded the shelter." Sylvia leaned forward. "When the case went to court, the chief had lots of character witnesses. Without prior arrests, the judge gave him only two years in prison, even after the hospital records proved he'd been beating his wife for years."

Scott had friends in politics and law enforcement to help him. He'd never allow his image to be ruined. Megan crossed her arms and rubbed the goosebumps.

"This place was established after that and is the safest transit house in the city. The cameras outside will catch anyone prowling around. When you're feeling better, and after we've secured new identity papers for you, we'll move you to a permanent location."

Megan stared a moment too long at the scar that ran down Helen's face.

The officer patted her deformity. "This is what my husband gave me as a going away gift. He tried to kill me, and in the struggle, I stabbed him. He's dead and won't ever hurt anyone else again. Too bad it had to end that way, but he never changed and kept coming after me."

Would only death stop a man from torturing his wife? Megan stopped crying and breathed easier. These women understood her and what she'd been through. She trusted them.

But she didn't believe for one minute she was safe.

CHAPTER TWENTY

When Scott marched into the police station, he shook hands with all the men as if he was on a campaign for re-election. He'd been on television every Sunday, so most people recognized him.

The officers escorted him into a room and read him his rights.

Scott's eyes filled with tears. "I lost my temper and hit my wife. I was worried and frustrated because it had taken so long to find her."

The female officer asked, "How many times have you hit your wife?"

"I'm so sorry." Scott didn't want to talk to the tough-looking female, but he needed to convince all the officers. "I hit her only one time. She fell against the table and landed on the floor." He wailed loudly, "I didn't mean to hurt Megan. I lost control."

Scott squeezed tears out of his eyes and sniffed. His interrogators lowered their eyebrows and uncrossed their arms. He had convinced them of his sincerity.

Later as he and Dan walked to the car, Dan pressed in a number on his cell and listened. "Thanks. Keep your eyes open." He slid the phone into his belt. "After the officers ushered you inside, I contacted my associate who has been tailing Ben."

"Great work. Where is he?"

"He was driving on the highway headed toward Memphis but stopped in a hotel to spend the night." Dan asked, "Where do you want to go?"

"Let's keep driving toward Memphis."

Dan shook his head. "I'm amazed at how quickly you were released."

"I know judges, police chiefs, and lawyers across the country, so it didn't surprise me when they let me go. What amazed me was how quickly Megan disappeared inside the police station. Did you see any signs of her? What did you hear when you looked around?"

"She didn't come out of any of the exits. I've called my associates to check it out. Looks like things are falling apart."

"No." Scott grinned. "Everything is falling into place perfectly."
*****

After spending the night in a hotel, Scott and Dan were on the road early the following morning.

Dan's phone rang and he answered it. Then he frowned as he ended the call. "My associate reported that Ben pulled into your church and is waiting in the parking lot."

Scott cursed the most despicable words uttered by man and profaned God's name.

"What's wrong?" Sweat broke out on Dan's brow. "Does he have a gang of men waiting for us at the church?"

"He follows the Bible. He's planning to confront me about sin."

"What sin are you talking about?"

"Some people expect Christians to love all brothers and sisters. Ben wants me to turn the other cheek when Megan angers me."

"What about disciplining wives so they repent to save their souls from eternal damnation?"

"Guys like Ben believe it's possible to do that without violence, but I don't. Force is the only way to keep a wife in place."

"My dad beat me every day, so I minded him. That's how to make women and children behave." Dan moved into the fast lane.

"Remember back in the motel when he advised me to seek professional counseling. That was a brother to brother warning."

Dan cocked an eyebrow. "Brother to brother?"

"Christian to Christian."

"Is there a law in the church that could force you to turn the other cheek?"

"Not the church," Scott laughed, "But God has laws about it."
*****

Ben sat in his Honda and studied Scott's colossal church, so much like King Solomon's Temple in Jerusalem. White marble walls shimmered with golden swirls. Sparkles ran down the length of the magnificent pillars supporting the roof over the portico. How much money had the extravagant building cost? Ben wasn't against a church being attractive to entice outsiders, but where did it stop?

And Scott had to be stopped, but the wheels of justice rolled slowly. It might take a long time before he was behind bars. Ben prayed Rev. Collins would repent and seek the professional help he needed.

Ben opened his Bible to the Sermon on the Mount and read. Then he flipped over to Matthew 18:15-17 and meditated on the words. Ben prayed. God confirmed what Ben needed to do.

Cindy phoned and assured him Helen Chalk had taken Megan to a safe house. Ben's job was finished, except to admonish Scott, the biblical way.

Lord, give me the right words.

Then he prayed for Scott's heart and soul.

*****

Scott cursed again as Dan pulled into the parking lot.

"You seem to know something that I don't." Dan stuffed the keys in his pocket. "Have you told me everything? Does Ben have his ex-army men inside who will take us out? Should I bring my heavy artillery?"

"Guns are useless in his kind of confrontation." Scott growled, "No one has ever pulled this trick on me."

"What's going down?"

"Let's go in and get this over with."

"I don't understand what's happening. What can I do?" Dan asked.

"This is between Ben and me. He'll not strike a blow or take out his gun. It would spoil the conflict." Scott opened the car door. "Men like him believe in two or more witnesses."

"I don't understand. We've got to keep things quiet."

Scott hesitated before moving. "Ben wants everything out in the open. If that's the way he wants to play it, I can go by his rules, too."

Dan checked his gun. "Let's go."

"You'll be my witness." Scott stepped out of the car and slammed the door. "We'll take care of him."

Scott and Dan marched up the marble steps between the massive pillars. They went into the wide circular foyer that ran around the gigantic church. The gold carpeting was supposed to make people feel they entered a celestial sanctuary, like Heaven. Scott thought the golden interior was necessary to keep up his image.

He nodded at the receptionist and secretary, who sat behind desks. Then he turned to Ben, who stood at attention as if he were still in the Army.

"Come into my office, Mr. Grant, so we can talk."

"I'd like the secretary and the receptionist to hear our conversation." Ben held up his phone with the photos he snapped of Megan. He showed the pictures first to Scott and then turned to the ladies. "This is what Mrs. Collins looked like after her husband beat her."

The receptionist started crying. The secretary hung her head and sniffed into a handkerchief.

"I'm a private investigator." He showed them his credentials. "I found Megan Jane Collins in a motel room with her face smashed and bloodied. She was crawling away from her husband and this man. I drove her to the hospital for treatment. Then she filed an assault charge against Rev. Collins."

Dan raised his fist and took a few steps toward Ben. "You have no right to accuse Rev. Collins."

Scott put his hand out and stopped Dan. "There's no need for fighting. Everyone knows I'm a man of peace. I abhor violence."

"Do you know why I've come?" Ben asked.

"Yes, you've come to warn me, brother to brother, with a scriptural admonition."

"We can all lose our temper at times. I've done it, but I praise God I didn't hurt anyone. I wrecked my car, smashed the television, and broke my phone. These could all be replaced, but the life of a loved one can never be restored." Ben lifted his palms in supplication. "I'm begging you as a Christian to stop, step down from the position of senior pastor, and seek counseling before you do something you'll regret."

"I appreciate your concern." Scott moved closer to Ben and extended his hand. "Thank you for your visit."

After Ben left, Scott spoke softly to those in the foyer. "You are witnesses that I, as a good Christian turned the other cheek to that man who is trying to ruin me. And he, too, was in the motel room with my wife." Scott headed to his office. "Come with me, Dan."

After they were inside with the door closed, Scott yelled, "How dare that hypocrite judge me, the man of God. He seduced my wife and now he's threatened to take my church. He must be stopped."

CHAPTER TWENTY-ONE

Ben drove to the neighborhood where he'd grown up. He parked in the driveway outside the attached garage to the brick home. He spent a moment admiring the thick, lush lawn that he mowed a few days earlier.

His mom opened the kitchen door and hugged him. "Come in and have some coffee. I've leftover apple pie from the church potluck."

He sat at the table. "Thanks, Mom."

She set the plate and coffee in front of him. "The national news was terrible. I'm glad you warned me. They showed a picture of Mrs. Collins's face after her husband beat her."

"Rev. Scott Collins hired me to find his wife. By the time I reached Mrs. Collins, he'd already found her and hit her, so I drove her to the hospital." He dug into the pie.

"My friends at the Bible study were shocked that Rev. Collins would mistreat that cute little wife of his. On television, they hold hands all the time."

His mother's innocence never surprised him. He took a sip of coffee. "I helped her file a police report."

"That's good. He'll be arrested and not hurt her again."

"The police questioned Rev. Collins and released him." Ben shook his head. "He's angry and threatened me. Promise me you'll keep the doors locked all the time. Your security system is sound. If anyone calls and asks for me, you don't know where I am. Hang up. Don't stay on the phone. Call me and tell me that someone asked for me, and I'll be right over."

His mother wrinkled her brow. "Does this mean the pastor has some way of listening to our calls?"

"It's possible, so we shouldn't talk in detail on the phone. We've done this before. God took care of us. If you need me to come right over or believe you're in danger, what do you say?"

"I watched Jeopardy."

"Why do we use that as our secret code?"

She giggled. "Because I never watch Jeopardy."

"Would you do something for me, Mom?"

"I love helping you in your work." His mother's brown eyes sparkled and she leaned closer, like a co-conspirator. "What would you like me to do?"

"Watch all the news, so you can update me. Rev. Collins is a popular preacher, and I want to know what he tells the public. I might be busy protecting Mrs. Collins, so I'll depend on you to keep me updated."

"I'll be glad to do it."

Ben leaned back in the chair and put his hands behind his head. His mother would stay closer to home. She'd keep the doors locked and watch the news. He appreciated her sharp mind. She had used the code only once, and that had been a false alarm. He'd been grateful he'd always told her as much as he could about dangerous cases he worked on.

Mrs. Grant finished her coffee. "Why did she marry him if he was so bad?"

"I had the impression Mrs. Collins didn't know him well before the wedding, and Rev. Collins wanted to marry quickly."

"Your father waited four years for me. If a man loves a woman he's willing to spend time with her and wait, no matter how long." She pushed her cup away. "Girls rush right into a relationship without paying attention."

"You're right about that." Ben finished his coffee and went to the door. He checked the lock and the security code. "If you're in danger, what's the word?"

"I watched Jeopardy." His mother laughed. "I don't have old timers' disease yet."

"I'll see you tomorrow." He bent and kissed her cheek.

*****

Scott stared out the window of Dan's old car as they tailed Ben out of the suburb where Mrs. Grant lived. "Run him off the road." Rage rushed through Scott energizing him.

"That's foolish. You'll be in more trouble."

"Haven't you ever been so angry you wanted to kill someone?" Scott pounded his fist into the dash.

"Yes, and the judge ordered anger management classes." Dan stayed a few car lengths behind Ben.

"I'm paying you, so run him off the road."

"I don't want to go to jail and would rather beat him up in a dark alley one night."

"That works for me, but right now I'm mad and need to hurt him. Bump him a couple of times."

"Will you pay for the damage to my car?"

"We'll ditch this vehicle. You can report it stolen. I'll buy you a new one."

Dan's car sped faster down the road and crashed into Ben's Honda. Bam!

"Do it again."

"It looks like he's calling someone on his cell." Dan shook his head. "We need to leave before the police arrive. We can't be caught in this car."

Scott screamed. "Do it again!"

Dan crashed into the back end of Ben's car a second time and pulled away. A siren wailed. "Let's get out of here."

Scott glared. "I'm still angry. Teach Ben a lesson and put him in the hospital for a long time."

*****

Ben glanced in his mirrors and recognized Dan's old Chevy right behind him. Ben dialed 911. The second crash echoed louder. He pulled onto the shoulder, jumped out, and reached for his gun.

Dan's vehicle roared past him and drove off the exit ahead. As Ben waited for their return, a state trooper pulled up behind Ben's Honda.

An officer stepped out and approached Ben. "What happened?"

"An old brown Chevy, license number ZA561 crashed into me twice. I recognized the driver, Dan Fuller, and the passenger, Rev. Scott Collins."

The trooper walked around the damaged vehicle and ran his fingers over the crushed back end. He rubbed off paint chips. "Brown.

Can I see your identification to complete the report?" After the trooper finished the paperwork, he returned Ben's documents. "I heard you were the one who found Mrs. Collins and drove her to the hospital."

"I resigned from Rev. Collins employment when I suspected he hurt her. Then I felt responsible for locating her for him. By the time I'd reached her again, he'd already beaten her."

"Someone started a rumor at the station that you were after Megan Collins for yourself, so you left Rev. Collins's employ." The officer frowned. "My former partner knows you from the army. Your reputation is solid and you're well liked. Be careful. Rev. Collins has friends and associates in places you'd never imagine."

After the officer drove away, Ben called his mom. He didn't want her to hear the news from a stranger.

When she answered the phone, he asked. "Mom, are you locked inside?"

"What kind of a greeting is that?"

"Rev. Collins followed me and tried to run me off the road. I'm fine, but my car's banged up. Keep the doors locked. I'm on my way there. I love you."

Scott's anger was escalating, so what was his next move?

CHAPTER TWENTY-TWO

Jane drove Mrs. Baker to the beauty shop for her weekly shampoo on her first day of caring for the older woman. While her patient sat under the hair dryer, Jane ran next door to the pharmacy. She pulled out her new driver's license and studied the photo. Then she reached for a box of brown hair color and a tube of matching mascara. After paying, Jane walked back to the salon to pick up Mrs. Baker and drive her to the doctor.

On the road home, Mrs. Baker asked, "Do you think you'll like it here in Pigeon, Arkansas?"

Jane turned into the quiet suburb. "Yes, it's a nice little town."

"My daughter is on the board of governors for the support group. I'm happy she found you to care for me."

"I'm glad I was sent to you." Jane patted the older woman's hand.

When they arrived at the house, Jane colored her hair. She rinsed it and lifted strands through her fingers. Studying it from all angles in the mirror, she smiled. It resembled her original shade before Scott turned her into a blonde. She wrapped a towel around her head, so she wouldn't frighten the older woman when she woke from her nap.

The phone rang and Jane answered it. "This is Cindy. We hired our private investigator to interview former members of Scott's church. Several of them contributed large quantities and never received income tax statements of their giving at the end of the year. If we find enough evidence, we'll turn it over to the IRS. They can audit the church's books."

"Scott always had a deacon check out the financial records."

"He should have hired an outside auditor. I don't like to stay on the line too long, so we'll talk again. Use your innocuous e-mail to send names and addresses of members who might be willing to help. Be careful and stay safe."

"I'll e-mail that information to you."

The recliner squeaked, indicating Mrs. Baker was awake.

Jane ended the call and dashed down the hall to the living room. "Mrs. Baker, are you ready for supper?"

"Did you wash your hair?"

Jane unrolled the towel. "Yes, I wanted to change it back to its original color."

The older woman grinned. "It looks nice."

"Did you have a good nap?"

"Yes, I always sleep well after I've been out. I like to go somewhere every day. I hope you don't mind."

Jane had minded, but Scott would never find her in Arkansas. Nor would he kidnap her while she was in the company of someone. Not unless he'd become so desperate he'd carry her off no matter the circumstances, but she'd keep Mrs. Baker's schedule as diversified as she could. No regular trips anywhere.

"What do you want for supper?"

Mrs. Baker leaned forward. "Do you like fried chicken?"

"I do, but I don't know how to make it."

To keep her figure, Scott wouldn't let her cook or eat fried foods. He wouldn't even allow her a plate of them at a church social.

"It's late and I don't want you slaving over a hot stove. Run down to Kentucky Fried Chicken and buy two dinners. I'd like the original fried chicken, mashed potatoes, gravy, biscuits, and coleslaw. You order what you want, Jane dear."

Scott had never allowed her to go out at night, except to church with him. She wasn't comfortable driving in the dark by herself, even just a mile down the road to Kentucky Fried Chicken. What if he found her there, alone?

Jane smiled. "Let's go together, Mrs. Baker. It won't take more than thirty minutes to drive there, wait for the order, and come back with it. It's a lovely night. We'll go in the drive-thru and watch the stars while we wait."

"You sound like a romantic." Mrs. Baker sighed. "I love going out, but I don't do it often, especially at night."

By seven o'clock they had returned home and were sitting at the dining room table feasting on fried chicken.

Mrs. Baker wiped her mouth. "That was fun. We'll have to do it more often."

Jane wanted to do it less, but it hadn't been scary going with Mrs. Baker. They'd stayed in the car with the doors locked. Jane lowered her window to pay and collect food at the drive-thru.

"I enjoy having you here with me." Mrs. Baker finished her iced tea. "It looks like there will be leftovers for lunch. Does that sound good?"

"Yes, it does. What would you like to do tomorrow?"

"I like to play bridge. If you take me after lunch, my lady friends and I play until supper time."

"Would you like me to leave you and pick you up later?"

"Yes, you'll be free from one o'clock until five. You can do whatever you like."

That would give her four hours of library time to research nursing classes.

*****

Scott Collins sat on his wife's side of the bed. He held a cashmere sweater to his nose and breathed in her fragrance. "Megan, Megan, why did you leave me? Why are you causing all these problems? I tried to love you even when you were bad."

He had received a court summons. The church members were suing him to give them access to the accounting records. Scott had phoned his attorney, who told him that the members were within their rights. His attorney promised to file an opposition and have it delayed as long as possible.

The telephone rang and Scott answered. "Hello."

"I found Benjamin Grant's weakness." Dan chuckled. "It's his mother."

"Tell me about her."

"She had two surgeries last year, but she's doing better. She lives alone, but her son stops by every day to see her unless he's away on a case. He has two older sisters, but they're both married and live across the country."

"When can you pick me up?" Scott folded the sweater and put it in the drawer.

"I'll be there in thirty minutes."

When Dan arrived, Scott was pacing in front of his house. He climbed into Dan's Chevy. "You got here fast. I'll charm Mrs. Grant into telling me where Ben is, then we'll have Megan."

"I programmed Mrs. Grant's address into my GPS. It'll take us fifteen minutes to reach her house. What'll be our approach?"

"I'll introduce myself and hope she has seen my pleas for Megan on television. I'll tell her how much I love my wife and want her back. I'll appeal to her maternal sense and beg Mrs. Grant to ask her son to help me find Megan."

Nodding, Dan turned into a middle class subdivision. He glanced at a mailbox on the side of the road. "It looks like this is Mrs. Grant's house."

Dan parked in front of the brick home. He and Scott stepped out of the vehicle and strolled up the cement walk to the front door. Scott rang the bell.

*****

When Ben's phone rang, he answered. "Hey, Mom. How are you?"

"I watched Jeopardy."

"I'm on my way."

Ben hung up and dialed 911. He reported a possible intruder at his mother's house. When Ben arrived, he spotted the black and white police car in front of his mom's home. His heart raced as he pulled into her drive and limped to the steps. Using his spare set of keys, he unlocked the kitchen door.

He hobbled inside and smiled at his mother, who served coffee and cookies to two officers.

"Are you okay?" Ben hugged her. "What happened?"

She handed her son a cup of coffee and started to explain. "The doorbell rang. I looked through the peephole and saw Rev. Scott Collins from television and another gentleman, so I called you."

One policeman set his empty cup down. "We received a call that a possible intruder had entered your mother's home."

The second officer stood and put his police cap on. "We need to go. Thanks for the refreshments, Mrs. Grant."

Ben walked them to the door. "I appreciate you coming. Rev. Collins threatened my family and me. I was afraid he'd carried out his threat when he came here."

"We were in the area and didn't mind stopping to check on your mom." He saluted. "See you around, Captain."

After Ben walked the officers outside, he went back in the kitchen. "It's close to supper. Let's go to Long John Silvers."

"Give me a moment to pick up these cups and get ready."

"I'll take care of the dishes while you change."

A few minutes later, Mrs. Grant came out of the bedroom wearing a flowered dress and carrying her purse. She held up a brown sweater. "Is it cold outside? I haven't been out all day."

"Bring your wrap. It might be a little chilly in the restaurant."

He checked the windows and locked the doors. Then he reached for his mother's arm and walked her to the car. After she was seated, he limped to the driver's side. Sliding behind the wheel, he groaned as a spasm shot through his leg.

His mother clicked her tongue. "You need to take care of that knee and see a doctor."

"I'm planning to do it as soon as Megan is safe."

"Speaking of Megan, I was surprised to see her husband standing outside my door, ringing the bell as if he came to call. But why?"

"He wants to use you to get to me. He hopes you'll tell him everything about me and learn where Megan is hiding." Ben pulled into traffic. "The man is a bully. He'd rather hurt a woman than come after me, man to man. I'm the one he wants because I stopped him in the middle of beating his wife."

His mother scowled. "I got a good look at him and that other fellow through the window. Rev. Scott isn't as handsome as he is on television. I guess they put a lot of makeup on him in front of all those cameras."

Ben chuckled. "Did they show any signs of aggression?"

"What do you mean?"

"Did they pound on the door or shout ugly words to you?"

"No, they ran to the car when the siren sounded."

"Thank God for that."

"Do you think they'll come back?"

"I'm not sure. They may, but Rev. Collins might call you first. If he telephones, tell him that you don't know where I am."

"That's the truth. I never know where you are. You and those policemen sure got here in a hurry."

"I'm glad. I'd like you to move in with me. Or would you prefer if I stay with you?"

"I'd love to have you live with me, but you do what's best."

Ben parked his car and went around to the passenger side. Cupping his mother's elbow, he accompanied her into the restaurant. He had offered to take her to the best seafood restaurant in Memphis, but she always wanted Long John Silvers.

Ben settled his mother in a booth before ordering their meals. After setting a plate of shrimp and fish in front of her, he handed her plastic ware, napkins, and a lemonade.

He sat opposite her and prayed. Then he picked up his napkin. "I've met some bad characters on my jobs and moved out of your place because I didn't want to put you in danger." Ben swallowed several bites of fried fish.

"That's why I worry about you." His mom sipped her drink.

"Don't worry. Keep praying. Rev. Collins wants me to take him to Megan. Let's stay in our own homes a couple of nights until he makes his next move."

"I like living in my own home."

"I know, Mom, but if I think you might be in danger, I'll move you to a secure location."

"Are you talking about a safe house with Megan? I'd like to meet the girl."

"I don't know where she is." Ben wiped his mouth.

Hopefully, Scott didn't know where she was either.

CHAPTER TWENTY-THREE

Ben hobbled into his driveway and waved to his next-door neighbor. As he headed to his car, sheer agony, like an electrical charge, burst through his knee and leg. He tottered and tumbled to the ground.

The neighbor lady ran to him and knelt by his side. "What happened? Can I help you up?"

"My leg slipped out from under me. I don't think it'll bear my weight." He groaned, "Now I need surgery whether I have time or not. My phone slipped out of my hand. Do you see it?"

She picked it up and gave it to him.

"I need to call a friend to take me to the hospital."

"I'm free and can drive you."

"Thank you."

On the way to the emergency room, Ben phoned his assistant. George had been his friend since their tours in Special Forces. They had watched each other's backs so many times they'd lost track. Ben often employed his former sergeant to help him with cases.

A few minutes after Ben arrived in the ER, George stepped into the cubicle. Ben waved his associate forward. An older nurse assisted Ben into a wheelchair. He rubbed his knee. "I'm going to a private room. One of the orthopedic surgeons had a cancellation, so I may have surgery as early as tomorrow after they run some tests."

"What will the surgeon do?"

"I've agreed to a total knee replacement. It never happens this quickly, but the doctors have been urging me for the last year to have it. They've kept everything up to date and taken it for granted I'd agree." He exhaled loudly. "I never thought it would come to this, but I can't walk anymore."

The nurse pushed the wheelchair into the hall. "We're going to the second floor, Mr. Grant."

George marched beside Ben. "Captain, it looks like it's got to be done."

They stopped at the elevator and George held the door open for them. His scarred face and huge nose intimidated most people, but underneath that rough, homely exterior was the heart of a saint. The corners of George's big lips opened to reveal an even set of white teeth. His wide grin put everyone at ease.

The nurse pushed the chair out of the elevator on the second floor and into a vacant room. She transferred Ben to the bed and left.

"I'm glad I kept you informed about the Megan Jane Collins case. Once I started searching for Megan, it didn't take long to find her. Then the evidence indicated her husband had hurt her, so I removed myself from the case. Now that she's installed in a safe house, maybe I won't be needed again. Scott Collins threatened me and went to Mom's house, but she didn't open the door to him." He whispered, "I can't protect Mom if I'm here in the hospital."

George patted his concealed weapon. "You have my word. I'll keep her safe."

"I'll phone Megan's contact and tell her what's happened to me. If Megan needs to be moved, you can do it for me." He shook his head. "I haven't called Mom to tell her I'm in the hospital. Can you see her and let her know? I don't want her coming here by herself."

"Sure." George stood. "Anything else, Cap'?"

Ben mumbled, "The meds they gave me are kicking in and I'm rambling."

"I've never known you to wander, even under duress." George paused in the doorway. "How much does Reverend Collins know about you?"

"He knows everything including my time overseas in Special Forces, which means he can hire equally trained professionals to come for me. After I resigned, Reverend Collins commissioned Dan Fuller. Try to learn everything you can on Dan."

"Don't worry. I'll take care of it."

Ben could trust his friend no matter what happened, so Ben let the medications take over and closed his eyes.

*****

Three days after surgery, Ben packed up to go to his mother's house. He shoved the crutches under his arms and clumped over to the closet to collect his clothes. He layered the garments in his suitcase. Then he opened the bedside table, tossed his toiletries into his overnight bag, and zipped it closed. He would put all his energy and focus into getting back on his feet. His goal was to resume work in six weeks.

George came into the room and reached for the suitcase. "Are you ready?"

"Yes. How's Mom?"

"Eager to have you home."

The nurse rolled a wheelchair to his bed. Ben sat in the chair. Then she pushed him outside and applied the brakes to the wheels. Ben slid into the passenger seat while George stowed the crutches and bags in the back.

"Mom will take me to physical therapy every day until I can drive. Twice a week she'll be at her Bible study. Would you mind taking me Monday and Thursday?"

"Glad to do it."

After a short ride, George parked in Mrs. Grant's drive and collected the crutches. Ben had already stepped out of the car and stood, using the door for support. Taking the crutches, he clomped into the kitchen.

Mrs. Grant threw her arms around her son. "I'm so glad you're here. Dinner is ready. George, I hope you're staying to eat with us. I cooked prime rib, mashed potatoes, and peas."

"We're hungry, aren't we George?" Ben hobbled to the table and pulled out a chair. He enjoyed being with his mom, but he didn't want her to wait on him.

"I'm glad you came to your senses and had the surgery. I'm thrilled you'll be staying here so I can look after you. It'll be like you're a little boy with mumps again."

"I can hardly wait." Ben rolled his eyes at George. Then he turned back to his mother. "Has anyone stopped or called?"

"Just my friends from church. I didn't think you'd want to know about them." She went to the oven. "I baked a blueberry pie for dessert."

"You shouldn't have gone to all that trouble, Mom."

"It's fun cooking for men who have good appetites."

After dinner, Ben limped to the living room and sat down in his dad's old lazy-boy. Raising the foot rest, Ben reclined to elevate his leg. Megan was safe, and there had been no other visits from Rev. Collins. He closed his eyes. Physical therapy exhausted him, but he was determined to recover in record time and get in better shape.

The phone rang. Mrs. Grant answered it. "Hello." Her jaw dropped, and she shook her head as she handed the phone to her son.

Ben reached for the receiver. "Hello."

The voice sounded pleasant. "This is Rev. Scott Collins."

"How can I help you?" Ben pressed the speaker button.

"I heard you were staying with your mother after surgery."

George went to the window and pulled the curtain to check outside. He shook his head slightly.

Rev. Collins enunciated each word as if he preached to a crowd. "I must apologize for Daniel's wild driving. I tried to stop him, but he was angry. I'd like to pay for the repairs."

"Thank you. I'll send you the bill."

"I'm calling about my wife. I lost my temper, and I'm sorry I hit her. I'd like to see Megan so I can apologize."

"I left her at the police station."

"Where is she?"

"I don't know."

"Isn't she looking after you?"

"Looking after me?" Ben furrowed his brows. "I don't mix business with my personal life."

"You aren't working for me anymore and she's an attractive woman."

Glaring at the phone, Ben breathed deeply to control the level of his voice. "Megan is a married woman, and you are a former client. I keep those relationships professional."

"I apologize if I offended you."

"No problem." Ben paused. "Is there anything else?"

"No. Good night."

After the call ended, Ben turned to his friend. "Would you help me to my room?"

"At your service, Captain." George walked behind Ben down the hall. "This reminds me of when you were shot in that knee years ago and shuffled around on crutches."

When they were in Ben's room, he sat on the bed. "Close the door."

George shut it without making a sound. Good old George had been the best scout Ben ever had and could creep up on the enemy without anyone suspecting.

Ben's mouth twisted in worry. "I don't trust Scott Collins. He knows about my surgery and that I'm here with Mom. I may not be able to drive, but I can threaten an intruder and defend Mom." He opened the drawer of the bedside table and reached in the back. He lifted out a box of ammunition. "Would you go to my car and bring in all my weapons? Put them in the overnight bag that's in the trunk to carry them into the house so Mom won't see them."

George returned with the sack and set it on the bed. "Anything else?"

"Take a look around the perimeter when you leave and see if anyone is watching the house. Call me and let me know if someone follows you."

"I'll keep you informed."

"I'm depending on that."

After George left, Ben loaded his guns and placed them within easy reach.

He could shoot well enough to wound an intruder without killing. Ben hoped he wouldn't need to injure anyone.

CHAPTER TWENTY-FOUR

Jane spread icing thickly on the chocolate cake. Then she licked the knife, her fingers, and lips. She'd always enjoyed baking, but Scott had tried to keep her thin by forbidding her from making desserts. Since leaving him, she savored the freedom of baking pastries and licking a bowl of frosting. Cooking for Mrs. Baker's sweet tooth satisfied both of them. Jane's dress size increased to an eight, and she was comfortable with it.

Whenever she drove Mrs. Baker to the beauty shop, her sister's home, or a bridge party, Jane went to the library to study nursing. No one checked the GPS to make certain she'd traveled the right number of miles. She stopped saving her receipts because no one demanded them. Her new independence was intoxicating and nothing could make her go back to Scott.

She'd bought soft-pleated skirts, matching blouses, and loose sweaters at the Goodwill. Scott would never look for her there. She'd despised the form-fitting dresses he'd forced her to wear. The uncomfortable, straight skirts had showed off her hips and emphasized her legs for Scott's viewers. Never again would she let any man tell her how to dress.

"I enjoy going out to lunch with you, Mrs. Baker."

"It's fun to dress up and eat at elegant places." Mrs. Baker powdered her nose. "I'm so glad we're going to Sally's today."

After a short drive, Jane parked and accompanied Mrs. Baker inside. Jane settled the older woman in a chair at the linen-covered table. She handed Mrs. Baker a menu and then admired the antique tables, old paintings, and heavy brocade drapes. "I love these renovated homes. They give me ideas for when I can have my own place one day."

"The owners worked hard turning this into a restaurant. They have a lovely gift shop downstairs if you want to buy home décor."

"I'll check it out some other time." Jane looked down at the menu again. "What would you like, Mrs. Baker?"

"My usual, egg salad on white bread. What are you having?"

"Turkey salad with cranberries, apples, and pecans on whole wheat. I like to try different foods."

"The way you go about living reminds me of someone who got out of prison and suddenly experienced freedom."

"That's how I feel."

"I've never had to go through that, but my daughter did. I saw what that monster did to her. I'm glad you got away from the brute after you."

"I feel so free today I'll order a spinach salad on the side."

"Yuck." Mrs. Baker wrinkled her nose and then grinned. "But I like your style."

Jane was learning to like herself as God made her. That was hard to do after being told how stupid, selfish, and ugly she was for so many years.

Sometime after they arrived home, Cindy called. "Our investigator has been checking the contacts you sent, and lots of figures don't add up. Your husband's personal income is not tax-exempt. If he's embezzling money, he's putting it someplace. We'll find it."

"Scott did all the income taxes and filed them jointly as a couple. He forced me to sign papers, but he wouldn't let me see them."

Cindy exhaled loudly. "Would it be too painful to write down everything Scott did to you?"

"It might be cathartic. I'll start and see where it goes."

After Jane hung up, she got out her pad and pen. She tapped her chin with the pen. There had been so much cruelty. Where should she start?

*****

When Jane woke each morning, she checked on Mrs. Baker, who liked to sleep late. But a few weeks later, when Jane went into the bedroom, an unknown chill stirred the air. She rubbed the goose bumps on her arms as she went to the bed. Staring down at Mrs. Baker's chest, Jane saw it no longer rose or fell. Her mouth fell open as she searched for a pulse, but the cold body had no signs of life.

Mrs. Baker had a smile on her face and looked as if she was in a wonderful place. Jane looked around the bedroom. Everything seemed to be in place, like it always was. The bell and the phone were in easy reach, so Mrs. Baker hadn't tried to get out of bed or call anyone. The elderly woman must have died peacefully in her sleep.

Jane dialed Joyce's number. "Hello. When I woke a few minutes ago, I went into your mother's room as I do each morning. She wasn't breathing. I'm sorry, but she's gone."

"What?" There was a pause on the other end of the line, followed by a sob. "I'll be right there."

By the time Joyce arrived, Jane had finished her morning chores. She accompanied Joyce into the bedroom.

Joyce kissed her mother's cheek. "You look happy, Mom. I'm sure you're in Heaven with Dad."

After Mrs. Baker's body was taken, Joyce sat down at the table and started sobbing again.

Jane poured tea. "I'm so sorry. I loved you mother, too, and enjoyed her sweet personality. What can I do to help?"

Joyce's shoulders shook. "The arrangements for mother's funeral were completed last year when she nearly died. I need to call her sisters. I'd like you to get the house ready and make the beds for them."

"Would you like me to go to a motel?"

"Goodness no, I need you to stay here and take care of my aunts. They can't drive, so you'll have to use mother's car to buy anything you or my aunts need. I'll give more details later."

*****

Benjamin's phone rang. He answered. "Hello."

"This is Cindy. How's it going since your surgery?"

"I left the crutches long ago, but I'm still in rehab. I can drive but haven't been released by the doctor."

"Jane's employer, Mrs. Baker passed away in her sleep. She was well-liked, and her family is expecting lots of guests at the funeral. I don't think Jane's husband would try something in front of a crowd, but I like to be cautious."

"I'll send my colleague to keep an eye on Jane."

"Our organization will pay for bodyguard services."

"Great, the man I'm sending is a family man and will appreciate it. What's the address?"

"345 South Main Street, Pigeon, Arkansas. The service is the day after tomorrow at 2:00 at Smith and Waters Funeral Home."

When Ben ended the call, he phoned George and explained the situation. "I'd like to go with you and stay in the car to keep watch."

"You shouldn't travel anywhere yet. You need to take care of yourself. If you return to work before the doctor releases you, then you could injure yourself." George hesitated. "And we don't want your mother to worry."

"You're right, but I hate to admit it. The doc says I can increase my walking to fast pacing next week. He told me that jogging would be a good compromise for later since it's between low impact walking and high impact running."

"You'll soon be in great shape, but for now, I'll go and keep Megan safe."

His sergeant was the best and would protect Megan.

*****

Jane glanced in the full-length mirror and studied her black dress, which she'd bought at a thrift store. The conservative outfit seemed perfect for Mrs. Baker's funeral. Most of the guests who attended would be dressed in dark colors, so Jane should blend in well.

She went into the living room where Mrs. Baker's two sisters waited. "Is there anything you need before we leave?"

"No, Jane. You've done a great job taking care of us."

"It's time to go." Jane picked up her purse and took out her car keys.

She helped the two older women into Mrs. Baker's ancient Buick and drove to the funeral home. Then she pulled into the parking lot and escorted the ladies into the building. They walked to the front toward the open coffin and stayed there for the visitation. Their shoulders slumped as sobs shook them, so Jane suggested they sit down. Family and friends came up and talked to them. The aunts needed help moving around, so Jane stood nearby with a walker to assist.

Before the service started, Jane turned her head to see the visitors that packed the sanctuary. There were too many people. She couldn't tell the strangers from the guests of the family.

At the end of the ceremony someone came and escorted the two sisters with the other family members to the back to shake hands with everyone. Then Jane accompanied them to the gravesite. Reaching the cemetery plot, she glanced around at the crowd of people who attended the funeral. After family and friends were gathered, the elderly sisters sat under the awning with the other relatives.

Jane stood off to the side with several members of Mrs. Baker's church. The clouds covered the sun. She shuddered at the dark sky as a creepy sensation swept over her. An unexpected gloom from the horizon sent tingles up and down her spine. She couldn't shake the feeling that an evil presence had taken over. Looking at the relatives and church friends, Jane didn't see any threat. Still the spine-tingling sensation of menace made her shiver again. In slow motion, she moved her head from left to right to see everyone who had come to the gravesite.

He was there. Her heart raced. No, it couldn't be him. Her breath came out in ragged gasps as she struggled for air. She was seeing things. No she wasn't. She saw her husband standing with a group of men opposite her. He wore his suppressed angry look and the smile that said he was about to punish her. She couldn't stop shaking.

Run Jane, run.

CHAPTER TWENTY-FIVE

Jane's leg muscles tightened as she slipped out of her high-heeled shoes. Where was Ben? Cindy had called and told her that Ben would provide protection, but he wasn't there. Megan had started to believe him, but no man could be trusted. When would she get that through her thick head? She was on her own again.

Scott wouldn't do anything as long as the ceremony went on, but the graveside service was about to finish. His cold, blue eyes sent quivers up and down her backbone. She spotted the goon, Dan, who had held her while Scott hit her in the motel room. She searched the cemetery for a path of escape through the crowd.

Not far to her right, she caught a glimpse of a stocky African-American, who seemed out of place among the expensively dressed white men. He appeared particularly dangerous as he patted the bulge under his arm and beamed with perfect, white teeth, but lots of assassins smiled on television before they killed. Her heart pounded.

Lord, give me strength to outrun these men.

When the service ended, Scott took a step in her direction, and so did Dan. Fear clawed at Jane's heart and dropped to the souls of her stocking-clad feet. The dark-skinned man's jacket flew open as he turned to Dan. Seeing the holstered gun, Megan shivered. Shrieks filled the air. "He's got a gun. He's got a gun." Men knocked over chairs and shouted. "He's got a gun. He's got a gun." Women scattered around her and darted off in every direction.

The African-American knocked out Dan and another guy, and then the heavy-set man screamed. "Run Jane, run."

And she ran. Jane sprinted toward the cemetery entrance. When she reached the first paved road, the asphalt nicked her feet. She thanked God the blacktop wasn't hot. She didn't care about her hose, but the longer she ran, the more the pavement sliced her soles and slowed her down. Hearing a struggle to her right, she glanced in that direction. Her guardian angel wrestled with another goon, who dropped to the ground. How many men had her husband brought?

She'd hesitated a moment too long. Scott had nearly caught up to her, but her rescuer was right behind Scott. As her husband reached out to grab her, she swerved away. Out of the corner of her eye, she saw her angel punch Scott with one hard blow. Wham! Her husband fell to the ground.

The angel yelled, "Go to your car. I'll hold them off until you get away."

Jane had parked in the nearby handicapped spot for the elderly sisters. She reached in her purse and found her keys as she ran. She pressed the button to unlock the door and jumped into the driver's seat. Then she remembered she was supposed to take Mrs. Baker's sisters back to the house. She opened the window and looked around for Joyce.

Her employer waved at her and yelled, "Go."

Jane's hands shook as she jammed the key in the ignition and started the engine. She kept looking in the mirror during the drive to Mrs. Baker's house. Fifteen minutes later, she pressed the remote for the garage and drove inside. When the door closed, she crossed her arms and put her head down on the steering wheel to catch her breath.

Why, Lord?

After her heart rate slowed to normal, Jane dashed into the house. She had been collecting nursing books and extra clothes but she stuffed only the bare necessities into her backpack. How could she run? Mrs. Baker's car and a taxi could both be traced.

The phone rang and kept ringing. Where had she put it? She had carried Mrs. Baker's cell with her in case she was separated from the older ladies, and they needed to contact her. She found the phone in her black purse, which she had dropped on the kitchen table.

"Hello." Jane's voice wobbled.

"Are you okay?" Joyce asked.

Jane held the phone with both hands to stop it from shaking. "Yes, I'm at the house. How are your aunts?"

"I'm bringing them back. Four men are lying in the grass. Mr. Grant sent the guy with the gun, so he is coming with us." Joyce paused. "Since your husband knows where you are, it's no longer safe to stay here. You'll have to move again, and I'm sorry. Keep the doors locked and the security system on until we arrive."

Jane's heart plummeted as she paced up and down the hall. She should leave before they came, but where could she go?

Twenty minutes later, the bell rang. Jane jumped. Then she took a few deep breaths to calm herself. She went to the door and peered through the peep hole. Jane let Joyce, her aunts, and her black angel inside.

"I'm glad to see you're safe." Joyce put her purse on the table.

Jane wasn't out of harm's way. Her husband was only a few miles down the road. She wanted to trust her Lord and not be afraid. She recalled a verse from her grandmother's Bible. *Put your trust in the Lord. Do not be afraid. What can mortal man do to me?*

One of the aunts announced. "We're going to our rooms to change out of our church clothes." They both left.

Joyce hugged Jane. "I told my aunts that your husband is a bad guy and had hurt you. They knew my own husband beat me."

Jane smiled at her angel.

The African-American man saluted. "George Washington Cunningham, the third, ma'am, former sergeant under Captain Benjamin Grant, at your service. Ben sent me to protect you because he's recuperating from emergency surgery."

"Please sit down." Joyce smiled. "Would you like some coffee?"

"Yes, thanks." He sat. "Ben's been putting off surgery until he collapsed and couldn't walk. He's had a total knee replacement."

Jane gasped and covered her mouth. "He was in pain the last time I saw him."

George reached for the cup Joyce offered him. "I couldn't secure any associates to help me guard you. When I arrived, you never left my sight. I stayed hidden so I wouldn't stand out among all those fancy dressed folks."

Jane blinked quickly to suppress the tears. "I thought Ben had abandoned me."

"Captain Benjamin Grant is the most faithful guy I know. He'd never walk out on anyone. If he couldn't keep his promise he'd send someone like me to take his place." George grinned.

"How long will he be laid up?" Jane asked.

"He's recuperating at his mother's home so she can look after him. He didn't want to call and tell you because he thought you'd worry about him, especially after Scott and his hired man showed up at his mother's home when she was home alone."

Jane's mouth fell open. "Scott went to Ben's mother's house?"

"Yes, ma'am."

"Is his mother alright?"

"His mother is fine."

Jane put everyone around her in danger, and she had no right to do that. She should go off someplace by herself so no one would be hurt.

George's smile disarmed her again as he handed a pair of black heels to her. "I picked these up after I'd taken down those guys."

He had knocked out four guys bigger than he, helped her escape, and then went back for her shoes. He really was an angel. "Thank you. I'm sorry to put you to so much trouble." Taking the heels, she noticed his wedding ring and smiled.

"It's no trouble. Glad to help out while the captain is recovering. It's hard to keep Ben down. He wanted to come but the doctor hasn't released him."

"My husband must have waited until everyone arrived at the graveside before climbing out of his vehicle."

"I had my eye on him and Dan the whole time, but I didn't know any of the men with him."

Tears filled Jane's eyes and she sobbed. "What chance do I have of ever being free of him?"

When the doorbell rang, Jane leaped out of her chair. "Oh no. It's Scott. He's found me."

The blood pulsed in her temples as she glanced toward the door and listened to the voice inside her.

Run Jane, run.

CHAPTER TWENTY-SIX

Jane put a hand on her chest hoping to slow her racing heart.

"Stay here. I'll take care of it." Joyce left the room. A few minutes later she returned with an elderly gentleman. "This is Mr. Smith. He's come to take you to your new home." She hesitated. "I need a moment to speak to my aunts. Would you excuse me?"

George pulled out his phone. "Ben's been worried about you and is at home praying."

"May I speak with him?" Jane leaned forward.

"We don't know if the calls are monitored so talk briefly. Don't give him any details. When I see him, I'll explain everything."

Nodding, Jane took the phone. "Hello. How are you? I'm sorry about your knee. Are you feeling better?" She paused to listen. "Thanks for sending George. He saved my life. I'll be praying for you. Goodbye." She handed the phone to George.

He opened his briefcase and lifted out Megan's grandmother's Bible. "When Ben searched your bedroom for clues, he found this."

She reached for it and clutched it to her chest. Tears filled her eyes. "Thank you."

"Don't thank me. Ben collected it from Scott."

Joyce came back with pillows, clothes, and a wig. "We'll disguise you as an elderly woman so you can leave in Mr. Smith's vehicle." She tied a couple cushions around Jane before slipping an old-fashioned dress over them. Joyce shook out the gray curls and then adjusted the wig on Jane's head. "Mom wore this one when she didn't have time for the beauty shop."

Jane glanced at her caring friends in the room who had helped her. She thanked God that she hadn't run by herself. She wouldn't have escaped.

"It's time to go." Joyce pushed a wheelchair toward Jane. "Sit down. I'll go with you to Mr. Smith's car."

"She's my wife, so I'll do it." Mr. Smith winked at Jane.

Jane hugged Joyce and her aunts before sitting in the wheelchair. "I appreciate your help."

Joyce put Jane's backpack behind her in the chair, wrapped her in a shawl, and covered her with a blanket.

Mr. Smith rolled the chair out to his truck and helped Jane into it.

Then he climbed into the vehicle and backed out of the driveway. "It doesn't look like anyone is following us."

He drove the rest of the afternoon. At dark, he pulled into an old barn next to a country house and turned to Jane. "Leave your disguise on until we're inside. We don't know who might be watching. You'll spend the night here. My wife has our guest room ready for you."

After helping Jane into the wheelchair, Mr. Smith rolled it up the walk and into the kitchen. He closed the door and slid the bolt. Then he kissed the gray-haired woman on the cheek and said. "This is Myra, my wife."

The older woman smiled at Jane. "It's nice to meet you."

Jane stood from the wheelchair. "I forgot my bag."

"I need to go out and check around before I lock the barn, so I'll bring it." Mr. Smith opened a drawer and picked up a flashlight. He turned to his wife. "Lock this after I leave."

"I'm sorry to be so much trouble." Jane frowned.

"It's no bother. We volunteers expect a few problems."

They may have planned on a little difficulty but certainly not all the trouble Jane brought. Myra put her arm around Jane's trembling shoulders as they peered out the window into the dark. Jane prayed that no one hurt the sweet old man as he walked around the house.

A few minutes later, Jane shuddered at the click of locks. How many more people would she place in danger?

Mr. Smith came into the kitchen. "There's a car parked down the road." Taking out a phone, he punched in a number. He put the cell to his ear. "I think we were followed," and hung up.

When the phone rang, Mr. Smith listened and handed it to Jane.

Cindy said. "Your husband broke the restraining order you filed, but he and his accomplices had left the cemetery before the officers arrived. Scott's becoming more desperate and behaving irrationally."

Jane asked, "What if he's in that car down the road?"

"Don't worry. Mr. and Mrs. Smith are experienced workers."

Could the elderly couple deal with violent men like her husband? She shivered.

"I'll call back in the morning with a plan, but we'll keep you safe until your husband is behind bars for a long time." Cindy ended the call.

"You look tired. I'll show you to your room." Myra led the way.

If Scott waited down the road, he might lose his patience and break into the house. Jane should put on a disguise and sneak away so no one else would be in danger, but where could she go? The old farmhouse and barn were the only buildings on a large plot of land out in the country.

Jane examined her feet during her shower. Several deep cuts on her soles still bled. She dried off, slipped into her nightgown, and put a dress on over that.

The clatter of dishes in the kitchen told her Myra hadn't gone to bed, so Jane tiptoed there. "Excuse me, do you have some antibiotic cream and bandages for my feet?"

"How did you hurt them?"

"I slipped out of my heels to run faster on the asphalt and get away from my husband."

Myra handed Jane a first aid box. "Sit down. Clean and bandage them while I make some herbal tea."

Jane lifted the cover and picked up an antiseptic swab to clean the wounds. She spread antibiotic ointment on the cuts and covered them with bandages. She slipped on a pair of socks to hold the dressings in place.

Myra set the cup of tea in front of her. "This will help you relax."

As Jane sipped on the hot drink, she started yawning. Exhaustion slowed her movements. She wouldn't have gone far on injured feet that night. Limping to the sink, she set her teacup down.

"Good night. I'll pray that God blesses you." Jane treaded lightly to her room to avoid shifting the dressings on her feet.

Before she fell asleep, she stroked her grandmother's Bible. Opening the book, she turned to a well-marked passage. *In God I trust.*

I will not be afraid. What can man do to me? Lord, protect and bless everyone. Amen.

The Lord had taken care of her, keeping her one step ahead of Scott. Sliding under the covers, she shivered at the thought of him catching her. Jane tossed and turned. Her mind raced through her near capture in the cemetery.

Scott was probably waiting down the road for her.

*****

Voices came from the hall. Jane's eyelids flickered open to sunshine that lit up her room.

She examined her feet, much improved but still sore. After dressing, she applied concealer on the dark circles under her eyes. Then she patted on foundation and brushed on some mascara. She tiptoed to the kitchen and stopped in the doorway. Jane stared at a woman in a security guard uniform with a holstered gun and another lady.

Why the security? Jane shuddered. Were they expecting a shoot-out? She'd never liked guns, but Scott had several of them hidden in the house.

Mr. Smith poured coffee. He pointed to the second female, who resembled him in height and features. "This is our daughter, Maryanne. She clerks for a judge."

Maryanne took butter and milk out of the refrigerator. "It's nice to meet you. This is my friend, Peggy, who's a security guard." She handed Jane a paper bag. "This is your new disguise."

"Thanks." Jane reached for the sack. "I'll get ready."

"No, sit down so you can eat breakfast." An apron-clad Myra stood at the stove. "By the time you finish your first cup of coffee, the food will be ready."

Jane needed caffeine to wake up and stay alert. So she did as she was told and took the hot drink.

Maryanne asked, "How long did you know Scott before you married him?"

"Just a few months. He wanted to marry right away so he could apply as a pastor for a church. The committee wouldn't approve a single minister. I wanted to spend more time getting to know Scott, but he became upset when I suggested it."

"We've learned from others it's best to spend at least two years with a man to observe how he treats others before getting involved."

"That sounds safer than marrying someone after a couple of months." Jane sighed.

Maryanne lifted the cranberry muffins out of the baking tin and set them on a platter. "You'll be leaving with us. The vehicle from last night is still parked down the road. If the driver follows, he'll think twice before going into a government building."

"I don't want to put anyone in danger."

"We understand, but sometimes you have to let other people assist you, so you can help others. Like when you helped the little girl in the culvert at the pharmacy." Peggy grinned. "Did you know you were on television that evening?"

"No, I didn't. What happened to the child?"

"The doctor treated her for dehydration and a head injury. Her stepfather hit her, so she hid in the sewage pipe. You saved the girl's life. The police thought you had stolen Megan Jane Collin's driver's license. The anchor woman announced an unknown woman rescued the child."

Maryanne teased, "You should be more careful when you stop to save someone's life. You were on the news again when you gave CPR to the gentleman having a heart attack."

"Jesus would have stopped to help." Jane smiled.

Peggy sipped on her coffee. "It's good you disappeared after both incidents."

Myra set platters of ham and eggs on the table before sitting next to her husband. He took his wife's hand and prayed aloud.

Then Peggy passed the muffins. "Rev. Collins has a lot at stake. When this is over, he'll have lost his wife, his church, his work, his career, and his livelihood. He may go to prison for a long time."

"He's convinced everyone that I suffer mental breakdowns." Jane took a muffin. "Sometimes, it looked like I had a problem from the drugs he gave me."

Maryanne gasped. "He gave you drugs?"

"Yes, he claimed the doctor prescribed them." Jane wiped away a tear. "No one forced me to marry him, so I reaped what I sowed."

"That's a lot of reaping for making one mistake by marrying the wrong guy." Mr. Smith scowled.

"No one deserves to be mistreated. Our organization is compiling a manual to help women avoid these blunders." Peggy sighed.

Mr. Smith brought the coffee pot to the table and refilled the cups. "Ephesians chapter four says we shouldn't be deceived like little children who are tossed about by every lie and false doctrine, by the sleight of men and their craftiness. Jesus talked of men who show signs and wonders to deceive God's children. Some might pretend to be Christians to meet a nice girl."

The doorbell rang. Everyone at the table jumped up.

"Come with us." Maryanne grabbed Jane's hand.

Peggy pulled out her gun. Jane stiffened.

Mrs. Smith moved a cupboard away from a wall. "We're going down into the basement."

Jane's heart pounded. No. No. No. Not the basement.

CHAPTER TWENTY-SEVEN

Jane's heart thudded so loudly, she feared it would give away their location. Gripping the rail, she stumbled behind Mrs. Smith and her daughter down the stairs. Jane had no reason to be afraid of the basement. It couldn't be anything like Scott's cellar.

The door banged shut behind her. Jane tripped and would have fallen forward if Peggy, walking after her, hadn't reached for Jane to prevent her spill.

A loud click, and then bright lights illuminated wall-to-wall carpeting, cushioned furniture, a large television, refrigerator, microwave, exercise bicycle and treadmill. They had stepped into a safe haven not a torture chamber.

Seeing a bathroom off to the left, Jane asked, "May I use your restroom?"

"Yes, make yourself at home." Maryanne smiled.

Jane went in and splashed cold water on her face. She breathed deeply several times to calm herself.

When she returned to the group, she saw that Mr. Smith had joined the ladies.

Maryanne patted the empty place next to her. "Sit down. Your husband and another man came to the house."

As Jane sat, she shook from head to toe. Even her lips quivered. Jane breathed easier when Myra hugged her.

Mr. Smith leaned forward. "Don't worry. I left the chains on the door when I spoke to Rev. Collins, who claimed that you are dangerous to others and yourself and need to be admitted to a mental hospital."

"Your husband and his men are watching all the doors, but we have to leave." Peggy checked her gun. "We're carrying out the original plan, and you're coming to work with us."

"I'll take Jane upstairs and help her get ready." Maryanne stood. "Bring the van to the side door."

In her room, Jane slipped into the pair of tight jeans and a low-cut tank top that Maryanne handed her. Jane put her sneakers on and tied them.

After adjusting the red wig on Jane's head, Maryanne picked up Jane's bag. "Peggy knows how to use that gun and will do it if someone is in danger. We won't let your husband get you. Don't worry."

But Jane worried an innocent person might be hurt. Maryanne took Jane's hand and led her to the kitchen where the others gathered. Peggy went to the side door. "The vehicle is five steps from the house. I'll lead the way and unlock the van. It's good that you're short, Jane, so when Maryanne and her parents surround you, no one will see you. Go inside and stay on the floor."

Jane walked the few steps to the van and got in. When the door slammed shut and the locks clicked, Jane let the air out of her lungs. When would she ever be safe?

The motion of the van jolted Jane backward. "Is the car still parked there?"

Maryanne had taken the front passenger seat and glanced back out the window. "I see the license plate, so I'll call a police friend to stop the car so we can get away."

Peggy looked in her mirrors. "It's turning around to follow us. Are you okay back there?"

"Yes." Jane pressed her sweaty palms together. "How soon will the police be here?"

Maryanne chuckled. "A cruise car is pulling the vehicle over now."

A half hour later, Peggy parked in the employee lot behind the courthouse. "We'll escort you inside."

When they were in the building, Maryanne led the way down the hall. "Peggy needs to report in to work, so I'll help you change." They went into the ladies room. Maryanne locked the door. Then she handed Jane a brown wig, red lipstick, and a purple and pink dress.

Maryanne changed into her clothes and glanced in the mirror. "We look like a couple of gypsies."

Jane adjusted the wig and straightened her skirt. "I've worn so many disguises to escape from my husband, I forget from one to the next. I always discard them so I don't mistakenly wear the same one twice."

"That's smart."

They left the restroom and strolled past Peggy, who whispered, "Drive carefully. Call me when you arrive."

Maryanne escorted Jane to an old Chrysler. Jane climbed into the passenger side and buckled her seatbelt. Then Maryanne slid behind the wheel and pulled into traffic.

After they were on the interstate, Maryanne turned into the slower lane. "We found a new job for you. One of our supporters has an elderly father who had a heart attack. The doctor released him from rehab yesterday. He needs someone to cook, clean, and drive him to doctors' appointments."

"It sounds like a position I'd enjoy. I've had lots of experience caring for the elderly." Jane kept her eyes on the side view mirror. "I thought someone followed us earlier, but I was mistaken."

"Someone was, but I lost him. No one's been behind us for the last hour." Maryanne turned off the expressway. "Most of our volunteers were either rescued from brutality or had family members and friends who were."

"I'd like to help one day if I ever am free of Scott."

"You will be."

They arrived in St. Louis, Missouri, at dark.

Maryanne pulled into the driveway of a wooden-framed house in a quiet suburb. "Several lawyers are working hard on your case."

"I appreciate it. Scott is powerful." Jane shivered. "He has money, colleagues, and position."

"That doesn't matter. God is with us. Our lawyers are smart and on the side of the law."

Jane shuddered at what Scott could do to her as long as he was free. But even in prison, he would find a way to harm her. Unless he changed, as long as he lived, he could hurt her.

******

A male groan woke Jane in the middle of the night. Where was she? She wasn't gagged and handcuffed, so Scott hadn't caught her. She switched on the light and looked around the lilac bedroom. The loud moan came again. Sliding out of bed, she opened her door.

A man shrieked. Jane raced down the hall. Dashing through the open door of Mr. Adler's bedroom, she followed the beam of the night lamp to the bed. The older gentleman wrestled with the bedsheets, so she untangled them.

Touching his shoulder, she whispered, "Mr. Adler, wake up. You're having a bad dream."

His eyelids blinked open. "Who are you? Are you an angel?"

"No, Mr. Adler, I'm your new caregiver. I arrived last night. You nodded off, so your daughters helped you to bed. Then they went home."

"May I have a drink?"

Jane poured water from the pitcher on the bedside table and put a straw in the glass before handing it to him.

When he finished, she reached for the tumbler and set it on the stand. "Good night. I'll see you in the morning."

"Good night, angel."

Relieved to be in a safe place, she went back to bed and slept well.

At eight Jane woke and needed coffee. She went to the kitchen to make it. She picked up the jar of instant on the counter and read the note. "For Dad. He can't have any caffeine."

Hearing Mr. Adler's snores, she peeked into his room to check if he grappled with his bed covers again. He slept soundly, so she went into the kitchen and searched in the cabinets for regular coffee. When she found it, she opened the can and brewed a small pot. Mr. Adler's daughters told her to make herself at home and eat anything in the house, so she made cinnamon toast.

Jane had just sat down to eat when Mr. Adler, still in his pajamas, ambled into the kitchen.

"Good morning, angel."

"Good morning." She stood up. "How did you sleep?"

"Slept like a log."

"What would you like for breakfast?"

"Grits, scrambled eggs, sausage, and coffee." He turned away. "We get dressed first."

Without a housecoat, Jane had been accustomed to slipping into her clothes while in someone else's home.

Her older patients often needed more time to dress, so she sat back down and finished her breakfast.

Two hours later, she turned her head to the doorway where the scent of Old Spice cologne grew stronger. Mr. Adler stepped into the kitchen and sat at the table.

"I'll make your breakfast." Jane rose. "Would you like your coffee first?"

"Coffee is supposed to come with the food."

"What's the plan for today?"

"Angel, can you drive me to my brother's house?"

"When would you like to go?"

"Ten o'clock."

"That gives me time to wash a load of clothes and clean the kitchen."

"You truly are an angel, aren't you?"

After Jane finished her chores, she checked out the car.

Mr. Adler joined her in the garage and ran a hand along the shiny finish of his vehicle. "I love this Cadillac. I wish I still had my license."

"Don't worry. I'll drive you wherever you want to go."

When they were buckled in their seats, Jane gripped the wheel with both hands. "This is a big car." She drove out of the garage.

"I like large cars. They're safer."

During the ride home, the older man laughed. "I didn't think I'd enjoy having a caregiver, but I like having a pretty chauffeur, gorgeous cook, and an angel to bring me water in the night."

Turning into the driveway, Jane asked. "What would you like for supper? I can make baked chicken, fish, or meatloaf."

"I'll eat anything you cook."

After they were inside the house, he turned on the television. "I like to watch the Big Valley before supper." He sat down in his recliner in the den.

If Jane had been born fifty years earlier, she might have married a nice man like Mr. Adler. His brother and friends had been just as accommodating and pleasant.

Where had all the gentlemen gone?

*****

Scott slammed the receiver down, yanked the church phone out of the wall, and hurled it across the room at a bookcase with glass doors. Splinters flew on the furniture and carpet.

"How dare that judge order me to produce the church accounting records?" He strode up and down the room and screamed curses.

The church secretary ran into the office and squatted to pick up the sharp fragments. "Can I do anything for you?"

"Just leave me alone," he shrieked.

She tiptoed out of the office.

Sometime later, two men in dark suits marched into Scott's office. They showed their badges to Scott. "We're from the FBI and have a subpoena to seize both the church's accounts and your personal records."

"You have no right to do this." His jaw clenched.

"The independent auditor found evidence that someone embezzled funds from the church." The FBI agent put his badge away.

"My wife stole the money."

"There is no indication she had access to any of the accounts."

"I didn't do anything. Everyone knows my wife is mentally unstable, and I can prove it."

"Some of your church members reported they never received the tax receipts for many of their donations."

Gritting his teeth, Scott turned to his secretary. "Give the church records to these officers."

The younger agent reached for the books. "We need to follow you to your home to collect your personal accounts."

After they left Scott's house, he speed-dialed a psychiatrist. "Are the papers for Megan to be committed to a mental hospital ready?" he yelled, "If you don't want me to tell your wife about your girlfriend, you'll bring them to me now!"

CHAPTER TWENTY-EIGHT

Scott strolled into the foyer and handed a memo to the receptionist. He glanced at the official car parked in front of his church. Now what? He clenched his fists behind his back, so no one would see his anger.

Two men in suits stepped out of the vehicle, climbed the steps of the sanctuary, and came inside. Both showed badges. "We're from the FBI," The older one stepped forward. "Scott Collins, you are under arrest for the embezzlement of church funds."

The other agent handcuffed Scott and read him his rights.

As they led him toward the front door, Scott yelled to the secretary. "Call my lawyers."

He slid into the back of the car and whispered. "Megan, Megan why are you doing this to me?"

It wasn't all her fault. Benjamin Grant had been responsible, too. If Ben hadn't taken up with Megan, Scott would have found her and brought her home long ago.

When the car parked in front of the FBI office, Scott turned his face away from the photographers and news cameras. Several of them held microphones, while others darted through the crowds to come closer. "Rev. Collins, did you embezzle the money?"

Scott kept his head averted and mumbled. "No comment."

They escorted him inside and to an interrogation room, where his lawyers waited.

Two FBI agents sat across from Scott and his attorneys. "We have evidence that you've been taking the donations of members for ten years."

"I didn't do it."

"Keep quiet." A lawyer put his hand on Scott's arm. "Don't say anything."

"My wife stole the money. Everyone knows that she's mentally unstable."

"Keep your mouth closed." The lawyer turned to the agents. "Can you give us a few minutes alone?"

Nodding, the FBI agents stood and left the room.

One of the lawyers shook his head. "There's no evidence that your wife stole the money. If you keep blaming her, the public will turn against you even more than it already has."

"I'm the pastor. If I say she did it, people will believe me." Looking at the two-way mirror opposite him, Scott smoothed his hair down. Then he smirked. "You could make sure an 'unnamed source' leaked the information that Megan did it. But I love her so much I'm willing to go to jail in her place. No jury would convict me if they thought I sacrificed my life for my mentally-ill wife."

Scott could pull it off. He was much smarter than Megan, who betrayed him. He'd make certain that stupid witch cooperated.

*****

For two months after surgery, Ben worked out at his physical therapy session every day except Sundays. He had more agility and stamina than before the knee replacement. Bicycling and swimming helped him shed twenty pounds and get rid of his stomach. Ben thanked God the doctor released him to resume work.

At his age it was harder and harder to keep weight off. He wanted to avoid desserts, but his mother would feel hurt, if he always refused her pastries. Limiting himself to one a day, not taking second helpings and not snacking seemed to work for him.

His mom handed him a bowl of mashed potatoes. "I overheard you refuse a couple of jobs."

Ben set the dish down without taking a second helping. "I feel obligated to keep an eye on Megan until Rev. Collins is stopped. If I hadn't located her, maybe Scott would not have found her and hurt her."

"That wasn't your fault." His mother handed him the roast beef.

"No, thank you." He returned the platter to her. "Megan is a married woman, but I care about her."

"You can't stop your feelings, but acting on them in the wrong circumstances might be a sin. Trust God in all things. He'll work it out in His time."

"I'm praying."

"Waiting is hard, but look at poor Megan. It must be difficult for her." Mrs. Grant took a sip of iced tea. "Our Bible study prays for Rev. Collins and his wife every week."

"There have been a lot of stories in the newspapers and on television about him beating his wife and the police arresting him. I'm worried the bad publicity will make him angrier."

When they had finished eating, Ben cleared the table and then dried the dishes for his mother. He went to his room and started packing. He looked forward to going home but would miss his mom. He folded his underwear, socks, and the last of his shirts. Then he packed them in the suitcase. After closing and clamping the lids, he carried his bags to the kitchen door.

His mother sat at the table reading the newspaper. "Oh, no."

Ben leaned over her shoulder to see the article. "How could Rev. Collins do this?"

"I don't think he's a Christian." Mrs. Grant shook her head.

Ben picked up the paper she'd discarded and frowned. "He's accused of embezzlement but says Megan stole the money. Then he claims to have been protecting her throughout the years because she is mentally unstable." Ben tossed the newspaper on the table. "I'm worried about Megan."

"She couldn't have taken the money."

"No, she didn't. If she had stolen it, she would've disappeared completely instead of working. Her husband beat her up, which supports her story and makes Scott less credible. Based on everything I've learned of Megan she doesn't have it in her to be dishonest."

"Then why are you worried?" His mother cocked an eyebrow.

"Her husband is so angry that he might plant evidence to frame her."

"After all she's been through," his mother's voice wobbled, "I'd hate to see anything more happen to her. So we'll keep praying for her."

Outside of prayer, Ben couldn't do much for Megan. "You're right, prayer is best." He was ready to leave, so he inspected his mom's security system.

His mom watched him. "Nothing is different since yesterday when you checked it."

He laughed. "No it hasn't changed, but I like to make sure."

"You worry too much."

"I like to think I take after Dad who was a cautious man. I know you're in good health, but I'd like to sign you up for a medical alert service."

She put her hands on her hips. "Those necklaces are for someone who's disabled, which I am not."

"You're seventy-five and live alone. What if you had chest pain or collapsed?"

She clicked her tongue. "I appreciate your concern, but I'm not ready for it."

It sounded like she wasn't ready for chest pain, but no one ever is. How could he convince her? He scanned the room, satisfied nothing could trip her. All electrical cords lay close to the wall, none of the corners of furniture stuck out, and there were no loose throw rugs she could stumble over.

Ben's shoulder muscles tightened. "If you had a medical alert necklace, you could use it if Rev. Collins or his men tried to harm you. I'd never get over the guilt if you were hurt because of my job." He kissed her cheek. "I love you. I want you to be safe and well. Thanks for everything. Keep the doors locked."

"Not a day goes by that you don't remind me, so I'll remember."

After he arrived home, he checked his security system. While he read his mail, his phone rang. After answering it, he called his assistant.

When George arrived, he kept his voice lowered. "Someone is watching your house. I wrote the car make, model, and license number but didn't recognize any of the men."

"We'll take care of them when we leave." Ben handed a cup of coffee to George. "Cindy called. Megan volunteered to make a statement about the missing funds, but she's terrified of her husband. She's convinced that Scott bribed the judge and police officers, which wouldn't surprise me. I promised Cindy and Eileen we'd protect Megan."

"You haven't worked since your surgery. Do you feel up to being a body guard?"

"Yes, I'm in great shape." Ben sipped his coffee. "Eileen will call and let us know where to meet them. We'll check into a hotel in St. Louis tonight. Tomorrow we'll investigate Megan's location and accompany them to the station."

"I'll go home and pack. After I rent a vehicle, I should be back in forty-five minutes." George put his empty coffee cup in the sink and left.

Ben phoned his mom and told her as much of the situation as he could. He asked her to stay in the house with the security system on and not open the door to anyone until he returned. Then he called a friend and asked him to keep an eye on his mom.

When George came back, Ben set the security code in his home and climbed into the rented car. Driving out of the peaceful suburb, George glanced in the mirrors. "Now there are two cars behind us."

"Pull into this gas station and pretend to buy gas. I'll sneak up behind those cars and get the license numbers."

George stopped in front of the pump. Ten minutes later, he had washed the windows and mirrors, and checked the engine.

Ben returned with the makes, models, and plates of the vehicles. He phoned his friend at the police station. "This is Benjamin Grant. My colleague and I are protecting a witness. We have two tails." He asked, "Can you check them out for me?" He ended the call and turned to George. "They're sending someone to detain them."

When Ben and George were back on the highway, George checked his mirrors and laughed. "Thank God for friends among the police. They've pulled both vehicles over."

George turned off the next exit and stayed on side roads for sixty miles. "If we've lost them, we'll be fine. We'll rent a different vehicle in the next town."

Ben studied his notepad. "When we brought that guy in to testify against the terrorists' group, those bullet-proof vests saved our lives."

"Can you get them by tomorrow?"

"I'll make some calls."

After stopping for supper, they drove to their hotel. Ben parked the gray rental in front of the office and went in to pay for a room.

George called his wife and boys.

Ben phoned his mom. When he ended the call, he sighed. "Mom's mind is still pretty good, but I worry. At her age lots of folks' memories have already started to deteriorate. She's seventy-five. She might forget to lock up and set the alarm."

CHAPTER TWENTY-NINE

Early the next morning, after Jane had washed the dishes and swept the kitchen floor, the doorbell rang.

"I'll answer that."

"No, let me. It must be my friend from church." Mr. Adler left.

A few minutes later, he accompanied a gray-haired woman into the kitchen. She picked up an apron. "I'll finish cleaning up for you so you can dress."

"Thanks for coming on such short notice." Jane put the laundry detergent in the machine and closed the lid.

"Mr. Adler and his wife were close friends of my husband and me for many years. Now go, get ready. When the clothes are finished, I'll put them in the dryer."

In her room, Jane changed her clothes and put on makeup.

When she was ready, she went into the living room. A tear slid down her cheek as she hugged Cindy and Eileen. "I'm scared. Thank you for coming. I could never do this without your help."

"We won't leave your side." Cindy reached for Jane's hand. "George and Ben have been scouting the area. After they make another trip around the block, they'll come inside."

The doorbell rang. A few minutes later, Mr. Adler escorted Ben and George into the living room. The men set boxes on the coffee table.

"It's good to see you again." Ben shook everyone's hands.

"I'm happy to see both of you." Jane smiled. "How's your knee? It looks like you've lost weight. Are you okay?"

"I'm in shape again and glad to get back to work. I like having something to do." Ben hesitated. "I don't expect any trouble, but I'm a cautious man. George and I have been in situations where an assailant shot at us to reach our client, so all of us will wear these vests." Handing her one, he spoke in a soft voice. "Put it on."

Her stomach fluttered as her mouth went dry. If it was so dangerous, she should stay in the house and not go out there. Her heart pounded so fast the room began turning.

She shook from head to foot. Her breath came out in ragged gasps. The weight of the heavy vest pulled her arms down. She couldn't do it, but she had to, if she was ever going to be free. Jane lifted the vest, but it slipped out of her hands to the floor.

A vest wouldn't stop Scott from killing her, and everyone with her.

*****

Ben picked up the vest Megan dropped. Her eyes widened and terror flashed across her face. She'd paled. Sweat glistened her temple. Her hands shook. Was she about to faint?

He spoke in a soft voice. "We're trained to protect you and have done this many times." He lifted the vest over Megan's head and fastened the straps. His fingers brushed her waist, and she jerked away. He dropped his hands and stepped back but remained close enough to catch her if she passed out.

Cindy reached for Megan and hugged her. "It's okay. Take a few deep breaths."

When everyone had their vests on, Ben closed the empty cartons. "Would one of you ladies like to pray?"

After the prayer, Ben smiled. "It's time to leave." He looked Megan in the eye. "You'll be fine. Walk right behind me in my steps. Cindy and Eileen, stand on each side of Megan and take her arms. George will be behind Megan."

During the short walk to the vehicle, Ben searched for unusual movements or threats but saw nothing. He helped the ladies into the windowless van and closed the door. He stood outside looking over the area until George was in the driver's seat and had started the engine. Then Ben jumped inside.

No one spoke during the brief drive to the police station. Megan licked her lips and her hands shook. Her white face worried him. He wanted to lift her in his arms and carry her into the building, but his touch might frighten her more. Would he ever hear the rest of her story? After what Scott did, was Megan terrified of all men?

They took their former positions, with Eileen and Cindy holding Megan's arms, as they marched into the police station. An officer escorted them to an interrogation room and asked, "Would you like some coffee?"

The ladies shook their heads.

An FBI agent and two officers entered the room and introduced themselves.

Ben left and returned with bottles of water. He handed one to Cindy and another to Eileen, and then he unscrewed the lid of one and set it in front of Megan. "Take a sip."

She picked it up with shaking hands. After a few gulps, she turned to the others. With their prompting and encouragement, Megan gave her account of the missing church funds.

An hour later, Megan signed her statement.

Ben asked, "Could two men escort us back to the van?"

When the officers arrived, Ben's group returned to the vehicle.

George drove to Mr. Adler's house and stopped at the end of the driveway. Cars filled the length of the private drive.

"It looks like Mr. Adler has more company from church." Cindy laughed. "I love those Christian bumper stickers."

George parked the van in front of the house along the street.

Ben stepped out of the vehicle and lifted his binoculars. He scanned the area and then went to the cars in the driveway and peered inside of them and under them. After walking around the house, he rang the doorbell and spoke to several older ladies.

He returned to the van, opened the door a little bit, and poked his head inside. "It appears safe to go into the house. No one even called while we were gone."

Ben turned to help Megan out of the van. "After you're out, stay behind me. Then Cindy and Eileen will be by your side." He stood in front of Megan as she stepped down. Then he moved away from the door with her, so the other ladies could get out.

Suddenly the blast of a gunshot filled the air. He shoved Megan to the pavement and landed on top of her.

Both men cocked their guns.

"Megan, are you okay?"

She whispered, "Yes."

"George?"

"Yes, Captain. Glad the women are still in the van."

*****

Rev. Collins scrunched down next to Dan on the hill across the road from the van. Scott lowered the weapon and let loose a stream of profanities.

"What do you think you were doing?" Dan wrestled the rifle out of Scott's grasp. "You were supposed to look through the site not shoot. We were going to use the gun to threaten them later. If they arrest you again, they'll refuse you bail."

"Money buys a lot of friends. No one will ever deny me bail." Scott looked down and across the road at the house. "Where did she find all those people to take her side?"

"You should be careful."

"I need Megan out of the picture, so I can be free."

Dan pulled a rag out of his pocket and rubbed the rifle. "We have to lure her away from those men. That black guy is as dangerous as Ben. They served together in Special Forces."

"The little witch has no money. The only way a man would help her would be if she gave him a personal favor." Scott hissed. "I want you to help me get rid of my wife."

"I'm not going to prison for murder." Dan removed the ammunition from the rifle. "We can make it look natural, like suicide. She can leave a note of regret saying how sorry she is for taking money from those good people." Dan lifted the gun scope to his eye.

"That would be the perfect ending to her."

"You fool. You may have already ruined everything by shooting at Megan. Too many witnesses."

"Megan makes me crazy. I've no patience with her anymore."

"Do you hear that?" Dan whispered.

Scott turned to the sound of the wailing sirens. Then he looked back to where Megan lay with the bodyguard on top of her. No one had moved. He grabbed the rifle from Dan to peer through the scope. If Scott had hit both Ben and Megan, all his problems would be over.

*****

Megan couldn't move. She was grateful Ben's weight restricted her, or she'd be trembling from head to foot. Ben had pushed her to the ground so fast, she thought he'd been hit. What if he was dead weight on top of her? No, he had aimed his gun and spoken, but he didn't move.

Ben raised and slid in front of her. She breathed a sigh of relief that he wasn't hurt.

"See anything, George?" Ben whispered.

"There was a glint on the hill in the wooded area across the road just after the shot, but it's gone."

Two police cruisers arrived. One vehicle parked parallel to George's van with a four-foot space between the cars. Two officers stepped out and approached. One asked, "Is everyone okay? An ambulance is on the way."

"Everyone seems to be fine." Ben stood from his prone position.

Megan let him take her shaking hand and help her sit up. She tried to smile, but her lips didn't quite make it. "Thank you." She leaned back against the front passenger tire.

"Were you hurt when you landed on the pavement?" Ben asked.

"No, I'm fine."

Ben reached for a bottle of water in the van and unscrewed the cap. He leaned down and held it out to Megan. "Take a sip and relax."

Had Scott really tried to kill her? She had always been terrified that he would kill her. So why was she surprised he had shot at her?

She glanced at Ben. He had looked at her as if he cared about her welfare. He helped her every time he was with her and put her safety above his, kind of like Christ did.

*****

Ben gave the officer his statement and then squatted to talk to Megan. In the closed quarters between the police car and the van, he lost his balance. He grabbed the fender to stop from tumbling into Megan.

She reached out with her free hand and steadied him. "How's your knee?"

"The physical therapy helped me get back in shape. Sometimes I forget and move too fast. Well, you saw what just happened." Ben didn't like discussing his weakness, but it kept Megan talking and her mind off gunfire.

"Thank you for risking your life." Megan gulped down some water. "That's more than you bargained for, especially in your weakened condition."

To keep the mood light, Ben teased, "What do you mean, my weakened condition? I can bench press 350, and that's not bad for a guy who had a knee replacement. I can bicycle twenty miles an hour and swim so many lengths of the pool I stopped counting."

Her eyes widened. "That's impressive." She offered him the rest of the water.

Reaching for the bottle, he took a sip and handed it back to her.

A paramedic came up to them. "Who was shot?"

"No one, thank God." Ben remained next to Megan. "The sniper missed, but I'd like you to check this lady out. I pushed her hard to the ground out of the line of fire."

"I'm fine. There's no need to examine me."

The paramedic put his hand on her shoulder. "Stay seated while I check your vital signs." When he finished, he stuffed his stethoscope in the bag. "You're fine, but we can take you to the hospital for a more intensive exam."

"No, thank you."

Ben moved to George and looked across the street where the shot had come from. "I never thought he'd go to such extremes."

"Thank God you had the foresight to bring those vests."

"Did they find the bullet?" Ben asked.

"Yes, right there in that tree." George pointed toward it. "We should go into the house."

Ben sighed loudly. "Megan can't stay here. Cindy and Eileen are on their phones trying to find a new place for her."

"Let's take her back to the police station. Maybe an officer can sneak her out the side door." George shrugged.

"We've done that before." Ben sighed.

"I don't think much frightens Scott. He tried to shoot her in broad daylight in front of all of us."

"That's what worries me." Ben ran his fingers through his hair. "He might be so desperate he'll attack her no matter what the risk. Men who torment women escalate their assaults toward them. I should have kept that in mind."

Scott's next attempt would be worse.

CHAPTER THIRTY

Megan lowered her face into her trembling hands and sobbed. She shuddered. Then warmth covered her, and her tremors slowed down. She lifted her teary eyes to Ben as he pulled the blanket around her.

He motioned the paramedic to them. "Can you drive us to the city morgue?"

Megan's mouth fell open. "I'm not dead."

"No, but maybe we can make Scott and his men think you are, at least long enough to get you away. Wait here while I discuss it with Cindy and Eileen."

She didn't want to go to the morgue, but how else could she escape if Scott watched her?

Ben came back and crouched next to her. "The ambulance will take you to the morgue and keep you in the vehicle until George and I arrive."

Cindy leaned out of the van. "We haven't been able to locate a place for you yet, but we won't give up."

Ben dialed a number. "We're fine, Mom, but someone shot at us. I didn't want you to worry if you saw it on the news this evening. Can I bring Megan over for a couple of days until we find a safe place for her?"

"I'd love to have her come." Megan smiled at the older woman's response coming from the phone.

"Mom, I'll be staying with you and Megan. It'll be this evening when we arrive. I'll need to smuggle her into the house, so no one knows. Please don't mention it to anyone as we're not certain who fired the shots. Keep the doors locked until we get there. I love you. Bye."

Eileen came around to the side of the van. "I've good news. The police have Scott in custody."

Ben drank some water. "Even if they don't keep him, it will give us time to hide Megan."

The paramedic and ambulance driver wheeled the stretcher between the police cruiser and the van.

"Scott's hired men could be watching, so we have to make it look real. George and I will meet you there as soon as we lose any tails." Ben nodded to Megan as she sat on the stretcher and lay down. He pulled the cover up over her face.

Megan couldn't stop her shakes as she was lifted inside the ambulance. Drops of sweat trickled down her neck under the cover. The doors banged shut and locked Megan inside. Darkness. Confined in gloom and deprived of light. Without Jesus, people lived in darkness forever. Thank God that she wasn't going to that hot, evil place. She kept her eyes closed but lowered the cover from her head. She pictured the glory of Jesus in Heaven, sparkling streets, and bright light.

But she might have been going to the morgue for real.

*****

Thirty minutes later, George pulled into the enclosed garage. He and Ben jumped out of the van and walked to the ambulance.

Ben thanked the EMTs for staying with Megan. Then he and George accompanied her to their vehicle.

George climbed into the driver's seat. When the garage door opened, he checked his mirrors and backed out. He turned to Ben and Megan, who were slumped in the back seat. "Are you ready?"

They both nodded.

"Sorry you had to go to the morgue." Ben suppressed an urge to take Megan's shaking hand. "Mom lives by herself and will enjoy having you as company. She pampers everyone, including me. She has three children, but I'm the youngest and her only son."

"Does she have any health problems?"

"Nothing that stops her. She has high blood pressure and arthritis. Taking an active interest in my life and church keeps her healthy. She was in her glory cooking and washing clothes while I got back on my feet."

"I hope my being there won't put her in danger." Megan sniffed. "Since that gunshot, I'm wondering if it's useless to run from Scott. He always caught me and dragged me back."

"Weren't you on your own the last time you tried to get away?"

She nodded.

"You're not alone now. You have the organization behind you and us to help. I read those verses you'd underlined in that Bible. Trust in the Lord." He grinned.

"I trust God, but it's been hard."

"Mom has wanted to meet you and is looking forward to your visit."

"I'd like to meet her, too." She hesitated. "If you're not working for Scott, who's paying you?"

"I'm working for myself right now and assisting the organization to protect you."

Six hours later George pulled into Mrs. Grant's driveway. "It doesn't look as if anyone followed us."

*****

Exhaustion slowed Megan's movements. She forced one leg in front of the other as Ben escorted her into the house.

"Megan, this is my mother."

"It's nice to meet you." Megan gave one of her real smiles. "I appreciate your hospitality."

"I enjoy having company." The older woman hugged Megan.

She caught a whiff of roasted chicken. Her mouth watered. The blinds and curtains were closed behind the breakfast nook in the corner. Blue tiles on the walls had been popular fifty years ago, but the hardwood floor looked more recent. It was a comfortable kitchen.

Mrs. Grant looked around. "Where's your bag?"

Megan had forgotten her backpack.

"Cindy packed your things." Ben smiled.

His mom asked, "George, will you stay for supper?"

"I'd love to, but Betsy is off work this evening. Since we're no longer on duty, I'd like to spend time with my wife and boys. So I'll say goodnight."

"I'll walk to your vehicle with you to collect Megan's bag."

He returned a few minutes later with the backpack. "I'll show you to your room."

"Don't be long. Supper's ready," Mrs. Grant called.

When they came back into the kitchen, Ben carried the serving bowls from the stove to the table while his mom poured water in the glasses. After they sat down, Ben reached for his mom's hand and offered his other one to Megan.

She hesitated so long that Ben put his empty hand in his lap, bowed his head, and prayed.

Mrs. Grant waited until Megan had filled her plate before speaking. "I'm so sorry for what your husband put you through. My friends in the Bible study and I prayed for you."

"Thank you." Megan swallowed a bite. "This meat is so moist, and the cheese potato casserole is delicious. Can you give me the recipes, Mrs. Grant?"

"Yes, I'd be glad to. But please call me Doris."

After they'd eaten, Megan put her fork down. "Thanks for supper. I'll wash dishes so you can rest."

"Let's do it together." Mrs. Grant filled the sink with soapy water. "I'm kind of old-fashioned. Ben bought me a dishwasher, but I don't use it."

He grinned. "I do when I'm here and there are lots of dishes."

"I don't mind washing them by hand." Megan took the offered towel from Mrs. Grant.

Megan had always worked alone in her kitchen. Scott had insisted Megan use the dishwasher for hygienic purposes. She watched Ben and his mom put leftovers in the refrigerator, wipe down the counter, and wash the table. As Megan dried the dishes, she admired the sweet teamwork of Ben and his mom.

After all the plates and pans were put away, the older woman scrubbed the sink and hung the dish rag while Ben carried out the garbage.

"What would you like to do this evening?" Doris asked.

"I don't want to intrude. What do you normally do?"

"Watch television."

"That sounds relaxing, but may I take a shower?"

"I'm sorry." Ben slapped his forehead. "I can be so thoughtless. Of course you want to bathe after I shoved you to the ground."

Mrs. Grant's eyebrows lifted. "You threw Megan to the ground?"

"Your son saved my life. When the gunfire started, he pushed me down and shielded me with his body."

Mrs. Grant smiled at Ben and then turned back to her guest. "Come, Megan. I'll show you where the towels and bathroom supplies are kept."

Ten minutes later, Megan came into the living room with her hair wrapped in a towel and wearing a short dress on top of a nightgown.

"Is there anything you need?" Doris asked.

"Please excuse my strange outfit, but I don't have a housecoat."

"I'll find something that one of Ben's sisters left." Mrs. Grant went out of the room with her son but returned alone carrying a green housecoat.

"Thank you." Megan reached for the robe. "Excuse me while I put this on." She went to her room.

When she returned to the living room, Ben still wasn't there. Where had he gone? Would he leave his mother and her alone in the house? What if Scott came back? She shuddered and crossed her arms.

Mrs. Grant pressed the television remote. "Ben doesn't care for old black and white films, but he'll watch them with me."

"I like them." Megan sat on the couch near Mrs. Grant's recliner.

The older woman turned to Megan. "Humphry Bogart and Katherine Hepburn are in the 'African Queen' tonight."

Before the movie started, the phone rang. Megan jumped and put her hand on her chest. "I'm a little nervous."

Mrs. Grant patted Megan's knee. "Don't worry. You're safe, and Ben's with us." She went to the phone. "Hello." Doris turned white.

Ben came into the room with wet hair and in fresh clothes. He went to his mother and took the receiver from her shaking hand. He wrapped his arm around her shoulder and pulled her close.

Megan's heart clenched at the sight of Ben comforting his mother. During the years she'd known Scott she'd never seen him hug his mother.

Ben pressed the speaker button. "Hello."

"This is Rev. Scott Collins. Did you receive the check I sent for your car repairs?"

"Yes, thank you."

"I want to apologize again for that inconvenience. Have you seen Megan?"

"Why do you ask?"

"She's my wife, but you've spent more time with her than I have over the last months."

"Good night." Ben punched the off button and slammed the phone into its stand.

Mrs. Grant lifted a shaking hand to her forehead. "I didn't tell anyone about Megan coming."

Ben hugged his mother again and then moved the curtain a little to peer outside. "Let's go downstairs to the den to watch the movie. Mom, you show Megan the way. I'll be there in a few minutes."

As Mrs. Grant went downstairs with Megan, the older woman exhaled loudly. "I nearly said the secret code."

"Excuse me?" Megan asked.

"If I'm ever in danger or someone comes who shouldn't be here, I call Ben and say I watched Jeopardy."

"Have you ever had to say it?" Megan followed Doris into a well-lit den.

"Once when Ben worked on a dangerous assignment, and some bad guys came." Doris sat down next to Megan on the couch and put her arm around her. "Don't worry. My son will keep you safe."

Studying the comfortable family room, Megan relaxed in the basement. Then she started worrying.

Had she put Mrs. Grant in danger?

*****

Ben walked through each room and rechecked the windows. He'd already closed all the blinds, so he looked out each side of the house and saw two vehicles.

Rev. Collins's investigators must have told him that Megan was there, but how did they find out?

He checked out possible places for a listening device and found one in a houseplant. He put the plant in the broom closet and went downstairs.

An hour later, his mom turned to Megan. "Let's take a break. I need to use the bathroom." She pressed the remote and stood.

Megan smiled. "Me, too."

Ben followed the ladies upstairs. His mother went into the kitchen for a glass of water, so he asked, "Who gave you the fichus?"

"One of my lady friends from church brought it to me while we were shopping. Is there something wrong with it?"

"No." Ben paused. "Did she bring it from her garden?"

"She bought it at a nursery because she knows how much I like them. A nice young man carried it to the car for her and wouldn't take any money." She frowned. "What is wrong?"

"Everything's fine." Ben hugged his mother. "Finish the movie downstairs with Megan while I take care of a few things."

Ben phoned George. "Scott put a bug in Mom's plant, that's how he learned what we were doing."

"I'll come right over and take care of it."

"Thanks."

By the time George left with the listening device, the movie was over. Megan and his mom came upstairs. Ben checked all the windows and doors again after Megan and his mom went to bed.

What kind of a man used a seventy-five-year-old woman to achieve his evil scheme? A bully, someone who hurt weaker people. Ben wanted to face Scott man to man, and maybe God would give him that day. Scott had to be stopped from oppressing and taking advantage of women for his own goals.

Frustrated, Ben went to his room. Lifting his weights and working out on his stationary bicycle released his anger.

It was better than pounding the walls or Rev. Scott Collins.

CHAPTER THIRTY-ONE

Megan colored her hair its original shade in the bathroom. She ran her fingers through it as she lifted and styled it. Maybe soon she'd have her own life back. Over the years with Scott, he had convinced her that he was making her into a better wife by changing her clothes, makeup and hair color. But she never liked his alterations.

She went into the kitchen. "Good morning. What can I do to help with breakfast?"

Ben's eyes widened. "I didn't recognize you for a moment. You look nice." He handed her a cup of coffee. "Everything is about ready." He set a platter of buttered toast on the table.

"I wish I had a proper outfit to wear to the courthouse today."

"It wouldn't be safe to drive you to the mall." Ben stroked his chin. "George's wife, Betsy used to be your size. Excuse me a minute while I make a call."

He came back with a smile on his face. "George is bringing some of his wife's clothes."

"I hope that's not inconvenient."

"Not at all. Betsy has closets full of outfits. Buying clothes is her major vice, so she justifies it by loaning them out."

Mrs. Grant came into the kitchen. "How are you today?"

"Scared and nervous."

As they finished eating, the doorbell rang.

"That was fast." Megan turned to Ben. "Does George live close by?"

"Yes, he's only about ten minutes away."

George carried a large carton into the kitchen. "Would you like me to take this to your room, so you can try on these clothes?"

"Why the box? I thought your wife was loaning me one outfit?"

"Over the years Betsy's gone from a size eight to eighteen and saves all her clothes. There's no room left in her closets, so she had this load ready to give the Goodwill. I understand they're all your size. Take what you like."

"Thanks. I can carry the box to my room and try them on there."

When she was alone, she lifted a black and white ensemble from the carton. The conservative outfit was one she would have selected herself, so she put it on. Then she slipped into high heels. She straightened the lace peeking out of the suit sleeve and glanced in the mirror. If only she could get rid of her jitters as easily as she discarded her older clothes.

Lord, please help me.

Trust me, your Lord.

Megan strolled into the living room and stopped in front of Mrs. Grant, Ben, and George. "Does this look appropriate for court, or is it too elegant?"

"It's perfect." Ben stood. "You look professional."

Mrs. Grant fluffed the lace at Megan's neck. "I like this feminine touch."

"Can I snap a photo and send it to my wife?" George asked. "Betsy loves to see the results of helping others."

"Sure." Megan checked her appearance again in the mirror. After George snapped photos, Ben opened one of the boxes on the coffee table. "As a precaution, we'll wear the bullet-proof vests again." He handed one to Megan.

She lifted it over her head and fastened the straps.

Then he turned to his mother. "You, too."

"It shouldn't be necessary. I'm staying with a friend."

"No arguments." He put the vest over her head and fastened it for her.

Ben led the way to the garage and helped his mom into the front passenger seat of the van. Megan climbed into the back and he sat next to her.

George backed out and drove a few miles before stopping and turning into a short driveway. He waited for Ben to escort his mother into her friend's house.

When they were back on the road, Megan started shaking. "I hate inconveniencing your mother."

"She had already planned on spending the morning with her friend today."

Reaching the courthouse, George parked and waited.

"Two officers are coming to escort us," Ben smiled at Megan.

"I prayed the judge will rule in my favor." Megan clutched her trembling hands together on her lap. Her heart pounded. The officers arrived and surrounded her as they marched into the building.

"The judge will see for himself how Scott has hurt you and refuse to let him go free on bail. He'll recognize Scott is a danger to you."

After meeting Eileen and Cindy in the hall, Eileen led Megan to a row of seats on the side of the courtroom but inside the railing. "Since there's no jury, you and I have permission to sit in the jury box."

Biting her lip, Megan followed. "I thought we'd sit at a table."

"The prosecutor represents us. He sits at the table."

When Scott entered the courtroom with his lawyers, he took a step toward Megan. His lawyers stopped him. One ordered, "Sit down."

Ben and George had taken seats in the gallery.

The clerk announced, "All rise for Judge Clinton Barnes."

*****

Ben clenched his fists when he saw the pictures of Megan's battered face and x-rays of healed broken bones. He forced himself to study every detail so if he ever had his hands on Rev. Scott Collins, he'd teach him a lesson. Ben wanted Scott to feel some of the pain Megan had suffered. Maybe then Scott would think twice before hurting someone again. And the minister would repent of his sins.

At the close of the session, the judge called for final arguments.

The prosecutor stood. "Your honor, Scott Collins is a flight risk. The missing six million dollars can buy the forged documents and transportation needed to disappear. He is a danger to the principle witness against him. As you heard from his wife's testimony, Scott Collins has a history of domestic violence. He flouted the law by violating a restraining order when he pursued her at a funeral. Somebody shot at her when he was out on bail. Her husband is the only one who has a motive for harming her. As long as he is free, his wife is in danger."

Then Scott's lawyer stood. "Your honor, my client is the well-respected and highly esteemed pastor of one of the largest churches.

His face is known to people across the nation. How could he possibly hide or run away?"

The lawyer continued. "Megan Collins's preposterous charge that her husband beat and shot at her is the product of a devious or deranged mind. Megan ran away after her husband secured papers for her to be committed for a psych evaluation. Her testimony is not credible. He is at his church every day counseling and helping others." He paused. "Finally, Rev. Collins has been slandered without reason or evidence, and he is determined to prove his innocence. The only way he can do that is through a trial where he can confront the chief witness against him. It is not in his interest to flee or harm his wife." The lawyer sat down.

"Thank you, counsel." The judge leaned forward and shuffled some papers. "I'll consider your arguments and rule on the matter tomorrow morning. In the meantime, Rev. Collins will remain free on the bond already posted."

After the judge left the courtroom, Ben went to Eileen. "George will make certain Scott leaves. Then we'll wait for two officers to escort us to the van. I don't know how many hired men Scott has, but he'd be foolish to try something here."

Eileen and Cindy hugged Megan.

Her lawyer said, "Don't worry. It may look like Scott is getting off now, but he will pay for his crimes."

After the courtroom emptied, the officers accompanied Megan to the vehicle.

George started the van and pulled into the road. A few minutes later he glanced in the rearview mirror. "No one is following us. Should I stop and pick up your mom?"

"No thanks. One of her friends will bring her home later."

George parked inside Mrs. Grant's garage and closed the door.

"Give me a moment to check out the house." Ben left, but returned in a few minutes. "Everything's secure. Let's go in."

When they were in the kitchen, Ben loosened his tie. "I'd like to change."

"Me too." Megan left.

She returned wearing brown capris and a striped shirt. George had taken off his jacket and tie. He rolled up his shirtsleeves while Ben brewed coffee.

When it was ready, Mrs. Grant and some ladies arrived with two cardboard boxes. "My friends cooked roast beef, mashed potatoes, and green bean casserole. Someone baked a chocolate cake." The women set the boxes on the table.

"I'll walk your mother's friends to the car before I leave." George opened the door for the ladies.

After they left, Doris asked, "How did the hearing go?"

"The judge has to think about it." Ben gave his mom a cup of coffee.

"What's there to think about? He beat up Megan and shot at her."

Ben's cell phone rang. After he answered it, he broke out in a sweat. He clenched his fists and ended the call. "Scott has a letter from a psychiatrist stating that Megan is mentally unsound and dangerous."

CHAPTER THIRTY-TWO

The next day, Ben went into the courtroom and sat on the other side of the aisle from the defendant's table. Keeping Scott's profile in his sight, Ben prayed the bail would be revoked.

Scott sat straight with his hands folded neatly in front of him. Slowly he turned to Ben and leered at him.

The clerk banged his gavel. "All rise for the Honorable Clinton Barnes." Then he called the first case. Scott and his attorneys rose and faced the bench.

"The jails are overcrowded, and I do not believe that Rev. Collins is a flight risk," the judge said. "Nevertheless, some restraint is appropriate. I order home confinement."

Scott banged his fist on the table.

Ben breathed easier. It wasn't as good as jail, but Megan should be safer if Scott was restricted to his house.

Honorable Barnes ordered, "The bailiff will take Rev. Collins to be fitted with an ankle bracelet before he leaves the building."

"No," Scott screamed as he struck the table again. "I won't do it."

The judge spoke to the lawyers. "Control your client or I'll have him removed from the courtroom."

Putting his hand on Scott's arm, the lawyer nearest him nodded. Then he whispered to his client before turning back to the judge.

"Your honor," the lawyer said, "may I say something?"

"Proceed."

"My client is the spiritual leader of a large congregation. His God-given duties include visiting the shut-in and praying for the sick in the hospital. He represents the church at community meetings and events. He cannot serve his congregation if he is confined to his home."

The judge rubbed his chin. "You've made your point. The Court will allow Rev. Collins to travel within a twenty-mile-radius from the church. The police will monitor his movements."

Scott hit the table again and started to get up, but the lawyer put his hand on Scott's shoulder, keeping him in his chair.

Bang! The gavel came down and the judge stared straight at Scott. "I've made my ruling. The bailiff will take you away now."

Ben waited until Scott left the courtroom before Ben went to his vehicle. Scott would still have freedom to call his goons to go after Megan. He had influence wherever he was, even in jail, to hurt Megan. Ben wasn't sure how Megan would take the news.

After parking in his mom's drive, he went into the kitchen. He filled a glass with water and sat next to Megan.

His heart lurched at the dark circles under her eyes. "How are you feeling this morning?"

"I tossed and turned well into the night before falling asleep. Even after praying, I couldn't recall why I felt so uneasy about the judge. If only I could remember Scott's connection to him." Megan's hand trembled so badly her drink almost spilled. "What happened?"

"Judge Barnes did not revoke the bail but ordered Scott to have an ankle bracelet." He started to reach for Megan's hand, but he pulled his back.

"I'd hoped the judge would put him in jail." Megan started crying.

"The police will monitor the bracelet. He can only go in a twenty-mile radius, and this home is outside his circle."

"Don't worry. My son will protect you."

"George will help me." Ben handed Megan his handkerchief. "I don't know of any other mistreated wife who has gone through as much as you have and come out of it as well as you have."

"I'm not yet out of it." Megan wiped her cheeks, but the tears kept flowing.

"You can stay here as long as necessary." Mrs. Grant reached for Megan's hand.

Ben gulped down his water. "I'm wondering what connection Scott has to Judge Barnes."

Megan's glass slipped out of her hand and fell on the edge of her plate, spilling water everywhere. Then it rolled off the table and crashed to the floor. She jumped up and looked down. "I'm sorry."

Ben leaned over and picked up the pointed shards while his mother reached for napkins from the table. He worried over Megan's near-white appearance.

*****

Megan shivered while she waited for someone to yell at her as Scott would have done.

"Don't fret about a glass." Mrs. Grant put her arm around Megan. "You're much more valuable."

Megan glanced at her ruined breakfast. "Would you excuse me?" She went to her room and removed her wet capris and slipped into some jeans. After splashing cold water on her face, she patted it dry and returned to the kitchen.

Her water-soaked meal was gone and in its place was another plate of food. They had forgiven and accepted her for breaking a glass, but the man who professed to love her would have punished her and sent her away hungry.

Megan ate a few bites and stopped. "Doris, this breakfast is delicious, but I can't eat now."

"It isn't even noon, and already you've had a difficult and stressful day. No matter what happens, God will take care of you and see you through it." Mrs. Grant patted Megan's hand. "Have you any plans for the future?"

"Eileen filed for my divorce. I'm not claiming any money or property. All I want is my freedom."

"A divorce after fifteen years of marriage should give you something to start over again." Ben leaned back in his chair.

"I used to believe divorce was wrong, but if a wife lives in terror of her husband and believes one day he'll kill her, how can God be glorified in that?" Megan wiped a tear off her cheek. "If I'm ever free of Scott, I'll stay single the rest of my life to keep my marriage vows, which are sacred and should be honored."

Mrs. Grant sighed. "It seems to me that's double punishment."

"What do you mean?"

"Being mistreated throughout your marriage is punishment enough, but if a good man comes along and you refuse his love so you can live alone, it seems like another penalty to me."

Ben set his cup down. "You must do what the Lord is leading you to do, but you're not to blame for who Scott is and what he has done."

Megan put her napkin on the table. "I've met Scott's family. He was raised with cruelty, which is all he knows. If a husband mistreats his wife and children, they grow up believing it is the normal way to handle anger. If the cycle isn't broken, it can continue for generations. I don't want to be a part of that."

Sadness crossed Ben's face. "I understand your concerns."

"God still might send you a good man who loved you and treated you well. Would you throw away that gift?" Mrs. Grant asked.

Megan's brow creased. "I hadn't thought of that."

Was it possible a man might love her and treat her well?

CHAPTER THIRTY-THREE

Megan screamed. Her eyelids flickered open. A moment later, someone pounded on her door.

Ben's agitated voice asked, "Megan, are you okay?"

She switched on the light and glanced around the room. Sliding out of bed, she put on her housecoat. Her heart pounded against her ribcage as she unlocked the door and pulled the knob toward her.

Seeing the gun in Ben's hand, she jumped back.

A pale Mrs. Grant with her hand on her chest stood next to Ben. "Are you alright, dear? We heard a shout."

Megan tried to unscramble her foggy brain. She glanced at the clock, two a.m. The shades were closed and the curtains drawn.

"I'm sorry for waking you. I had a bad dream."

"It sounded like someone was hurting you." Ben remained in the doorway but moved his hands behind him. "Just to be certain, may I come in and check out the room?"

Her heart rate returned to normal as she stepped aside for Ben to enter. Scott would have barged in and yelled how foolish she was.

Ben went to the windows. "They're still sealed, so it looks like no one got in."

"It was only a nightmare."

She stepped aside as he opened the closet door and pushed the hanging clothes back, and then he peered behind the curtains and under the bed. Megan went into the hall to give Ben more space.

Mrs. Grant put her arm around Megan. "I have some sleepy time tea with natural herbs. Would you like a cup?"

"No, thank you. I don't want to disturb anyone."

Ben joined them in the hall. "I need some sleepy time tea, Mom. I'll make it. You go back to bed."

"No, I'd like some myself." Doris reached for Megan's arm. "Let's go to the kitchen."

When they were at the table sipping tea, Mrs. Grant asked, "Do you often have nightmares?"

Megan nodded.

"I can't imagine all the horror you suffered with Scott. Maybe soon you can start trusting us." Ben sipped on the drink.

"I'm already trusting people more." Megan lifted her hand to cover a yawn. "Excuse me."

"It looks like that sleepy time is working." Mrs. Grant stood. "Are you ready to go back to bed?"

"Yes, thank you for the tea." She went to her room.

*****

Ben rechecked the doors and windows in the house. His mom followed him around the rooms.

He whispered, "I'm worried about Megan. I want to comfort her."

"Why can't you?"

"You've seen how she pulls away from my touch." He checked the security alarm. "Her husband hurt her badly, so it will take time for her to trust a man again. She might need intensive counseling."

"Be patient. Keep offering your hand for prayer. One day she'll take it." She hugged her son. "The way you look at her tells me you care a lot for her."

"I never could hide anything from you." He walked her to her room. "Megan has a lot to think about now, so there's no way I'd burden her with my feelings." He kissed his mom's cheek. "Let's go back to sleep. It's late."

Ben went to bed but tossed and turned. He hadn't exercised for a few days and needed a physical workout to tire him and help him sleep. His concern for Megan kept him awake. He worried about her mental wellbeing and safety. He'd do his best to prevent Scott from hurting her again.

Even with the help of the Lord, would she ever recover from everything she had suffered?

*****

The scent of frying sausages woke Megan the next morning. After slipping into her housecoat, she went to the kitchen to help with breakfast.

When they were at the table, Ben extended his hands to his mom and Megan to pray.

She took his hand and mumbled, "Amen." Then she picked up her coffee cup. "I'm sorry for waking you in the middle of the night."

"Don't worry. At my age I'm often awake." Mrs. Grant buttered her toast. "Did you go back to sleep?"

"Yes."

Ben passed the eggs. "There's plenty of food, eat as much as you like."

"I'm trying to cut back a bit. I've gained too much weight."

"Nonsense, you're the perfect size." Mrs. Grant turned to her son. "Do you think Megan needs to lose weight?"

"No, it doesn't look like it."

"Did you ever see me on television with my husband?"

Ben nodded. Mrs. Grant smiled. "Yes."

"I was very slender when I was with Scott. He wouldn't let me gain any weight. He claimed television added twenty pounds. I had to maintain a size four."

Mrs. Grant shook her head and clicked her tongue. "That's ridiculous. No man who loves his wife will force her to be a certain size."

"Scott was always telling me that he loved me. But I realized the other day when he shot at me that he never loved me. That was harder to accept than his cruelty." Tears filled Megan's eyes as she stared at her plate. "He gave me nice presents, but all of them had strings or threats attached."

Ben sighed. "That doesn't sound like love to me."

Megan fumbled in her pocket and pulled out Ben's handkerchief to wipe her eyes. "He always apologized but hurt me again. He told me if I hadn't been so bad or disrespectful, he wouldn't have had to punish me."

Mrs. Grant hugged Megan. "You cry all you want. Everything will soon be better."

But would it really?

*****

Ben watched the two women. Megan must be discouraged, and his mom looked exhausted. "We need a change of environment and some sunshine. It's a pretty day. Would you ladies like to go on a picnic?"

"I planned to work on my Bible lesson, but I can do it tomorrow." His mom sipped on her coffee.

"Will you excuse me while I make a call?" Ben left but returned a few minutes later. "What do you think about packing a lunch and going up to Lake Wallatussie? It's only an hour's drive and an easy place to lose a tail."

Megan mumbled, "Sure. If you think it's safe."

By the time Megan and Mrs. Grant filled the picnic basket, George and his boys had arrived in a black Toyota van. Ben and George carried lawn chairs, the ice chest, pillows, and blankets to the vehicle.

During the drive, Megan sat in the back seat. George's younger son sat next to her, and she asked, "Eli, how old are you?"

"I'm six, ma'am. Henry is ten. That's four more years than me. When I'm ten I'm going to be in the fifth grade like Henry. I have to be in the first grade now." He reached for Megan's hand. His grin showed several missing front teeth.

Megan liked George's sons. "What do you like to do, Eli?"

"Play with my trucks."

Henry sat in front of them in the middle seat with Mrs. Grant. The boy worked on a children's crossword puzzle in an exercise book.

Bright sunshine gleamed through the windows. Megan put on her sunglasses and relaxed at the spectacular view of hills, streams, and groves. Orange and scarlet trees covered the countryside.

She'd been alone for so long and terrified of being caught. But having new friends who helped her escape made a big difference. Her life was richer and happier with the people around her.

"Ben and I like to swim in the lake when it's warmer." George turned down a narrow road. "You boys are not to go in today. The temperature may be hovering around seventy, but the water has already turned cold." He parked in a small paved area a hundred yards in front of the lake.

Ben slid open the van door for his mom and helped her out. "I'll bring the ice chest."

George went to the back and collected the chairs. He handed a pillow and a blanket to each of his boys to carry.

Ben led the way to a small worn area near the lake, thirty yards from shore. He took the picnic basket from Megan and turned to his mom. "Have a seat and relax."

Megan admired the view of oak, elm, and maple trees that framed the lake. She let the gentle breeze blow through her hair. Scarlet and gold leaves dropped from the trees. The sun glistened on the blue water. A gentle breeze swirled the leaves along the edge of the lake.

While Ben scouted out the area, George took a soccer ball out of the van and tossed it to Henry. The boys started kicking it.

Ben returned. "We're the only ones here today."

Then an unfamiliar car parked in the road. The adults turned to look at it.

Megan shivered. Not again.

CHAPTER THIRTY-FOUR

Megan's fear left as she watched the boys play. The children kicked the ball, ran, and laughed together. George and his wife must have a very happy home. Megan regretted that she'd never been a part of one while growing up.

"I'll check out that car that pulled in and look over the perimeter." George turned to Ben. "Will you watch the boys?"

Ben nodded. "Always."

"It's a little windy." Mrs. Grant shivered.

"Stay put. I'll bring your jacket and be right back." Ben left.

Seeing the ball roll onto the pier, Megan held her breath. When the ball fell into the water, Eli ran to the edge of the wharf and leaned over. A second later, he disappeared.

Megan's heart raced as she sprinted toward the boy. He had not come up for air. Henry was about to jump in after his brother, so she yelled, "Stay here. I'll get Eli."

She dove off the end of the pier and quickly found him caught in an old fishing net. She struggled to free his arms and legs from the tangled ropes before she had to surface for air. The little boy fought her and the cords, but they tightened.

Eli stopped moving. Megan didn't have enough strength to untangle the snarl. Her arms dropped to her sides, and she couldn't move. A knife came near her and slashed through the ropes. A moment later Eli was free. A large arm wrapped around the child and another hand reached for hers.

Within a few seconds, she, Ben and Eli surfaced. She gulped in air. George reached down for his son and laid the child on the edge of the pier. Ben grabbed the wharf and hoisted himself out of the water. Then he turned to her, but Megan had already pulled herself onto the wooden platform.

George's lips moved as if in prayer. He started CPR by putting the heel of his hand over the lower third of the child's breastbone and counting, "1, 2, 3."

Megan's heart pounded.

Please, Lord, let Eli breathe.

After 30 quick chest compressions, George put a hand on the child's forehead and two fingers of the other one under the tip of the boy's chin. Silence filled the air as George tilted the child's neck back to open the airway.

Lord, please save Eli.

The child coughed. Water rushed out of his mouth. George turned the boy's face to the side and pointed it down. The child vomited.

Thank you, Lord.

A siren wailed in the distance. George raised Eli, so he wouldn't choke.

The little boy vomited again and then cried. "Daddy, I was scared."

Tears ran down George's face. "So was I, but Jesus kept you safe."

A police car and an ambulance arrived. Two paramedics leaped out of the emergency vehicle and ran to Eli in George's arms. Megan and Ben moved away so George could speak to the EMTs, and they could check out his son.

Megan shivered from head to toe and her teeth chattered. Then a warmth spread over her. She smiled at Ben's mom.

Mrs. Grant adjusted the blanket. "Pull it tight. I don't want you to catch pneumonia. I brought one for Ben, too."

He reached for the second cover from his mom and draped it around him. Then he nodded at George before heading toward the police officers.

Ten minutes later, the cruiser and ambulance drove away.

Mrs. Grant rubbed Megan's back and arms. "I wish we had brought a change of clothes for you."

"We keep overnight supplies in the vehicle in case we have to leave in a hurry. I tossed them in the rental." Ben went to the car. He returned with two bags and a folded pile of children's clothes.

George changed Eli's clothes. "I called Betsy. She's worried, even after talking to Eli. She took off work and is on her way. The hospital is closer to us than home, so she'll be here soon."

Ben frowned. "She could have brought some dry clothes for Megan."

"She can change into my extra set. They'll be too big for her, but they're clean and warm." George opened his bag and handed Megan some men's clothes. "I'll bring a length of rope for her to use as a belt for the pants." He put Eli on his back and left with his sons.

When they returned, Eli was walking beside his dad. Henry carried the rope, which he handed to Megan.

"Thank you. How are you feeling, Eli?" Megan asked.

"Good, but when are we going to eat lunch?" The little boy grinned.

"Nothing takes away his appetite." George turned to Megan.

"Where can I change?"

Ben pointed. "Go behind those bushes and get out of the wet clothes before you get sick."

"I'll go along to stand guard." Mrs. Grant kept her arm around Megan.

Ben laughed. "Great idea."

Megan giggled at the image of a seventy-five year old lady standing guard. Megan approached the cluster of bushes to use as cover and handed the blanket to Doris. Then Megan set the pile of clothes on top of a large shrub. Her body trembled as she removed her bra, blouse, and sweater. After slipping into the T-shirt, she put on the button-down shirt and lightweight jacket. The garments hung to her hips and warmed her.

Being chilled to the bone had been a new experience. Scott had never let her get cold. He kept her smothered. Not always with blankets, either.

Megan stripped out of the rest of her wet garments and stepped into the boxer shorts and trousers. Her hands shook as she threaded the rope through the loops of the pants and knotted it. When she moved away from the bushes, a warmth landed on her.

Mrs. Grant pulled the blanket tighter. "This should keep you warm."

Megan rolled up the long sleeves on George's shirt. Then she bent down and folded up the pant legs. She picked up her wet clothes as Ben, dressed in dry clothes, came away from some nearby bushes.

When they returned to the picnic site, George was holding Eli, who sipped on a coke. Henry sat on the blanket by his dad's feet.

Ben handed Megan a towel.

"Thanks." After drying her hair, she wrapped the towel around her head turban-style to keep the chill away.

Ben poured coffee and handed the cup to Megan. "This should warm you."

She gripped the hot mug with both hands and let the heat flow through her.

A few minutes later, the boys yelled, "Mamma. Mamma."

Everyone turned to the approaching car. An attractive, ebony-skinned woman in hospital scrubs parked and jumped out. The boys ran to her and George followed. She knelt and hugged her sons. Then the family walked hand in hand to the picnic site. George and Betsy each held one of their sons on their laps as they sat on the blanket.

Mrs. Grant opened the picnic basket. "Eli's hungry. How about a ham sandwich?"

Betsy's voice wobbled, "Elijah Benjamin Cunningham, why did you jump in the water when your dad told you not to?"

"I didn't jump in the water. I leaned over to look for my ball and fell in."

Henry looked at his mom. "I wanted to go in after him, but Miss Megan said to stay there, so I obeyed."

"I'm glad you did and both of you are safe." She stroked Henry's cheek and sighed, "I'm hungry, too, now."

As Doris passed out the sandwiches, Betsy turned to Megan, "We haven't been properly introduced. I'm George's wife. It sounds like you saved my little boy, Megan."

"No, ma'am. Ben saved him." Megan sipped her coffee.

Betsy roared with laughter. "Again, Ben?"

He shrugged and turned to Megan. "When Betsy was pregnant, the baby was in distress. George was delayed reaching Betsy because of a pile-up on the freeway, so I drove her to the hospital."

"Your action saved Eli's life that day." Betsy patted Ben's hand. "So thank you again."

"Just my duty, ma'am." He smiled at his assistant. "George saved Eli by starting CPR. He had Eli breathing quickly. There doesn't appear to be any permanent damage, the way Eli is eating and drinking."

"It sounds like a team effort." Betsy took another sip.

Megan grinned. "By the way, thanks for those beautiful clothes. They fit perfectly."

"I gave up trying to be a size 8 again. I'm now a comfortable size 12." Betsy chuckled.

George reached for his wife's hand. "That's right for me."

"I'm a little worried." Doris sighed. "I wanted to make sure Eli had medical intervention if needed, so I dialed 911, but I didn't want to put Megan at risk."

"I'm glad you called." Megan took the older woman's hand. "All of us might have needed help."

George asked, "What happened down there in the water?"

"Eli got tangled in a fishing net. Megan tried to free him but didn't have a knife, so I cut Eli loose."

As Megan drank her coffee, she saw herself caught in a web of Scott's ropes. The more she struggled, the more the cords tightened until she had nearly lost all strength and given up. If only someone could have cut away the net and set her free years ago, like Ben released Eli. Thank God she'd been liberated from Scott's net. But would he catch her again and tie her up in his web of control?

Ben poured the rest of the coffee and handed out the last of the soft drinks. "I talked to the police officers, who promised to do their best to keep this incident from the public. Scott shouldn't learn you were here with us." He passed the container of oatmeal cookies to George and his family. "It looks like Eli's no longer cold. Megan, are you warm?"

"Yes."

"Daddy, can we play again?" Eli asked.

George looked at his wife, who nodded and pointed to the area behind them away from the lake shore. "Right there."

"Yes, ma'am." George kissed his wife and tossed Henry the ball.

After George and his sons left, Mrs. Grant put her empty cup in the basket. "You're so good with children, Megan. It's a pity you don't have any of your own."

"It's not a pity." Megan stared over the lake. "I thank God Scott and I didn't have any. After what I suffered under his tyranny, I can't imagine what my helpless children would have endured."

Mrs. Grant exhaled loudly. "You're right, dear. It's a blessing in disguise."

Ben swallowed the last bite of cookie. "Megan, have you thought about working with children?"

"After I renew my license, I'd like to go into pediatric nursing."

"We need that specialty in the hospital." Betsy grinned.

Ben had intended the day to be relaxing, but so far it wasn't. Megan needed a diversion, and Ben wanted to take her away from the site in case Scott's men had learned she was there.

"Would you like to go for a boat ride on the lake?"

"Sure, but I'm not presentable." She lifted the towel from her head and finished drying her hair. Looking down at her outfit, she started laughing.

"What's so funny?" Ben cocked an eyebrow.

"Scott would never let me wear something like this, even during an emergency."

"It's the perfect disguise."

"You're right." Megan stood. "Lead the way."

The wide trail permitted them to walk side by side. Ben scanned the area for strangers or movement. "My friend has a home here on the lake, but he's out of town. I called, and he told me we could use his boat." Ben grinned. "While I was employed by your husband I investigated your background and learned you were an accomplished cross-country runner and swimmer. So when you and Eli didn't surface, I was uneasy."

"I'm glad you came to our rescue." She smiled.

When they reached the shed, Ben lifted a key from under an old flower pot and unlocked the door. He brushed away the cobwebs and stepped inside. "Stay out there. It's dirty in here."

A moment later, he pulled out the boat and shoved it into the lake. He handed Megan a life vest. "Put this on."

She slipped it on and fastened it.

Then he put his own vest on, took off his sneakers and socks, and put them in the boat with a pair of binoculars. He rolled up his pant legs. "You can climb in now."

She sat. Then he pushed the boat into the water and jumped inside the craft. A surge of pride for Megan warmed his heart as he picked up the oars. He'd never known a woman with as much spunk and compassion.

Ben rowed to the middle of the lake and lowered the oars.
He picked up the binoculars to scan the surrounding area. Spotting two men in suits, he phoned George. "We have company. Pack up. Have Betsy take the boys home. Drive the van with Mom to the east side of the water and meet us."

How had Scott's men found them? Ben should have searched his mom's house for another bug.

CHAPTER THIRTY-FIVE

Scott opened the front door and motioned Dan into the house. Paying off judges, doctors, and police officers ensured Scott would reap what he had sown. Most of the officials had already taken his side.

Dan put a fingertip to his lips and motioned for Scott to be quiet. He led the way through the elegant living room and dining area and up the stairs. Walking through the master bedroom, he headed to the bathroom. Dan turned the water on in the bathtub full blast. After lowering the toilet seat, he sat on it and pointed to the ledge of the tub.

"My men spotted Megan with Ben Grant out on Lake Wallatussie. They looked real cozy, alone in a boat in the middle of the lake." Dan opened his jacket and handed a stack of photos to Scott.

He took them and glared at the pictures. "I'm going to take care of Ben Grant if it's the last thing I do. Have your guys keep watching him and Megan. When you see one without the other, let me know."

"I'll take care of that."

"I hate this ankle bracelet." Scott ran his fingers over it. "I've figured everything out, so it'll be a happy ending. My friends are leaking word to the press that I'm sacrificing myself for Megan."

"That's not a good idea. Suppose it backfires."

Scott's plan would succeed. His church members had seen his protection of his wife after her supposed nervous breakdowns and failed health. They would see for themselves how much he loved Megan.

"I'll go to prison for my wife's embezzlement. My sentence will be reduced to practically no time at all. Everyone will applaud my deep devotion to Megan. It will touch people's hearts. They might even let me off without any jail time." Scott beamed.

Dan furrowed his brow. "It's risky."

"It will work."

"How will you escape the assault charge on Megan?"

"I have a proposition for you. How much money would you want to take that rap for me?"

"What?" Dan jumped up.

"We were both in the motel room with Megan. I'd like you to step up and confess that you were the one who beat her because you lost your temper and were so angry when she disrespected me. You can say that I tried to stop you."

"Why would I do that?"

"I'll pay you."

"It won't work. You've already confessed to it, so why would anyone believe me?"

"They'd believe you because I'd agree with it."

"It's too late."

"It's not too late. This falls in with my plans. I'll remind people of the times Megan disappeared and ran off with one of her lovers, who beat her up. She returned to me and I nursed her back to health."

"Give me two million dollars, and I'll take the fall for the beating. I'll set up an account in Switzerland. After you transfer half the money, I'll confess to the assault. Then you'll have two weeks to give me the rest. If you don't, I'll retract my confession."

"It's a deal."

They shook hands.

Scott's perfect plan would succeed.

*****

Jane sat in the passenger seat of the old station wagon and lowered her window. As they drove out of Memphis, she enjoyed the wind rushing through her hair. Freedom. She thanked God for the crisp breeze and sunshine. Red, gold, and purple leaves coated the countryside.

Her transporter, a cautious man in his fifties, checked the mirrors frequently. "No one's been following us."

She leaned back and closed her eyes. Thanksgiving with Mrs. Grant and Ben had been the best one she'd ever had. Doris taught her how to make homemade cranberry sauce and dressing. She had enjoyed working with Ben to stuff the twenty-pound bird. Too bad she couldn't spend Christmas with them.

After the feast, Jane had helped pack plates for needy families. As she delivered food with Ben and his mom, she hoped soon to have a ministry, but until then, she'd take pleasure in doing what she could with those around her.

Three hours later, she was surprised when the vehicle pulled in to Mrs. Sully's drive.

Peter came out of the house and reached for her suitcase. "I'm glad you're back. After you left, I investigated the support group and told them I wanted to volunteer, so arrangements were made for you to work here. Mom and I have missed you."

"I missed both of you, too." She had quickly learned to go from Jane to Megan and back again. Mrs. Sully knew nothing about her past and had only known her as Jane. So it was agreed that's what she'd be called.

She slung her backpack over her shoulder. "Thank you for hiring me again to care for your mother."

Jane started work right away, and the following week, she drove the older woman to the mall to buy Christmas presents. After parking in a handicapped spot, Jane helped Mrs. Sully into her wheelchair. "Where would you like to go first?"

Mrs. Sully clutched her purse on her lap. "The decorations are up, so I'd like to see the displays first."

Jane rolled the chair down the wide passageway and then halted in front of Macy's. "Do you know where they sell the men's toiletries?"

"Upstairs." Mrs. Sully fidgeted. "I hope they'll have the right aftershave for Peter."

Jane pressed the elevator button a second time and then patted Mrs. Sully's shoulder. "I've written down everything he likes, so I'm sure we'll find some nice gifts."

Entering the lift, Mrs. Sully asked, "How are your online nursing classes coming?"

"There have been lots of changes in the last fifteen years, so it's hard."

"I'll bet you're picking it up quickly. You're the smartest girl I've ever had taking care of me."

Having been badgered for years into thinking she could do nothing, it had been hard to concentrate on the first course. She'd started with a geriatric class since she had lots of experience caring for the elderly. When she received her first A, it gave her the momentum to keep going.

A couple hours later, Mrs. Sully tired, so Jane suggested. "Would you like to go to the food court and have a drink?"

"Yes, that would be nice."

Jane parked the wheelchair in front of a table and applied the brake. "What would you like?"

"My usual."

When Jane returned, she handed the iced tea to the older woman. Jane sat down next to Mrs. Sully and sighed in contentment as she sipped on her milkshake. Nothing could destroy her happiness now. She loved her job and worked on classes to renew her nursing license.

"Can we come back next week and finish your Christmas shopping? I think we're a bit worn out." Jane smiled.

"Of course, dear, if you're tired." The older woman yawned.

*****

Two weeks later, Jane and Mrs. Sully finished the Christmas shopping. Jane pushed Mrs. Sully's wheelchair to the car, helped the older woman into the vehicle, and drove home.

When Jane pulled into the drive, she spotted a florist box with a big red bow leaning against the front door. "I'll bet Peter sent you beautiful flowers." She jumped out of the vehicle and ran to collect the carton.

Seeing it was addressed to Megan Jane Collins in Scott's handwriting, she slowly turned around, expecting Scott to grab her. Her hands shook as she gripped the envelope. Her breathing quickened. She looked around frantically again. Would he kidnap her in front of Mrs. Sully? Icy terror trickled down her spine.

Jane stuffed the card in her pocket. "Maybe you have a secret admirer." She turned to Mrs. Sully and handed her the florist carton, but she remembered another time Scott had sent her a box of flowers that didn't have any blooms in it. Scott had wrapped a dead mouse inside an expensive negligee.

"May I take a peek inside first?" Jane confirmed roses were in the box, so with shaking hands she gave the carton back to her employer.

Then Jane drove the car into the garage and closed it. Her heart pounded as she helped the older woman into her wheelchair. Jane fumbled with the keys at the kitchen door. Nerves skittered around the base of her stomach. How had her husband found her? As she pushed Mrs. Sully's chair down the hall to her bedroom, Jane peered into each room along the way.

While Mrs. Sully napped, Jane tiptoed through the rest of the house and checked the doors and windows. Everything looked secure, but she dialed the security company to confirm that no one had entered.

Then Jane punched in another number. "He's found me again."

Peter arrived that evening for supper. After Mrs. Sully had gone to bed, Jane showed the flowers to Peter. "My husband sent these. I didn't want your mother to worry, so I waited until now to tell you." She handed him the card.

Taking it, he read aloud. "My dear Megan. I love you and miss you. I will soon bring you home so we can be together again."

"He keeps finding me." She shivered. "It's never going to end. He'll catch me and take me back one of these days. I called the support group. They're searching for another place for me."

"Mother will be disappointed that you had to leave again, but you must be safe."

Mrs. Sully's phone rang, and Jane answered it. When she ended the call, she turned to Peter. "Someone will pick me up at eight tomorrow and take me to a safe house."

Peter pulled out his wallet. "Let me give you a little extra."

"It's not necessary."

"You might be on the run again."

"Thank you." She accepted the cash. "I need a disguise so Scott won't recognize me. I don't want to go out alone tonight to buy one. May I borrow some of your mother's older clothes?"

"Take anything you need to get away safely."

"There's a bottle of black hair color in the hall closet."

Peter laughed. "Mom dyed her hair years ago. Take it and use it. Do you think it's still good?"

"Yes, it hasn't been opened and kept in a dry place. There's no expiration date. I've used so much hair color over the years, I'm familiar with it. It will be fine."

"Please come back when it's safe again."

"I will. I enjoy working for you and taking care of your mom."

After Peter left, Jane went to the bathroom to color and cut her hair again. She packed her bag, and then she wrapped some Christmas presents.

Early the next morning, she checked on Mrs. Sully, who still slept. Jane didn't want to leave. The older woman would be hurt if Jane ran out on her again without saying goodbye, but Jane had to leave. Peter would explain her disappearance to his mother.

Seeing someone come to the front door, Jane recognized the temporary aid and let her in. The worker went to the kitchen to make coffee.

Jane was so tired of running, but she had no choice. Her heart clenched. She went to her room and tied two old pillows around her, and then she pulled one of Mrs. Sully's dresses over her head. Glancing in the mirror, Jane saw an overweight, middle-aged woman whom Scott wouldn't look at twice.

She went into the living room and stared out the window at the snow that covered the ground. A drive over the white-capped mountains would be beautiful, but she might be going south and away from the snow. Jane walked to the garland-draped fireplace and let the heat warm her. Christmas was only one week away, and it would have been her second one free of Scott. She brushed a tear off her cheek and then ran her fingers over the gold and silver wrapping paper that covered the gift in her hand. Mrs. Sully would appreciate the bath powder and lotion.

Jane knelt under the magnificent Christmas tree and left the present. Then she went to the front door and peeked out the window. A dark van pulled into the driveway. Jane waited until the driver rang the doorbell. Jane recognized Peggy, dressed in her security guard uniform. She kept her hand on the gun in the holster at her waist.

Jane opened the door. "Come in. It's good to see you again."

Peggy stepped inside and stared at Megan. "I hardly recognized you in that disguise. I wish we could have met under more pleasant circumstances."

"Me too." Jane locked the door. "How are Maryanne and her parents doing?"

"They're well. Today's my day off. Your husband might think twice if he saw someone with a weapon come to the house." Peggy patted her gun. "Most tormenters give up and go after someone else. Your husband's cruelty and stalking have escalated to psychotic levels."

Jane shivered and rubbed her lower arms.

"We need to go." Peggy turned to the door.

"I'll wait for you to open the garage door and pull the van into it."

Inside the closed garage, Peggy put Jane's bag in the vehicle. "Get in the back on the floor so it looks like I'm alone in the van."

Jane scrunched below the windows, as Peggy backed out of the driveway. Suddenly the van stopped. Jane's heart beat faster when Peggy jumped out of the vehicle and ran off. Jane lifted her head and peeked out the back window. She immediately dropped down and curled into a fetal position. Peggy was talking to a man that Jane recognized as one of Scott's police friends.

Had he seen her?

CHAPTER THIRTY-SIX

Megan scrunched lower and stayed under the windows in the back of the van. She broke out in a sweat.

Trust in the Lord. *Those who know your name, Lord, will trust in you. For you Lord have never forsaken those who seek you.*

She breathed easier when Peggy climbed back into the seat and started driving.

"That officer is a good friend of your husband." Peggy shifted gears. "He's looking for you, but I don't think he knows I came here to help you. I told him that I'm collecting donations for new equipment."

"Did he believe you?"

"I don't know, but the police car turned around and left, so it's safe to come up here and sit. I'll stay in the right lane so no one will see you in the passenger seat."

The van was warm so Megan left her coat in the back, crawled to the front seat, and fastened the safety belt.

Peggy drove south. Several hours later she pulled into a gas station outside of Memphis. "Go to the back and stay low. I'll let you know when it's safe to come out."

A few minutes later, the van stopped. Megan lifted her head and peeked out. They were parked in front of an elegant gold brick home. Megan recognized the neighborhood but not the house. "Do you think I'll be safe this close to Scott?"

"Come up here and wait. The leaders have a plan. You will be quite safe." Peggy tapped in a number and spoke. "We're here."

A few minutes later, Fred and Louise Sparks marched out of the house and approached the van. Fred opened the door. "Mrs. Collins, it's good to see you again. I hardly recognized you in that disguise."

Megan's heart pounded. She lifted trembling fingers to push her hair behind her ear. She was seeing things. No, she saw Fred Sparks, Scott's head deacon and closest friend in the church. Megan's husband had to be hiding in the house and waiting for her.

What could she do? Where could she go? Her adrenaline rushed. It didn't matter, but she had to get away.

Run Jane. Run.

*****

Megan jumped out of the van and sprinted down the street in the opposite direction of her old home with Scott.

"Come back." Peggy yelled.

Tears blurred Megan's vision. She searched frantically for an alley between homes in which to hide. She jogged faster, swerved to the left, and darted between two houses. She hid from the road and looked back. Her heart plummeted as Peggy turned the van around and headed toward her. It looked like Scott sat in the vehicle. He was hunting her down like an animal, but she couldn't see well through her tears and the falling snow.

Where now? Who could she trust? Of all the people she'd met, she had the most confidence in Mrs. Grant. The older woman would never betray her. Megan didn't think Ben would betray her either, but she hadn't learned to trust any man completely yet.

Trust in the Lord with all thine heart.

Megan raced down the alley and came out at the adjacent street. She jogged across the road and into another lane. After ducking behind a storage shed, she caught her breath and leaned back against the building before slumping to the ground.

Why hadn't she given up long ago? It would have been easier to let Scott kill her. She leaned forward, pulled up her knees, and wrapped her arms around them. Then she let her head fall in her lap. Too bad she hadn't thought fast enough to grab her coat and backpack, but it didn't matter anymore. Her life was over now. Even if she wanted to call someone, she didn't have a phone.

Give up.

Why had she tried so hard to leave Scott when he always found her and took her back? Tears ran down her cheeks. She tried to wipe them, but her fingers were too stiff. Her shoulders shook. Freezing to death couldn't be a horrible death.

Several minutes later, her fingers were redder and too stiff to move. She stuffed her hands between her stomach and the pillow tied to it.

She no longer wanted to live in a cruel world where men could torture women and get away with it. Deep sobs shook Megan's shoulders. Best to let nature take its course and freeze to death. She shivered as icy snow flakes beat down on her. Her teeth chattered. She shifted her weight to sit on her feet, closed her eyes, and surrendered to the inevitable.

Lord, please take me to Heaven.

Trust me, your Savior.

I trust you Lord, but I'm not sure who else I can trust.

Ben couldn't have betrayed her. He had rescued her from Scott and risked his life by shielding her when Scott shot at them. If only she had a phone to call Ben's mother.

Lord, thank you for saving my soul. If it's your will, spare my life.

"Are you lost?" A teenage girl stopped in front of her.

Megan lifted her head and stuttered. "Can... can... can I use... use ... phone?"

The girl handed her cell to Megan, who put her index finger in her mouth to warm it enough to press the numbers. "Hello... I...I... I played jeopardy."

Everything went black.

*****

When Ben answered his phone, his mother panted, "Megan called. She's in danger and she sounded hurt."

His heart clenched. Sweat broke out on his brow. "I'll be there in five minutes."

When Ben walked into his mother's house, he found her pacing the kitchen floor. A pile of folded blankets covered the table.

He hugged her. "What happened?"

"Megan called and whispered, I played jeopardy. I had told her once about our secret code."

"Where is she?"

"She must have dropped the phone because a young girl told me a homeless lady sat in the snow without a coat and had gone to sleep. Here's the address. I tried calling back, but no signal."

Ben glanced at the paper and memorized the location. Then he picked up the blankets. "Keep praying, Mom. She is close to Rev. Collins's church." He kissed his mom and left.

How could Megan have been abandoned in an alley with a blizzard heading that way? Scott must have found her and taken her there hoping she'd die. Ben shuddered.

Lord, help me reach her in time.

Ten minutes later, he found the alley and a teenager covering a giant snowball with a blanket. His heart lurched. It had to be Megan. He parked close by and introduced himself. "Hello, I'm Benjamin Grant. Thanks for bringing a blanket."

"I wish I could have come faster." The girl jumped in place and blew on her hands. "This lady needs an ambulance. I should have called one when I went home to bring a blanket, but I was too upset to think about it. When I returned, my cell had died. I didn't want to leave her."

Ben knelt next to Megan and searched for a pulse. He found a slow, weak one. The icy snow fell hard in the thirty-one-degree temperature. Even without a wind, the cold penetrated. He picked her up and slid her onto the back seat of his Honda. Then he covered her with the blankets he had brought.

"Thank you." Ben returned the girl's blanket.

Lord, please don't let it be too late.

He turned back to the seat and lifted Megan's short, black hair away from her face. After he increased the heat, he removed his coat and sweater and added them to the heap of covers on top of her.

"We'll take care of her now." He shook the girl's hand. "I appreciate your help. You probably saved her life."

"It's what Jesus would have done." The girl clutched her blanket and left.

Gently he pulled Megan's hands out from under the pillow. Ben had some experience treating men found in snow drifts. He examined her fingers, which were cold but not frozen. They were red and not white. He saw no signs of frostbite. Should he take her to the emergency room? Without knowing who had hurt her or left her in an alley to die, she might be in more danger at a hospital. His mother's home was closer. They could have her in warm clothes and a bed much quicker.

After pulling into his mother's garage, he closed the door and ran into the house. "I've brought Megan. We need to get her warm."

"Her bed is ready."

As he carried Megan to the guest room, a moan escaped her lips. "I think she's coming around." He put her on the bed.

"Son, you wait outside while I undress her."

"I'll be here in the hall. Call me the minute you're done."

Five minutes later, his mom opened the door. "I put a flannel nightgown on her and covered her, but you can help me with socks and gloves. Her hands and feet are cold. She had pillows tied to her and an extra layer of clothes over that. Why was she dressed as a homeless person?"

"I don't know." He stepped back in the room with his mother and put two pairs of socks on Megan's feet while his mom put gloves on Megan's hands. She would live, but would Scott find her again?

*****

Megan woke up and looked around trying to place her surroundings. She was safe and warm in Mrs. Grant's home. *Thank you, Lord.*

Seeing Mrs. Grant on one side of the bed and Ben on the other, Megan asked, "How did I get here?"

Mrs. Grant pulled her chair closer and took Megan's hand. "You called me and said, I played jeopardy."

"How do you feel?" Ben clasped his hands together and leaned forward.

"A little cold."

Mrs. Grant stood. "I'll bring you some hot tea and toast. You need something inside to warm you."

"Please don't go to any trouble. I'm sorry to be such a burden to you." Megan started crying.

"You're not a burden. We love you." Mrs. Grant smiled before leaving the room.

"We care about you and want to help." Ben reached for the box of tissues on top of the dresser and handed it to her. "Can you tell me what happened?"

She closed her eyes and squeezed more tears out of them. Taking several deep breaths, she tried to compose herself. "I can't believe it. Everyone betrayed me. I thought you did, too."

"Me?" Ben asked.

His mom returned with the tray and poured Megan a cup of tea.

Cradling the mug in both hands, Megan brought it to her lips and sipped. "This is so good. Thank you."

Ben lowered his voice, "Can you start at the beginning and talk about it?"

"I was in Nashville, taking care of Mrs. Sully. I drove her home from shopping and found a box of red roses with a note from Scott. I was so scared." She started crying again.

He leaned back in his chair as if he had all the time in the world. Ben clasped his hands and put them behind his head. "Go on."

"I called Cindy and told her about the roses. She sent Peggy to pick me up this morning and drive me to my new location. She stopped at a house about a mile from Scott's. But then ... then..." Megan gasped for air. "Fred Sparks, my husband's closest friend, who is also the head deacon, came out of the house. It was a trap. Scott must have paid everyone off."

Ben asked, "What happened?"

"I ran into an alley. After I collapsed, a girl came, so I used her phone. It started snowing. I couldn't stay warm and must have passed out." She sniffed. "How could everyone I trusted have deceived me?"

"We didn't. We love you." Mrs. Grant patted Megan's arm.

She believed Ben and his mother, but would she ever be able to trust anyone else?

CHAPTER THIRTY-SEVEN

Ben didn't think the organization had betrayed Megan. Someone must have written the wrong address or received incorrect information.

He went into the kitchen and called Cindy on his cell phone. "This is Benjamin Grant. Do you know where Megan is now or where she should be?"

"One of our associates picked her up this morning and drove her to a new location. When they arrived at the home, the hosts came out of the house. Megan looked at them and ran so fast she didn't take her coat or bag." Cindy's voice wobbled. "We don't know where she is."

"Megan called my mom. Megan thought you had betrayed her by taking her to the home of her husband's friend. She was terrified Scott would come out of the house."

"Where is she now?"

"Somewhere safe."

"I want to fill you in, but I'd like to talk to our lawyer first. I'll phone back."

After the call, Ben returned to the bedroom. "How's the patient doing?"

His mom smiled. "She's better."

"How can I ever thank you?" Megan gulped down the last bite of toast.

Mrs. Grant picked up the tray. "We thank God that you called."

Ben sat in the chair next to the bed, facing Megan. "You could have died. Why did you decide to trust us?"

"You saved my life. That's something Scott had never done." Megan covered a yawn. "Excuse me."

"God calls us to lay down our lives for others. When we love people it shows the world that we're Christians." Ben took the tray from his mother. "I'll carry this to the kitchen."

"Take a nap." Mrs. Grant plucked the pillow from behind Megan and tucked in the covers. "Stay warm and call if you need something."

Alone in the kitchen with his mother, Ben set the dirty dishes in the sink. "It's time for lunch. I'm hungry. Do you have any leftovers?"

"There's plenty of roast beef and gravy, rice, green beans and corn in the refrigerator for you, me, and Megan when she wakes."

When they sat down to eat, Ben told his mom about Cindy's call.

"Megan has gone through enough. She can stay here until her husband is put in prison." His mom put her napkin in her lap.

"Her husband is dangerous. This is the first place he'll look for her. God forbid, but he could come with a gang of his hired men and try to take her by force and hurt you and her in the process."

"She's my guest, and she's staying until that organization finds another safe house. Your father would have agreed with me."

He laughed. "If Dad were alive, Rev. Collins would think twice before coming here."

When they finished eating, Ben dried the dishes for his mom. After hanging the towel, he turned to the hall. "I'll go check on Megan."

Seeing her read her grandmother's Bible, Ben tapped on the open door. "I'm glad you're awake. How are you feeling? Are you warm?"

"Yes, thank you. I want to take a hot shower and then help your mom."

"Are you hungry?"

"No, I'm full from the tea and toast."

"May I sit down?"

She nodded.

After he sat, he leaned forward. "I called Cindy and told her what happened. They're checking it out, but I don't think the organization betrayed you."

Megan started crying. "Freezing to death in an alley would have been better than living in a world where everyone I started to trust had betrayed me."

"You have us and people like Peter Sully and his mother."

"Yes, I do. I appreciate your coming for me. A verse I read reminded me to trust in the Lord with all my heart and lean not to my own understanding." Megan bent forward and put her hand on top of his.

Ben liked the feel of her palm on his hand, but it would take time for her to trust him.

His phone rang and he answered it. After ending the call, he said, "Cindy and Eileen are coming over to explain what happened. I'd like to hear what they have to say. You can stay in your room with the door open, so you can listen without being seen."

His mom had turned up the heat and put on a summer dress. Ben changed into a short-sleeved cotton shirt and pants but still felt hot.

After Megan had taken a hot shower and dressed in wool slacks and two sweaters, she went into the living room. Then the bell rang.

"That's probably Cindy and Eileen."

Megan went into her room.

Ben brought the ladies into the living room. After a few minutes of drinking coffee and eating cookies, Cindy fanned herself with some documents. "We're sorry about the mix-up this morning. We try to keep everyone safe by telling only what people need to know. Even Peggy didn't know of our plan."

Eileen unbuttoned her sweater. "The less people know of our safe homes and transporters the less information there is to get into the wrong hands. We're set up similar to the Underground Railroad when people transported slaves to freedom. No one knows the next station or the names of the people who help them escape."

Ben asked. "How did Megan end up a few miles down the road from Scott?"

Cindy rolled up her sleeves. "We planned it."

Hearing a faint gasp from the bedroom, Ben wondered if Cindy and Eileen had noticed, but they didn't flinch or turn toward the sound.

"Why?" He asked.

"Since the photo of Megan's battered face and the news about the missing six million dollars appeared on television, more people have come forward with accusations." Eileen lifted a paper out of her briefcase. "Two young girls alleged that the pastor made improper advances to them. A number of people claimed they gave the pastor large sums of cash because they didn't have their checkbooks. Reverend Collins promised to give them a receipt, but he didn't."

Eileen handed Ben a note. "Fred Sparks came to me after the hearing and passed me this."

Ben opened it and read it out loud so Megan could hear. "My name is on the church account with Scott. I'm afraid people will think I'm an accomplice. I want to help, but I don't know how to do it without making Scott suspicious. Please call me."

"If Megan stayed with Fred and Louise Sparks, how would that help?" Ben asked.

"She and Fred could go through the records the auditor gathered. Fred knows church business and Megan knew her husband's schedule and the days away from home."

He asked, "How do you know you can trust Fred?"

"It's a risk. I'm inclined to believe Fred. The auditor reported that even though Fred's name is on the church account, he never signed any checks."

Silence filled the room until a white-faced Megan stood in the doorway. Ben started to stand but Megan motioned him to stay seated. "So the Sparks and I would be spies?"

Eileen stared and then smiled. "If you and Fred confirm discrepancies and record them, it would give us specific amounts and times to investigate more thoroughly. It's bewildering that Scott has no offshore accounts anywhere. Where is the missing money? No one's been able to locate it." Eileen handed a sheet to Megan. "Here's an outline of specific dates and incidents to look for."

Megan sat. "Scott disappeared lots of times, but I don't know where he went."

"We think he went to the bank or to meet someone."

With trembling fingers, Megan lifted her hair away from her face. "Do you think I'd be safe? Fred has been Scott's close advisor and treasurer all the years that Scott has been the pastor. Fred is compliant and passive. His wife is docile. Fred has followed and obeyed Scott in everything."

"We planned on discussing this with you before we sent you there, but when Scott found you at the Sully's house, we needed to move you quickly. We had no other options on such short notice."

"If that's the case, I'll go over there, but I've a feeling that Scott may have found out about my arrival there."

Ben leaned forward. "Would you ladies consider a compromise?"

"What do you suggest, Mr. Grant?" Eileen asked.

"Let Megan stay here with Mom until Christmas. It's only a week away and will give her time to adjust to the idea of going to the Sparks home."

"I like that, and I have another request." Megan smiled.

"What is it?" Eileen asked.

"Can I meet Fred and Louise someplace alone in the next few days? Then I can talk to them and maybe sense their intentions."

"That would work, but you can't meet in a public place or Scott might hear about it. If someone saw you, it could put you in more danger." Cindy frowned.

"We can invite them here for dinner." Mrs. Grant beamed. "Megan, you can help me cook."

"I'd like that. Thank you."

Ben's eyes narrowed. "All right, but George and I will be here, too."

Closing her briefcase, Eileen looked at Megan. "Three months ago I filed a petition for the dissolution of your marriage, and we served Scott the summons. We assumed it would be a simple divorce, since you wanted nothing from your husband, but Scott has refused to sign the papers."

"What reason did he give?" Megan asked.

"He claimed you'll stay married to him until death separates you. I'll have a judge rule in your favor, but it sounded like a threat. So be careful." Eileen picked up her briefcase. "One of us will call you after Christmas and ask how the meeting went with Fred and Louise."

Everyone stood, but Megan spoke. "I appreciate your concern and your visit. You've put my mind at ease and given me much to pray about."

Cindy smiled. "I hope it works out with the Sparks because it could be a way of proving beyond a doubt that Scott's an embezzler and help us find that money."

They walked to the front door and Megan looked out. "It's snowing again. I thank God that I'm not out there."

Ben mumbled, "Yes, thank you, Lord."

CHAPTER THIRTY-EIGHT

Megan zipped the pleated red and gray skirt and then tugged a black sweater over her head. After pulling on a pair of hose for warmth, she slipped into her black heels. She stuffed her gloves and scarf in the pocket of her coat, and then she picked it up with her grandmother's Bible and hugged it.

She had no idea how Ben managed to collect her bag and coat. But her heart warmed at his constant care and thoughtfulness. It was so opposite that of her husband's behavior.

The out-of-style coat was worn and a bit large, but she thanked God it would protect her from the cold. She carried it into the living room. Ben stood and helped her into the garment.

His mom already had her coat on and reached for her purse. "We're ready, son."

Megan turned to Ben and smiled. "I'm looking forward to church."

After checking the locks on the windows and doors, he led the way into the garage. He opened the front passenger door for his mom and the back one for Megan. When the ladies were settled, he slid into the driver's seat.

Megan stared out the window. "I'm sorry for quarreling with you. I quickly learned with Scott, it would be a waste of time to argue. He was always right in everything and let me know it. I let him tell me what to do and never asked for anything. Ben, you're the first person, I've ever quarreled with. Thank you for letting me come to church."

"I was trying to protect you. I didn't think it was safe for you to be out in public with Mom and me."

"I appreciate your trying to keep me safe." Megan hesitated. "I didn't want you to miss this program because of me." She paused again. "The longer I'm away from Scott's control, the more I see that I have a right to speak and share what's on my mind."

A few minutes later, he pulled into the parking lot. "Going to church is probably best for all of us." Ben walked between them, took their arms, and escorted them into the sanctuary. His mother led the way down the aisle and into the pew. Megan sat next to Mrs. Grant, and Ben took the aisle seat.

After the presentation, the pastor stood. "Take the hand of the person next to you and let's pray."

Mrs. Grant slipped her hand in Megan's. Ben held out his, but Megan ignored it. When he started to lower his arm, she changed her mind and reached for his hand. Unlike Scott, he didn't squeeze so hard that ripples of pain ran up her arm.

When the prayer ended, Ben turned to his mom. "Let's go straight to the car and not stop to visit."

"That's fine. I'll call my friends later."

As they strolled to the vehicle, Megan sighed. "I needed a touch from the Lord, and Christ calmed my soul. After all you've done for me, I couldn't let you miss your annual Christmas cantata."

"We had planned to stay home with you." Mrs. Grant squeezed Megan's arm. "Love means sacrificing for others."

"Scott never made any sacrifices for me."

"True love means that you're willing to surrender your will for others." Ben lifted his car keys out of his pocket and opened the doors.

Harsh ice crystals had pounded Megan in the alley that morning. But that night gentle snowflakes caressed her cheeks and soothed her. Or maybe being in the presence of caring people filled her with peace.

When they arrived home, she went to her room and changed into her nightgown. Looking in the mirror, she removed her makeup. Black hair didn't become her, but it had been necessary to escape.

*****

Ben glanced at Megan as she, wearing her housecoat, came into the living room. He found it hard getting used to Megan's charcoal-colored hair. She smothered a yawn and rolled her neck from side to side. It had been a long, difficult day, and her shoulders were bowed.

"Mom is starting an old movie. Join us."

Mrs. Grant clicked the remote. "It has Debbie Reynolds and Frank Sinatra."

Megan went to the couch.

His mom smiled. "Lie down and relax."

Ben glanced at Megan as she stretched out. She rubbed her arms as if she were cold. He left and returned with a blanket, which he spread over her.

"Thank you."

In the middle of the movie, Megan's snore grew to a deafening roar. Ben and his Mom chuckled.

Mrs. Grant stood. "I'll wake her and send her to bed."

"Don't bother. I'll carry her."

His mom frowned. "I'm surprised her husband allowed her to snore."

"He probably didn't like it but would have needed to take her to a doctor to have it corrected. Those quick fixes from the drug store wouldn't quiet this snore." Ben lifted Megan from the couch.

Megan snored louder and more deeply. Ben and his mom laughed harder. He followed his mother into the room. She pulled the covers of the bed back, and he put Megan down. His mother covered Megan and tucked her in. Ben checked the seals on the windows, closed the blinds, and shut the curtains.

*****

Megan woke early the next morning and went to the kitchen. As she started the coffee, Ben joined her.

"How are you feeling today?" he asked, "Any side effects from the cold?"

"Thanks to you and your mom I don't feel like I spent time outside in a blizzard." Megan sat down at the table with him. "What does your mom want for breakfast?"

"I never know. It's best to wait for her. Some mornings she eats cold cereal." Ben sipped on his coffee.

"I should set a time to meet with Louise and Fred Sparks."

Mrs. Grant came into the kitchen. "Call and set the date so we can work around it for our holiday activities. We need to decorate cookies, deliver presents to the homebound, and see the lights."

Ben pressed in the Sparks number. "It's ringing." He handed the phone to Megan.

"Hello, this is Megan Collins."

After a long pause, Megan smiled. "What evening would be convenient to join us for supper?" She cocked an eyebrow at Mrs. Grant. "Tomorrow night?"

Mrs. Grant and Ben nodded. He pulled out a card, wrote on it, and handed it to her.

She glanced at it. "Would six o'clock be okay?" She gave the address from the card before ending the call. Then she turned to Mrs. Grant. "What should we cook?"

"Please call me Doris." She thought a minute. "Baked chicken or pot roast with potatoes would be simple, and most people can eat it."

"Can you teach me how to make your homemade apple pie?"

"Yes, of course, but breakfast comes first."

*****

Megan jumped when the doorbell rang at a few minutes to six.

"It has to be the Sparks. I'll answer it." Ben left.

Several minutes later he escorted Louise and Fred into the living room where Megan and Mrs. Grant waited.

Louise hugged Megan before sitting. "We're so sorry. When I saw the photo of your beaten face on television, I suspected Scott had hit you other times on occasions you were absent from church. When you returned, you looked in agony and could scarcely walk. Scott told us he had to give you medications for your emotional well-being, but you appeared drugged."

Fred sat next to his wife on the couch. "Scott had us all convinced you had mental problems."

"He always hovered over you." Louise frowned. "It looked like devotion."

The oven bell rang. Megan stood. Mrs. Grant mumbled, "Excuse us," and left the room.

Megan was grateful for the interruption to help Mrs. Grant with the food. She and Doris set the meal on the table. Ben escorted Mr. and Mrs. Sparks to the dining room.

After everyone sat, Ben prayed. Then he passed the roast to Fred and asked, "How do you intend to help Megan?"

"The lawyer suggested we compile missing amounts with the dates of Scott's disappearances from the office." Fred swallowed a bite of beef and gravy. "The sooner, the better. Scott told the church Sunday night that Megan has been stealing funds. He apologized for hiding it from us but wanted to protect his wife's fragile health. He is willing to take the blame for what you did."

Megan dropped her fork. She picked it up and shook her head. "Take the blame for me? But I didn't do anything."

Fifteen years of torture was bad enough. Now he accused her of taking church money. What more would Scott do to her before it was over? She shivered.

"Sorry to say it, but most members believe you stole the money and he is protecting you." Louise sniffed. "Scott's charming personality comes across as loving."

Megan's hands shook as she cut her meat. If people knew Scott hurt her, would it be a bad witness of Christianity?

Fred wiped his mouth. "He's convinced everyone to look for you and bring you back to him, so you can return the money to the church where it belongs. Louise and I don't believe him. Stay with us and help us find evidence to arrest Scott."

She still didn't completely trust Fred and Louise. Their concern for her seemed too convenient, but she would work with them since the organization suggested it.

"Scott's plan could backfire." Megan sipped on her water. "If you took me back, I couldn't return the money because I never stole any of it."

Louise smiled, "We'd never take you back to him."

Her response didn't seem genuine to Megan.

After coffee and apple pie, Fred took his keys out and stood. "We need to be going. Not all the roads are plowed." He helped his wife into her coat. "Would you like us to pick you up on December 26?"

Ben shook Fred's hand. "That's thoughtful of you, but I'd like to drive Megan over to your house so I know where it is in case something comes up."

Louise hugged Megan. "I'm so glad we'll be able to make sure Scott doesn't harm anyone else."

Megan shivered. Only God could stop Scott from hurting people.

CHAPTER THIRTY-NINE

Ben drove his mom and Megan to the shopping mall. Bright stars and garland-draped displays covered the outside buildings. Christmas lights and decorated trees twinkled along the passageways. Elves, reindeer, and peppermint poles surrounded Santa Claus. A long line of waiting children wound around the center of the mall. Ben didn't like the crowds, but surely Scott wouldn't kidnap Megan in front of shoppers.

"Uncle Ben!" A child yelled.

The voice belonged to one of George's sons, who stood in line with his father and brother to see Santa Claus.

Ben turned to the ladies. "Let's say hello."

They walked up to ten-year-old Henry, and six-year-old Eli. The boys jumped up and down as George herded them forward. His sons chattered about what they wanted for Christmas and wondered how Santa could come into their house without a chimney.

When they were nearly to Santa Claus, Ben said, "We've lots of shopping, so we'll say goodbye." He turned to his mom, "Where are we going?"

"Sears is the best place to buy gifts for the ladies in the Bible study and the homebound folks."

Inside the department store, Mrs. Grant headed to a clearance rack while Megan went down the neighboring aisle. Ben kept his eye on her as she picked out a garment, and went to the check-out. He glanced at his mom who searched through a display of dresses.

Out of the corner of his eye, Ben spotted Daniel Fuller at the back of the store. Then Ben noticed two more guys closing in on Megan. The larger one reached her before Ben got there.

The big man stepped behind her and wrapped his huge arm around her waist, making it appear romantic. He whispered in her ear.

Terror flashed across her face. Her eyes widened, and she nodded.

Ben put his hand on his gun and moved closer to them. "You're on camera. Let her go now or I'll have you arrested for attempted kidnapping."

The man released Megan. "Rev. Collins isn't happy you've taken up with his wife. You and this little lady aren't getting away from him, and neither is your sweet old mother."

"Leave now or I'll call security." Ben ordered.

"You can't get rid of us this easily." The two men turned away from Megan.

Ben grabbed the larger one's arm and twisted it behind him. "I'm a God-fearing man and don't like to be rough, but you'd be a lot better off if you stopped working for Scott."

After the hired men left, Ben whispered to Megan. "Let's check on Mom. She's at the end of the next aisle."

Ben went with Megan to his mom, who held up a dress.

"Do you like this, Ben?"

"It's perfect. Let me buy it for you."

Megan opened her bag. "No, let me pay for it as a thank you gift for letting me stay in your house."

Doris shook her head. "I'm buying it myself." She went to the cash register.

Ben kept an eye on his mom but asked Megan, "Did that guy hurt you?"

Her brows furrowed. "He only threatened me."

"What kind of threat?"

"It doesn't matter. We're safe."

Ben persisted in a calm, but firm voice. "How did he threaten you?"

"He told me if I didn't go with him quietly, Scott would send someone to hurt your mother and then kill you."

"And you had agreed to go with him?" Ben cocked an eyebrow.

She lowered her head and nodded.

He whispered, "Please look at me."

She raised her head.

Ben's heart clenched at her tears. "Over the years, I've dealt with bad characters and protected my mother. She trusts God to keep us safe but also follows my advice regarding security. Scott's men will say anything and use any means to persuade you to go with them. Promise me you won't listen to idle threats."

"I'll try not to." Megan sighed and turned toward an aisle. "I didn't finish my shopping, but you can't come with me because it's a surprise."

"I'll keep an eye on you."

Ben punched in George's number. "I just snagged some hired men away from Megan. What are your plans after the boys see Santa Claus?"

"I'm taking them to lunch."

"Could you run interference for us in an hour and follow us to the house? I wouldn't ask if I thought the boys would be in danger, but there's no record of Scott ever hurting anyone except his wife."

"I'll be right behind you."

As Ben, his mother, and Megan strolled to the car, Megan started shaking. Ben couldn't resist putting his arm around her shoulders. She didn't recoil at his touch.

*****

Ben drove to his mom's and parked in her driveway. After helping his mom and Megan out, he lifted several sacks.

George pulled his van up behind the Honda. When George's sons jumped out of the vehicle, he called, "Henry, Eli, help Uncle Ben carry the bags into the house."

Mrs. Grant smiled at George. "There's plenty of food, so you and the boys can have lunch with us. We've lots of cookies."

The boys yelled. "Wow, cookies. Can we stay, Daddy?"

"Wouldn't you rather go to McDonalds?"

The boys shook their heads. "They don't have Aunt Doris's snowman cookies."

After everyone had been seated at the table, Ben asked, "Whose turn is it to pray?"

"It's Eli's." Henry grinned. "I prayed last night."

The six year-old nodded and reached for his dad's and his brother's hands. Megan held her hand out to Ben. So he took it and bowed his head.

When they finished the meal, George turned to Ben and spoke to him in a low voice. Sometime later, George glanced at his sons and scowled at the empty platter. "How many cookies did you eat?"

With a milk-covered grin, Eli looked at his daddy. "We didn't count them."

Using the back of his hand, Henry wiped his mouth. "I counted six."

"You've had enough, and I want to be home before Mommy is off work."

Mrs. Grant handed a large shopping bag to George. "I made a lunch for Betsy and more cookies for everyone."

After George and the boys left, Ben locked up and set the security alarm. Then he carried a giant carton of paper and ribbons to the dining room table. "Mom's going to wrap presents."

Megan pulled out the chair next to Doris. "I'd like to help."

"I can't wrap, so I'll collect what you need and carry gifts for you." Ben sat across from the ladies.

"I'll write the card and give it to you, Megan." Mrs. Grant smiled. "Can you wrap the gift and attach the note?"

"Yes." Megan wrapped the first present.

The older woman beamed. "This is exquisite. Where did you learn to do fancy packaging?"

"I've always had a talent for gift-wrapping and it came in handy as a minister's wife." Megan folded and flipped the ribbon as she fashioned it into a tree which she centered on the next gift. "I worry about putting you in danger."

"Let's enjoy the Christmas holiday. My son can take care of our security. He's the professional." She smiled at Ben.

He prayed. *Lord, I trust you to take care of all of us.*

*****

On Christmas Eve morning, Ben cracked eggs in a bowl and beat them with a fork. To protect Megan from Scott's malicious accusations of her running off with men, Ben would keep his feelings for Megan to himself. After her husband was behind bars, the divorce final, and she was a free woman, he could tell her he loved her. His heart clenched. What if she couldn't love him the way he loved her?

Megan and his mom came into the kitchen.

Mrs. Grant poured the coffee. "Let's look at the Christmas lights tonight. Then we'll come home, make hot chocolate, and eat cookies while we watch, '"It's a Wonderful Life.'"

Megan laughed. "It sounds like fun."

Ben stirred the frying eggs. "George and the boys will be here after breakfast to help deliver the gifts to the shut-ins."

"I'm so glad you're with us." Mrs. Grant hugged Megan. "Thanks for suggesting the boys join us. It will be a good experience for them."

When George and the boys arrived, everyone carried gifts to the van. Megan sat in the back with the list of deliveries. At each stop, she handed the boys the designated packages which they proudly carried to the door with their father and Ben watching.

Halfway through their route, she smiled at the boys. "Isn't this fun?"

"Yes, ma'am." Eli grinned.

Megan wanted to work in her own ministries, not the religious programs her husband forced her to attend for his success. Maybe the New Year would bring her freedom.

*****

On Christmas morning Megan slipped into her robe and walked past the living room. Piles of presents surrounded the twinkling tree. Three bulging stockings dangled from the garland and holly-trimmed fireplace.

She and her grandma had simple holidays. Her Christmases with Scott had been dismal affairs.

After pouring a cup of coffee, she joined Mrs. Grant and Ben at the table.

"We're having a huge dinner, so only yogurt and a biscuit now." Mrs. Grant sipped her coffee.

"Yes, ma'am." Ben opened the refrigerator and set the butter on the table.

After breakfast, Megan joined Ben and his mom in the living room. Megan caught a whiff of the evergreen wreaths in the windows. She knelt in front of the old-fashioned nativity scene. Her fingers ran over each exquisitely carved piece.

Ben unhooked the red stocking with Megan's name on the cuff and handed it to her. Using her finger as a pointer, she traced the hand-embroidered name. She loved her Christmas sock, the first one she'd ever had.

"It's so beautiful. Thank you." She turned her stocking upside down and pulled out several pairs of earrings, an orange, some walnuts, plastic cookie cutters and a hand-embroidered handkerchief.

After Doris and Ben emptied their stockings, Ben handed Megan a large box. "Merry Christmas. We're pleased you can be with us. This is from Mom and me."

"You shouldn't have." She squealed in joy. "Being in your home over Christmas is gift enough."

Megan held the package on her lap.

"Open it." Mrs. Grant's eyes sparkled.

When Megan unwrapped it and lifted the cover, she gazed at the gift. Then she picked up the dark-brown coat and stood. "It's gorgeous. I love it."

"Try it on." Ben stood and held it open for her to put her arms into the sleeves.

She buttoned it and twirled around to show them. "Suede is so warm and fashionable. Thank you."

Ben helped her out of the heavy garment and put it on the couch. "I'm glad it fits."

Megan went to the tree and picked up two gifts. She handed one to Mrs. Grant. "Open this one first."

Doris unwrapped the box, lifted the tissue paper and picked up a large purse. "It's beautiful, Megan. How did you know?"

"Your bag's a bit worn. I thought you might like a new one."

"I do. Thank you."

Megan handed the other gift to Ben. "Merry Christmas."

He tore off the wrapping paper and held the green sweater to his chest. "Thank you. I'll wear it to church on Sunday."

After all the gifts were opened, Mrs. Grant served eggnog while Ben built a fire in the hearth and put Christmas hymns on the player.

Megan caught a whiff of sweet vanilla from the scented candles. Flames crackled in the hearth. Thankful to be safe and warm, she glanced out the window and smiled at the snowflakes drifting to the ground. God's love was the greatest she'd ever experienced. Outside of her grandmother's love, the love from Ben and Mrs. Grant was the only other one on earth she'd known.

They feasted on a meal of gourmet macaroni and cheese, ham, homemade rolls, sweet potatoes, and green bean casserole.

Megan wiped her mouth. "I'm so full I can't move."

"We can eat dessert later."

"I've been looking forward to tasting that chocolate mousse ever since I helped make it."

Ben's mother stood. "Let's rest before we tackle the dishes."

"Great idea, Doris. Take a nap in your recliner. You've worked hard."

After the older woman left the room, Ben and Megan carried the dirty dishes to the kitchen. Ben spooned the leftover food into containers and set them in the refrigerator.

Megan scraped the dishes. "Do you want to use the dishwasher?"

"No, I'm used to washing and drying dishes with you and enjoy it now."

His smile warmed her heart as she ran hot water and squirted soap in the sink to start washing. "You and your mom have made this a perfect Christmas for me."

"We love you and enjoy having you." He picked up the towel and began drying.

Megan finished with the pots. As she scrubbed the pans, she sighed in pleasure. She could stay there, washing dishes with Ben in the kitchen for the rest of her life and be quite content.

Why couldn't her marriage have been happy?

CHAPTER FORTY

Ben knocked on Megan's open door an hour after breakfast the next morning. "Are you ready to go to Mr. and Mrs. Sparks' house?"

"Yes." She folded a sweater and laid it in a large suitcase. "Thanks to you, your mom, and Betsy, I've more clothes now than I've had since I left Scott."

"After three children, Betsy seems to have settled into her present size."

"Three? I only met Henry and Eli."

"Their first child, a little girl, had a rare heart disease and died when she was three. George and Betsy were reluctant to have more children because the illness is hereditary. They trusted God, and He blessed them with the boys, both free of disease."

"The Lord is always faithful." Megan snapped the lid of the suitcase. "Sometimes it's hard for us to trust Him in everything."

"Yes, it is, but we must trust Him. I'll take your bags to the car."

Doris came into the room and put an arm around Megan. "I'll walk with you to the garage."

Megan hugged the older woman. "I'm going to miss you so much."

They walked arm in arm to the car while Ben carried the bags.

"Since you can't go to church with the Sparks, I could pick you up on Sunday mornings to attend the service with us. It would be safer than being alone in the Sparks' house." He'd make certain Scott's men were out of the way before he drove her to a service.

"I'd love that." Megan's eyes twinkled as she slid into the passenger seat.

Ben backed out of the garage and turned into the street. He caught a glimpse of George behind him and a strange car following both of them.

"We have a tail, but George will distract him." Ben shifted gears.

By the time they arrived at the Sparks' house, Megan was laughing at a funny story that Ben told. He got out and accompanied her to the front door.

Louise hugged Megan. "We're so glad you've come. Make yourself at home. Ben, you can take her bags to the first room on the left upstairs."

When Ben returned, Fred asked, "Would you like something to drink?"

"I can't stay. We were followed, and I need to leave before anyone sees my vehicle in your drive."

Fred shook Ben's hand. "You have our number in case you need to reach us."

"And you have mine. Don't hesitate if anything is wrong."

*****

Scott paced the length of his office as he talked with his attorney. "I want her back."

"It's too late. If you don't sign these divorce papers, her lawyer will take the case to court. The publicity would finish you."

"Megan belongs to me. She's mine."

"She wants nothing to do with you."

"That private investigator, Benjamin Grant, lured her away from me. I'll have him discredited."

"That's going to be hard. He has an impeccable reputation."

"He betrayed me, seduced my wife, and then left my employment."

"One of your investigators claims that Megan has been staying with him and his mom."

"I have some photos of them at the mall." He handed his attorney an envelope of pictures.

The lawyer frowned. "This one with his arm around her shoulders might help us."

"I've reason to believe that Fred and Louise Sparks have taken Megan in."

"If she's staying with your head treasurer, maybe she's coming back to you and asked Fred to pave the way. Then your problems will be solved."

"When Megan returns, I'll give a marriage seminar and charge ten thousand dollars a couple." Scott rubbed his palms together. "We'll tell the media that Megan spent the money she stole. I'll forgive her because she's my wife."

*****

Megan studied the accounts and dates with Fred and Louise Sparks, the retired couple. Together they reconstructed the times of church deposits and Scott's absences from home. They compiled the dates Scott left the house.

Unlike the Grants, Louise Sparks wouldn't let Megan lift a finger to sweep or wash a dish. She'd grown accustomed to carrying out chores with Mrs. Grant and Ben. Megan missed them and being part of a family. She looked forward to spending New Year's Eve with them, the perfect end to the year.

Louise didn't feel well on the Sunday between Christmas and New Year's, so they stayed home from church. By New Year's Eve the older woman's health had improved and she decided to attend with her husband while Megan went with Ben to his church.

Megan stepped into the kitchen. "I've nothing dressy enough for a celebration. Do you have any suggestions?"

"It's not safe to go shopping. Our daughter left some clothes behind in the guestroom closet. They're not as classy as the ones you wear, but maybe you can find something that will do."

"Scott dressed me up in what he liked. He never let me select my own clothes because my choices were far simpler. I'm sure one of your daughter's dresses will be lovely. Thank you."

She selected a blue gown, which fit perfectly. Then Megan slipped into black heels and checked in her purse to make certain she had the house key Fred had given her.

Louise knocked on her door. "Ben's here."

Megan carried her coat into the living room.

"Scott will be busy with his own New Years' service tonight." Fred looked up from his newspaper. "He insisted his private investigators attend his church to support him, so most of them will be there."

Ben helped Megan into her coat. "Eileen called and reported that Scott has stayed close to home over the last week. He's busy with holiday programs, so it's safe for you to come to ours."

"I've looked forward to it."

It would be the best New Years Eve of her life.

*****

Ben cupped Megan's elbow and escorted her to the car. "I drove Mom early to prepare the refreshments. We'll sit with her during the service."

When they arrived at the church, they walked into the sanctuary and found his mom. Ben made a security sweep and saw no strangers in church, so he leaned back in the pew.

After the singing, the preacher gave a short message and announced, "Come to the fellowship hall for a light meal. At 11:30 we'll return to the sanctuary to pray in the new year."

Ben escorted his mom and Megan to the hall. His mother stepped behind the buffet to serve while Ben led Megan to the end of the line.

Men and women came up to Ben to wish him a Happy New Year.

"It looks like everyone knows you." Megan smiled at him. "Have you always attended this church?"

"Mom and Dad belonged here while I grew up. I come when I'm not working, which isn't often enough."

He handed Megan a glass of punch. "Let's sit over there with some of Mom's friends. Then she can join us."

When everyone had been served, Doris joined them. "After you finish eating, can you bring the four boxes of quilt squares from your trunk?"

Ben wiped his mouth. "Yes."

His mother frowned. "Don't carry all four at once, you'll disturb the piles inside. It took me a long time to arrange them."

"Yes, ma'am."

"Bringing two at a time shouldn't shift the squares."

"Yes, ma'am." Ben rolled his eyes at Megan.

She put her napkin down. "I could carry two and we could bring them in one trip."

He didn't want to leave Megan and his mom alone for a long time, but he'd seen no strangers. Megan would be safer with him. They could bring the boxes in one trip. He glanced at the people in the fellowship hall. Everyone visited, ate, or watched children. No threats there.

"I'd be grateful for your help." Ben stood and helped her on with her coat. He led her to the front door. "Are you ready to brave the cold night?"

"With this warm coat, I can walk into a freezer."

Ben wished he could take Megan to church every week for the rest of his life. He took her arm as they crossed the parking lot. "It sure is a pretty night." He wanted to say he was with the prettiest woman in church, but he didn't say it. She was still married.

A few feet before reaching the Honda, four men darted out of the shadows and surrounded them. One grabbed Megan, but Ben knocked him out. Then Ben gave a couple of well-placed blows to another man, who landed on the ground.

Ben yelled. "Run Jane, run."

*****

Megan didn't hesitate. She kicked off her heels and sprinted across the parking lot. Maybe she could distract an assailant from Ben. She couldn't go back into the church. It would put those folks in danger. So she turned down the alley.

Footsteps pounded behind her. Bang! She jumped. Was it a gun? It didn't matter. Mrs. Grant assured her Ben could shoot expertly and take out a whole unit of bad guys.

Racing around the corner, she searched for a place to hide. Her feet hurt, but the blotches of snow protected them a little. She kept going. More steps thudded louder behind her as if several men chased her. The hair on the nape of her neck stood up. Her eyes adjusted to the dark, but it was still too dim to see the way clearly or find a hiding place. She kept running.

At the end of the lane, she turned right. If she jogged around the block she'd come back to the church. Ben had been smart to tell her to run so she could lead some of the men away while Ben knocked out the rest. But how many were there? More steps pounded louder behind her.

Her breath came out in ragged gasps, but she concentrated on the breathing she'd learned in cross-country running. Soon she'd meet Ben back in the parking lot. Bang! Another shot. She focused on the last right turn coming up ahead. A flash of lightning revealed the opening of the lane next to the church. She should reach shelter before the storm started unless it passed over them.

Another bolt of lightning filled the sky. She searched for Ben and spotted him on the pavement. Blood covered his head and face, and he wasn't moving. Her heart plummeted and she screamed. "No!"

She raced toward him, but someone grabbed her from behind. A voice snarled, "Your boyfriend's dead."

Megan kicked and twisted to escape his hold, but he tightened his grip on her. Her wrists were pulled behind her back and taped together. She quivered. Her life was over, so why fight? No, she should try to free herself to save Mrs. Grant.

Someone slapped her, and a second voice growled. "Stop struggling."

"No. No. No." Hysteria clawed at her throat and she shrieked, "Help!"

A third man stuffed a rough cloth in Megan's mouth before tying her feet together.

Tears filled Megan's eyes. She was responsible for Ben's death. He'd sacrificed his life to save her, but it had been for nothing. She'd soon be dead, too.

One of the men tossed her over his shoulder. "I'll throw her in the trunk."

Tears ran down her cheeks.

Lord, please don't let Ben die.

Ben might not have been killed but only hurt. His mother needed him. *He's a good man. Touch him, send help, and keep him safe.*

Scott would take her back to his torture chamber. No one would ever find her and her life would end. When she died, he'd bury her in the back yard and tell the world that she'd run away again. Everyone would believe her charming husband.

The man carrying her stopped walking. A trunk popped open. She landed with a thud but wasn't hurt. She thanked God for the thick coat that protected her. The lid slammed shut. She'd read about kicking out the brake lights so the police would stop the car, but she couldn't maneuver her feet into position.

A short time later, the vehicle stopped. When the trunk opened, one of the men carried her into the house she had shared with Scott and set her in a kitchen chair. It faced the black granite island. She remembered what had happened on that and began shivering.

Bang! Bang! Bang! She jumped and lifted her head to the kitchen clock. Midnight. Happy New Year. More firecrackers went off.

Scott pulled off her coat. He untied her feet and used the rope to bind her hands to the chair. "You've gained weight, Megan, shame on you. I told you what I'd do to you if you got any bigger."

The man who brought her said, "My men and I would like our money."

Scott opened his jacket, reached for a thick envelope, and handed it to them. "There's one more job for you."

Were they talking about her death?

Before leaving, the man scowled. "Be careful. The police might show up with a search warrant."

"That won't happen." Scott turned to Megan. "I've paid off all the police officers and they're always busy on New Year's."

"Call me when you need that last job. I'll make it look good." He turned to leave. "And Happy New Year. Have a good one."

Scott removed her gag. Megan shivered. Their house stood on an isolated ten-acre piece of land. It was useless to scream.

Her body shook. Tears ran down her cheeks. She wished he'd kill her. That would be less painful than one of his punishments.

"Happy New Year, Megan. We're going to celebrate. Lots of fireworks."

She lowered her head.

"No one leaves me, especially someone who belongs to me." He stepped behind her, pinched a cluster of nerves in the back of her neck, and twisted them.

The room went black.

CHAPTER FORTY-ONE

Ben woke up on a stretcher in an ambulance. The vehicle bounced down the road, and the siren wailed louder. Didn't they only use the alarm if a patient's condition was fatal? He jerked his hands up to massage his pounding head, but he couldn't move. Was he paralyzed?

"We've restrained you for your safety. Lie still. You've had a head injury. It looks like your skull is cracked. You need stitches, antibiotics, and an MRI."

Ben mumbled, "Stop the ambulance. Let me out. It's a matter of life and death." The paramedic adjusted the flow rate of an IV bag.

The ambulance went black.

He opened his eyes and moved his head a little to the left. Seeing his mom and George, Ben tried to sit up but groaned and fell deeper in the pillow. "Did Megan come back in the church?"

"No," his mom sighed. "When you and Megan didn't bring my boxes from the car, I got worried, so I asked my girlfriends to go outside with me and look for you. We divided into two groups of four. The other team found you and called 911."

George frowned. "If it hadn't been for the fireworks, someone would have heard the commotion. Your mom called me. When I reached the church, they were loading you in the ambulance. She and I came here."

His mom reached for his hand. "You'll be fine, but you must rest."

"We beat up bad guys and they hit us. But I didn't think anyone could crack that skull of yours, but the MRI showed it's fractured."

"I told Megan to run, and she did. I knocked a couple guys out and winged two of them, hopefully bad enough they wouldn't go after her. Then something whacked my head. I woke up groggy, saw a man carry Megan away, and passed out again."

"I'll check local hospitals for gunshot victims." George took out a notepad.

Ben licked his lips. "Is there water?"

"It's here. I'll get it." His mother poured a cup, put a straw in it, and held it to his lips.

After sipping half of the water, Ben looked around. "Contact your man with the computer. Check again if Scott has any property where he could hide Megan."

"The doc says you can't go anywhere." George wrote notes. "I'll see if Megan is at Scott's house first."

"After I sleep a couple of hours, I'll join you."

"Stay here and rest. I'll take a buddy of mine and go over there, but first I'll drive your mom home."

Mrs. Grant offered her son the rest of the water. "You don't need to take me home. I'm staying here."

Ben mumbled. "You'll be safer with me."

The pain medications had taken over and Ben nodded off and on.

"I'll take care of everything, Captain. I'll call and give you a report before they turn out the lights or sooner if I find Megan."

Ben whispered, "Lord help her."

*****

When Megan regained consciousness, Scott dragged her upstairs and into the bathroom.

He ripped off her clothes. "You're filthy. Get in the shower. I'm scouring that man's hands off every inch of your body before I teach you a lesson."

She shivered and kept her head lowered.

Lord, let it be over quickly.

When she stepped out of the bath, she dried off.

Scott tossed her a set of sweats. "Put them on."

Her hands shook as she struggled to dress. He'd always insisted she wear the outfit, so if anything went wrong, he could tell the paramedics she'd been working out. He blindfolded her and led her downstairs. He shoved her into a chair and handcuffed her to it.

With her eyes still covered, she quivered as ripples of electrical jolts shot through her. She saw stars from the shocks of the Taser. Then she passed out.

Sometime later, the footsteps on the stairs grew louder. She caught the scent of his aftershave and tensed. Would there be another round of electrifying bolts or a session alone handcuffed to the water heater in the basement. He unlocked the cuffs, pulled her from the chair, and fastened her hands together. Scott yanked the chain of the handcuffs. The iron bit into her wrists. There were twelve steps to the top of the stairs which she had counted every time and three locks that clicked behind her. With the blindfold on, she'd never seen his torture chamber, but one day she had found the secret door padlocked shut. She never mentioned it to anyone. Who would believe a pastor had a torture chamber?

He pulled the blindfold off, unlocked the cuffs, and tossed a transparent blue nightgown to her. "Put this on."

As she changed, her shoulders shook. She kept her lips clamped shut and her head lowered. Then he fastened the handcuffs to the bed post. Bruises were taking shape on her chest and stomach. She'd be black and blue and hurt in places that no one would ever see.

*****

Ben woke and rubbed his head. He looked around and spotted his mother, sound asleep in a cot next to his bed in the hospital room.

George stepped inside. "How are you feeling this morning?"

"Did I miss your call? Have you found Megan?"

"Betsy worked here last night, so I phoned her. She checked in on you. They gave you a sleeping pill and you were snoring. How are you?"

"My skull must be cracked. It's never hurt this badly."

"After I picked up my buddy, I went over to Scott's house and waited until he left. I understood his elaborate security system, so my buddy and I went inside and searched every room." George pulled up a chair, leaned closer to Ben, and lowered his voice. "Megan wasn't there. We found handcuffs attached to the bedpost as if she'd been there or was coming back."

Ben shivered. "Scott must have stopped and cuffed her to the bed while he made plans to take her somewhere else. Did you locate any other property he has?"

"He doesn't have any. If he does, it's not in his name."

"What about parents, a brother or friend who might have a home or cabin that he'd use? Is there anyone at church who'd loan him a place?"

"I checked it out. There's no other property he has ever used." George sighed. "Two guys were taken to the emergency room downtown for gunshot wounds. The hospital wouldn't tell me anything because of the confidentiality laws, but my friend at the police station got the information. They were shot around the time someone hit you, and the slugs taken out of them probably came from your gun."

"We have to find Megan. I've a bad feeling."

George reached for his cell phone, pressed a number, and asked, "Anything to report?" He listened for a few minutes and then hung up. "My men have been watching Scott's house. There's been no movement in there."

"Can you come back at noon and take Mom and me home?" Ben whispered.

A nurse entered the room. "It's time for your pain medication, Mr. Grant. What's your pain level on a scale of one to ten?"

"Ten."

The nurse poured some water and handed him the pills.

After she left, Ben lowered his voice. "If Scott has taken her someplace, wouldn't he have taken her with the handcuffs?"

George shook his head. "Scott might have a box of handcuffs."

"Or he might have already killed her, so he no longer needs them." Ben slumped back into the pillow.

*****

Megan practiced the lessons she'd learned from Scott. Don't look him in the eyes. Keep your head lowered. Answer in a soft voice only when spoken to.

Scott screamed, "You're a fat slob. You start your diet today. No food or water."

She wasn't hungry but wanted a drink. Then she remembered Ben and his mother, so she prayed for them.

"I hope you learned your lesson. You'll never run away from me again."

Tears filled her eyes, and she nodded.

Scott smirked. "Don't look so sad. I'll whip you into shape."

She knew he would. Megan shivered. She was at his mercy, and he didn't have any.

"I'm going back to the church to work on a sermon. You have a nice rest and think about what you did to me. When I return, it'll be like old times. I'm glad you're back." He laughed.

Her lips quivered and drops spilled from her eyes.

"Stand up and give the man who loves you a proper goodbye."

He yanked her to her feet. His teeth clamped on the inside of her lip as he brutally kissed and bit her mouth. Then he threw her roughly to the bed and glared down at her. "See you later. We're going to have fun."

Megan pressed the back of her hand over her mouth. Her tongue stroked the inside of her lip. "Lord Jesus, forgive me for all my sins. Forgive me for marrying this man. Take care of Ben and his mother. He risked his life to save me. I'd die happily if Ben and his mother were okay."

Lord, please help.
Please help.

CHAPTER FORTY-TWO

Megan sat on the floor and leaned back against the base of the bed with her right hand lifted and cuffed to the post. Scott had ordered her to stay down, and she would. If not, the punishment would be double.

She shuddered as the door inched open. One of Scott's hired men was returning to make her death look like an accident or suicide.

Lord, help me.

Trust in the Lord with all thine heart.

Ben and George with their guns drawn crept into the room. Was she dreaming or hallucinating? Ben put his finger to his lips. A sliver of white bandage escaped the cap on his head. He was alive. Her heart swelled with joy and gratitude.

They approached the bed and knelt in front of her.

"I'm so glad we found you. Thank God you're alive." Ben whispered. "Is there anyone in the house?"

Megan's voice wobbled. "Not that I know of."

George pulled out a slender steel instrument. "I'll have these cuffs off in a minute."

"Stop." Ben put his hand on Megan's. "We need evidence."

He and George snapped photos of Megan's bruised shoulders and handcuffed wrist.

When the cuffs were off, she still couldn't move. Her heavy limbs held her down, paralyzing her. She rubbed her wrist and numb arm. Ben and George reached for her hands and helped her up.

She ran her tongue over her lips to suppress her thirst. Better leave before Scott returned. She could have a drink later.

"My coat is on the chair."

Thank you, Lord.

Ben would be fine, and soon she'd be free.

But would Scott kidnap her again?

*****

Ben's heart clenched at the bruises forming on Megan's neck and arms. The transparent nightgown revealed splotches of black and blue on her back and sides. He went to the closet and returned with a pair of bedroom slippers, a scarf, and gloves. He stopped at the chair and picked up the coat he and his mom had given Megan for Christmas.

He held it open for her. She groaned as she slipped her arms into it. Her shaking fingers slid off the buttons.

"Let me." As he fastened the garment, Ben thanked God again she was alive.

If Scott had been there, Ben would not have turned the other cheek. He'd have inflicted excruciating discomfort on Scott, agony to remind him of what he'd done to Megan.

Her bruises looked painful. Would she be able to walk on her own?

"Would you like me to carry you?" Ben asked.

"I'll walk." She stayed between the men going slowly down the stairs, out the back door, and into George's van.

When they were on the road, Ben opened a water bottle and handed it to her.

After draining it, she lowered her head. Blood coated the rim of the plastic.

"Would you like another?" Ben asked.

She nodded. "Scott didn't give me anything to drink or eat." Her lips quivered.

Ben wanted to wrap her in his arms, but a man had hurt her badly. She probably wasn't ready for another man's touch. How could Ben help her? Ice would be good for her mouth. Should he take her to the hospital for x-rays or to a restaurant for food?

The heavy coat protected her against the cold, but she couldn't walk into a public place wearing a nightgown and bedroom slippers. "George, stop at Burger King and order ice water and a vanilla milkshake. After that, we'll take Megan to the hospital."

"Scott told me you were dead, and he sent men to kill your mother." She brushed away a tear. "I'm so glad you're okay."

George laughed. "It's hard to kill Captain Benjamin Grant. He's got a cracked skull and look how easily he rescued you."

Her eyes widened and she gasped. "You should be resting."

"I've already slept and taken pain meds."

George turned into the fast food restaurant and pulled into the drive-thru. He ordered five ice waters, two coffees and a milkshake. He passed one of the waters and the shake back to Ben.

Ben set Megan's drinks in the holders and stuffed a straw in each of them. He smiled at Megan. "George had a friend watch Scott's house. When he spotted two forms through the bedroom window, he phoned us." Ben took a cup of coffee from George and sipped it. The caffeine calmed his pounding head.

With trembling fingers, Megan picked up the ice water and wrapped her hands around the cup. She sipped the water alternately with the shake. "This is so good. Thank you."

Ben spoke in his gentlest voice. "At the hospital, they'll be able to examine you and check for internal injuries. A police officer will take photos. If we have more proof of Scott's torture, the judge might not be so lenient with Scott."

Tears filled her eyes, and she nodded. "Thank you."

George pulled up to the emergency room. "Wait here." He jumped out and went inside. He returned with a wheelchair.

"I can walk." Megan mumbled.

"I know, but this looks better. More proof that Scott hurt you."

Ben wheeled her directly into a cubicle in the ER. The doctor sent Megan to radiology for a series of x-rays. Then a female detective wrote pages of notes and snapped photos. She radioed in the report so the officers could pick up Scott Collins.

After they were finished at the hospital and back in the van, Ben handed Megan another ice water.

George pulled into Mrs. Grant's garage. The door closed, and he jumped out as Ben took Megan's hand and helped her into the house.

Ben hugged his mom and whispered, "Megan's husband hurt her again." Ben wanted to take Megan someplace safe, but the best place would be at the lake, and Scott's men had once found them there.

"I'm glad to see you." Mrs. Grant took Megan's hands. "Make yourself at home."

After Megan left to bathe, Ben handed George a slip of paper. "Would you pick up her prescription at the pharmacy? I don't want to leave her alone with Mom. I've no idea what Scott is planning."

Several minutes later, Megan came into the kitchen with wet hair and wearing a housecoat. "Do you have any aspirin?"

"I sent George to collect your prescription." Ben pulled a bottle of pills out of his coat pocket. "These are stronger than aspirin. If you're familiar with the drug and aren't allergic to them, take a couple."

Megan read the label of the container. "This is your medication, but it's the same narcotic the doctor prescribed for me."

"We'll share until George returns. Take the pills. Then we'll eat mom's wonderful cheese and broccoli soup. You'll sleep like a baby."

After swallowing the medicine, she sat down at the table with them.

George returned before they had finished eating and handed Megan her prescription. Then he joined them for a bowl of soup.

No one spoke during the meal. Ben noticed his mom's fatigue and the dark circles that rimmed Megan's eyes. They needed rest.

When they were finished, Ben stood. "Mom, Megan, we've had a difficult night, so let's take a nap."

Megan took a step closer to him and checked his dressing. "I hope you're going to rest."

"I will."

"How much do I owe you?"

"Owe me? For what?"

"For the pills."

"I'll give you the bill when everything is over."

Ben hoped that it would be soon, but would she ever be okay?

CHAPTER FORTY-THREE

"Megan."

She rolled over in bed. She'd only been asleep a few minutes.

Ben's voice came into the room again. "Megan."

She opened her eyes and glanced at the clock. Seven in the evening. She'd slept all afternoon.

Ben whispered again, "Megan."

She stretched and groaned, "I'm getting up."

"Louise and Fred are here and would like to see you."

"Give me a few minutes to freshen up."

She went into the bathroom and splashed cool water on her face. After patting it dry, she walked to the living room.

Louise came toward her. "Thank God, you're okay."

"We're sorry." Fred sighed. "Scott knows you're with Ben and Mrs. Grant. Scott called an emergency meeting with the elders. He announced that you are crazy and had been spending time with your lovers over the years. They were the ones who hurt you, but he nursed you back to health."

Ben scowled. "He can't refute Megan's bruises and broken bones, so he's blaming her for them."

Louise wiped her eyes. "Scott claims he is devoted to Megan. He always forgave her when she returned from one of her boyfriends. She and her last lover stole the six million dollars."

Megan heaved a sigh and sobbed, "Do people believe this?"

"Yes, he told everyone that you went back to Scott last night to confess your indiscretions and beg forgiveness. The church members believed him." Fred scowled.

Ben pulled out his phone and showed them the photos of Megan handcuffed to the bed. "If that's true, why did George and I find her like this?"

Louise's eyes widened as she clapped a hand to her mouth. "How awful."

"Scott claims your lovers are trying to ruin his ministry by framing him." Fred stood. "We need to be going. We only wanted to see Megan and assure ourselves she is safe again."

After Fred and Louise left, Megan started crying. "I don't see any hope."

Ben left and returned with her grandmother's Bible, which he opened and read. "Put your trust in the Lord. Do not be afraid. What can mortal man do to me?" He closed the book and handed it to her. "We must trust the Lord no matter what."

Mrs. Grant frowned. "If people think you're both here in the house alone, not knowing that I'm here, they might believe that Megan's been unfaithful."

Megan nodded and wiped her eyes.

"That would give Scott more ammunition to use against you." Ben exhaled.

The phone rang and Ben answered. "Yes, I'll tell her." He turned to Megan. "The organization found a safe house for you. I'll drive you to your contact at Sugar Hill Mall at ten in the morning. They want you to dress in your most unusual outfit and go into the restroom in the food court."

Mrs. Grant stood. "You both slept through supper. You need to eat something before you go to bed."

"Go to bed? I just got up." Ben grinned. "But I'm hungry."

"You've a fractured skull." Megan stood. "We should both eat, take more pain pills, and rest."

"You sound like a nurse." Ben smiled at Megan and then turned to his mom. "What leftovers do you have?"

"My friends brought casseroles, fried chicken, roast beef, scalloped potatoes, corn, beans, and rolls while you were in the hospital."

"Let's eat and take our medicine." Ben chuckled.

*****

Ben almost dropped his coffee cup the next morning when Megan stepped into the kitchen. She wore an orange and purple flowing skirt with a ginger-colored blouse. A gold scarf served as a head band around her short black hair.

He laughed. "No one will recognize you in that."

"I hope not." She smiled.

Ben noticed her face held no traces of her ordeal the previous day. He suspected there were bruises under her conservative outfit. As he took her bag, he hefted it like a weight. "It's not heavy."

"I'm leaving most of my clothes and books here. Your mom promised to keep them for me." She paused. "How's your head?"

"Much better. I slept well. How about you?"

"The pills helped me rest." She took the cup he offered her.

He enjoyed the sweet companionship between them. Ben finished scrambling the eggs as Mrs. Grant joined them. Megan toasted the bread and buttered it.

After eating, they washed and dried the dishes. Ben had warned his mom not to hug Megan because of her bruises.

His mother reached for Megan's hands. "I hate to see you go. I always miss you and hope one day you'll stay."

Megan wiped away a tear. "I'll miss you too."

During the drive to the mall, Megan's silence filled the van. Ben glanced at her trembling hands as he slowed to make a turn. "Your new safe house sounded quite hush, hush. I can't imagine Scott finding you again." He pulled into the mall and drove to the store next to the food court entrance. "Let's wait five minutes for George to get in place."

Megan reached for his hand. "Thank you. I can never repay you."

He wanted to tell her he loved her, but he remained quiet. It wasn't the right time. She was still a married woman. "Mom and I love you and care about you. Be careful."

Ben waited for her to step inside. Then he parked the vehicle and went into the food court. He sat at a table not far away from George. They both faced the restroom.

Unscrewing the top of a water bottle, Ben drank. A couple of minutes later, Scott marched up to the table. Ben thought he saw things or Scott's double.

Ben asked, "Can I buy you a coffee or coke?"

Scott sat across from Ben, so both men faced the restroom. "No thanks. Megan will be out any minute."

"Aren't you supposed to be in jail?"

"The judge is convinced I'm being framed. How can I do anything with this ankle bracelet?" He lifted his pant leg. "Fortunately this is within the twenty-mile radius. My associate reported she's in there."

Ben scanned the food court to see how many men Scott had brought. Ben didn't see any thugs in the area. A mother pushing a stroller walked past them and into the restroom.

"The restraining order prohibits you from coming any closer to her."

"Who made you her body guard?" Scott glared.

"Do you think she needs one?" Ben kept his eye on the door of the ladies room.

"She has nothing to fear from me. I'm her husband and love her."

"What do you love most about Megan?" Ben could list the reasons he loved her. He loved her compassion, determination, and the sweet way she put everyone around her at ease. He loved her friendship, her help in time of trouble, and her encouragement. Megan's smile and laughter brightened his day. He loved how she sacrificially served others. He admired her passion to secure her nursing degree and help children. Ben even loved her snoring. There was so much to love about Megan. How could her husband not see any of it?

"I've trained her to be the perfect wife." Scott crossed his arms.

"Wasn't she a good one when you married her?"

"Megan had a hard time submitting to me, so I taught her."

"What kind of instruction?"

"You're not married are you?"

"No."

"Then you have no way of understanding how difficult it is for a husband to teach his disobedient wife to mind him."

Ben glanced at the mother coming out of the ladies room. As she pushed the stroller past them, he recognized the build, height, walk, and shrug of Megan's shoulders, even in her disguise. She had a habit of hesitating a brief moment before turning or opening a door.

Scott didn't notice her. A narcissistic man, like Rev. Collins, never saw anyone, but himself.

A blonde stepped out of the restroom. Scott leaned forward. "There's Megan." He stood and followed her. Scott's twisted mind hadn't seen the difference between his wife and a blonde in a low-cut blouse and tight pants.

Ben chuckled as the woman sashayed and thrust her hips forward, so unlike Megan. He turned slightly to the front door. Through the line of glass windows, Ben watched Megan wheel the stroller to a gold Nissan and then open the back door. No men chased her. So Ben ambled behind Scott to make certain he didn't hurt the blonde.

Scott ran closer and reached for the woman's arm. She turned her head to him and hurled a stream of curses. Then she shook off his arm and marched away.

Thank God Megan had escaped.

Lord, keep her safe.

CHAPTER FORTY-FOUR

Megan lifted the baby-doll and fastened it in the car-seat. The trunk popped open, and she removed her bag from the rack under the pram. She folded the stroller and put it inside the trunk.

The young man behind the steering wheel didn't frighten her as she slid into the passenger seat. She trusted him, a stranger. A year ago, she would have run in the opposite direction if she had spotted a man in the car.

"Hello, I'm Aaron." He pulled out of the parking lot. "My mom's one of the ladies in charge and asked me to help out since this is my day off."

"Are you a college student?"

"Look in the glove compartment."

Megan leaned forward and clicked the latch. She pulled out the ID but ignored the gun. "You're a police officer?"

"Yes. I went into law enforcement because of what my dad did to my mom." A look of disgust crossed his face.

Megan closed her eyes and leaned back. She was safe.

*****

Scott kept no records of cash that admirers sent him in the mail or handed him after services. The foolish auditors had no idea he'd taken over fourteen million dollars but paying off judges, lawyers, and police officers had depleted a chunk of it.

In the eyes of God, Megan was his wife and he'd never be free of her unless she died. He thought about giving Megan another chance, but she'd been running her own life for over a year and might not be pliable. But training her again might be easier than starting all over with another woman. And if he spared her, he could frame her for stealing the money. Then he could disappear and start over again leaving evidence to suggest Megan had killed him.

It had been hard to suppress his jealousy over her when his church members and television viewers had liked her. She made a good impression on his followers. She had served a useful purpose. Outside of that, there were no other reasons to keep her. At first, he thought he might love her, but he had never loved anyone but himself.

God created the man first and gave him authority over all creatures including women. Why couldn't they be content? Why did they fuss when a guy did what he should do and take charge of them?

*****

Megan shared a house with Barbara, an older nurse in Clarksville, Texas. As Megan bustled about the kitchen, she sang *"Amazing Grace, how sweet the sound that saved a wretch like me.'* She sighed in pleasure for she would soon be free. *Thank you, Lord, for helping me run away from him.* She had much to be grateful for. *'Thro' many dangers, toils, and snares, I have already come;* The Lord had brought her through several near-death escapes. *Tis grace hath brought me safe thus far, and grace will lead me home."* God was good and she loved Him.

When Barbara came home from work, Megan had supper ready and set the bowls of food on the table. "I hope you're hungry. I made steak, baked potato, and vegetables."

"Starved." Barbara set her purse on the counter. "Why are you so happy tonight and what are you celebrating?"

"I'll tell you during supper. Sit down. Dinner's ready." Megan filled the water glasses. "I drove your dad and mom for blood work today. They handled it well."

Barbara sat across from Megan. "Thanks for looking after my parents each day while I'm working."

"I'm glad to do it." Megan grinned. "I passed all my nursing courses and qualified to renew my license, so I baked a cheese cake."

"Congratulations. If you didn't need to stay hidden from your husband until the trial, you could work in the hospital and make real money."

"I know, but it's safer to hide until Scott's behind bars." Megan took her time eating. "Your mom is excited about the anniversary party we're planning."

"I ordered the food and cake today and sent a hundred invitations. Not many people stay married to the same person for sixty years." Barbara reached for second helpings.

"Your parents told me that commitment is the secret to a solid marriage. It's also important to love unconditionally and forgive in spite of hurt feelings, disappointments, and when everything goes wrong."

"Do you think men today are different from what they were like fifty years ago?" Barbara asked.

Megan laughed. "I've taken care of older men. All of them were sweet gentlemen. They shared fond memories and happy times of their marriages."

"We don't have much choice. Either take one of the men available or stay single. Would I have been better off staying married to a man who beat me and my boys?" Barbara shook her head. "I haven't met any honorable men. Let's face it. Men are jerks and scoundrels. Women don't need them and would be better off without them. Children would grow into good citizens without the influence of a cruel role model."

"You have a point. With artificial insemination, a woman can find the perfect father of her child." Megan hesitated, not sure how much she should say. "The thought of us not needing men troubles me."

"Why?"

"If I believe we don't need men, am I dishonoring God who created them?"

Barbara shrugged. "I hadn't considered that."

Hating all men felt like hating God. Megan couldn't do it. Some men were tyrants. Others were bullies. A few were narcissistic, while some were incapable of admitting when they were wrong and blamed everyone else for their problems.

But Benjamin Grant wasn't any of those things. He wasn't manipulative or selfish. He'd never use a female to meet his own needs. She missed Ben, but she had never missed her husband. If only Scott would sign the divorce papers so she could move on with her life.

Then what would she do? She wasn't good enough for Ben, and he could never be interested in her. He deserved a woman who didn't have fifteen years of emotional baggage.

CHAPTER FORTY-FIVE

As Megan collected the garbage for pick-up, she read through the junk mail. A brochure advertised online courses towards a master's degree in pediatric nursing. She would do it after she was free of Scott.

Barbara lifted the heavy sack. "I like taking out the trash, so I can visit with the neighbors."

A few minutes later, Barbara, out of breath, barged through the front door. She put her hand on her chest and gasped. "I always take a good look around when someone is staying with me. There's a vehicle not far down the road. Two men with binoculars are sitting in it." She double-locked the door behind her.

Megan's heart beat faster. "What are we going to do?"

"I'll call our contact. We have a friend in the police station, who can drive by to check them out."

When the phone rang, Barbara answered and nodded. Then she hung up. "Daniel Fuller and another PI are in the car."

Megan broke out in a sweat. Scott had friends and contacts across the states, and he offered lots of money for her return. He always found her.

Barbara opened the hall closet and dug out an old bag. "We're having a prayer meeting. You'll need to change your appearance by adding twenty pounds, reading glasses, and gray hair."

Megan tied pillows around her stomach. She slipped into an older pair of pants and shirt. After putting on the wig, she adjusted the reading glasses.

Barbara handed her a stuffed purse. "I collected your makeup from the bathroom."

"What about the rest of my things?"

"Don't worry. I'll take care of them."

The doorbell rang and Barbara opened it to eight different-sized ladies ranging in age from twenty to eighty.

"Collect your clothes and books from your bedroom and put them on the table. The ladies will divide them and stuff them in their purses. You can't leave a prayer meeting with a suitcase."

Barbara led them in prayer, and one of the ladies put her arm around Megan. "We're sticking close and surrounding you as we go to the van."

The ladies picked up Megan's belongings from the table. With the group of women around her, Megan walked to the vehicle and got in. The youngest one started driving.

The elderly woman sitting next to Megan introduced herself. "I'm Mrs. Steel and you're welcome to stay with me until your husband's trial in two weeks. The leaders of our group feel you'll be safer there."

"I appreciate it, but I don't want to put you in danger."

"We'll stay inside and be just fine."

Inside the van they removed Megan's things from their bags and stuffed them in two big grocery sacks, which they handed to her.

She looked out the back window. The car wasn't following. She had escaped again.

For an hour, Megan recognized the circuitous route. The young lady who drove the van pulled up in front of an older wooden-framed house that sat by itself on a large plot of land.

Mrs. Steel smiled at Megan. "This is my place. We're getting out here."

Megan carried the two grocery bags and followed the older woman out of the vehicle and up to the house.

The elderly woman unlocked the side door. "Come in. It's not fancy, but it's home. I've lived here fifty years."

She removed her disguise, looking forward to the day she'd never need to wear a costume again. Soon Scott's trial would take place, and he'd be sent to prison.

"The spare room is at the end of the hall and the bathroom next to it. Make yourself at home, take a shower, and relax. You can come to the living room to watch television with me."

"Thanks for your hospitality."

She showered and dressed in her housecoat. When she came into the living room, Mrs. Steel was watching the national news.

The anchor woman announced, "Rev. Scott Collins, pastor of one of the largest churches in Tennessee, will be on trial for beating his wife."

Photos of her face, arms, and neck flashed on the screen. She leaned closer to watch the rest of the news. "I've a bad feeling he'll be freed again. He claims my lovers beat me up."

"Your lovers?" Mrs. Steel gasped. "I didn't think you had any."

"I don't. My husband lied and told everyone that I did."

Would she ever be free of him?

*****

Megan drove Mrs. Steel to her eye doctor's appointment a few days later. Since the older woman didn't have an enclosed garage, Megan parked the vehicle next to the house in the driveway when they returned and collected the grocery bags, while Mrs. Steel unlocked the side door.

An arm wrapped around Megan's waist and a large hand clamped over her mouth. She twisted, turned, and bit the man's hand. He didn't loosen his hold but tightened his grip.

Mrs. Steel yelled into her phone. "Hurry, officer. A man is attacking the young lady staying with me. He's throwing her into the trunk."

Megan landed with a thud. When the door banged shut, she smiled. The thug hadn't taped her hands together. Ben had told her how to escape from a locked trunk. Since 2002, American cars had an emergency release, but she didn't know the year of the car. So she searched, but the release catch had been disabled. She lifted the carpet, searching for the cable line that ran from the dashboard to the trunk. There was none. Her heart plummeted, but she didn't give up. She searched for a weapon. Nothing. So she pulled out the wires to the brake lights.

Her abductor would take her back to Scott in Memphis, but no vehicle could travel fourteen hours without fuel. The driver would need to stop. When he did, she'd leap out. If she hadn't been maintaining a low profile, she would have found a gym and mastered kick fighting or karate. Self-defense classes would have been good, but

Ben had given her some helpful tips to free herself. For the first time, she wasn't afraid.

But what if Scott ordered the driver to abandon her someplace along the road or kill her? She prayed. A verse popped into her head. *Trust in the Lord with all your heart. Lean not to your own understanding.*

After what felt like hours, the car stopped. The trunk lock clicked, but the lid remained closed. She pounded on it, but it didn't budge. Then it flew open. A hand grabbed her arm, yanked her out, and twisted it behind her. She moaned.

She blinked to focus on a man who wore a ski mask and reeked of beer. He was bigger and stronger than Scott with massive muscles popping out of his arms. He tied a rope round her neck. Was he planning to hang her there in the woods and make it look like suicide? An icy tremor ran down her backbone. She used to pray to die so many times. But over the last few months she realized she wanted to live.

Then he handed her a bottle of water. "Drink."

She gulped down the cool fluid and thanked Jesus for it.

"If you need to use the toilet, go behind those bushes. You won't get out again for another six hours."

Stumbling forward, she hoped he wouldn't stand there and watch her.

She cocked an eyebrow. "Aren't you going to turn around?"

He laughed. "Who do you think you are?"

Over the years with Scott, she'd learned to keep her mouth shut. Her head dipped to her chest.

He yelled. "I have to watch you."

She lowered her pants and did her business. When she finished she thanked God for the brief rest and a drink. Her captor had been kinder than Scott.

The thug wound the end of the rope around his hand and led the way back to the car. If she didn't walk at his pace the cord choked her.

"Get in." The man yelled.

She took a good look at the car, an ancient, unremarkable model. She prayed for courage and strength. "I'll pay you three times what

Scott is giving you not to take me back there. He's told everyone I stole the money and hid it. So I can pay you, whatever you want."

Never had she stood up to any man in all her life. She couldn't believe the words that had shot out of her mouth.

"Get in the trunk."

"My husband's going to prison. How can he pay you?"

"He's already paid me real well." He pushed her into the trunk.

Her heart clenched. The lid banged shut. She didn't give up but searched again for a weapon or a way to break through into the back seat.

Hours later, the car stopped. The trunk popped open. She expected the police to rescue her. Surely, they had seen the vehicle didn't have brake lights in the pitch dark.

She caught a whiff of Scott's aftershave and shivered. He wore a red wig and glasses. She'd never seen him without his business suit in public. It looked like he bought the old plaid shirt and torn jeans at the mission. She glanced around and tried to place her surroundings, but they were somewhere out in the country.

He reached for her hands and tugged her out. "We're taking a second honeymoon, you and me, sweetheart."

She shuddered. The temperature had dropped to below freezing, but she'd been warm inside the trunk. She spied a vacancy sign about five hundred yards down the road.

"I told the manager we wanted to be far away from others for privacy." Scott twisted her arm behind her back.

The cold wind chilled her to the bone. Too bad she couldn't zip up her jacket.

Scott maintained his hold on her as he unlocked the door of the last room and marched inside. Taking out his handcuffs, he fastened her wrist to the iron leg of the bed.

"You've let yourself go, but I'll have you in shape before you go on television." He grabbed her hair and ran his fingers through it. "What's this color, mousy brown? It's hideous. Why did you dye it this shade?"

The hard glint of his icy, blue eyes, shot through her. She spoke softly and kept her head down, so she wouldn't set his rage into motion. "It's my natural color."

"I'll run to the store and buy blonde coloring and a decent dress for you to wear for the camera. By the end of the week, you'll be a size four again."

She shivered from head to toe, not because he hadn't turned on the heat in the room. Starving her and not giving her water would be the beginning of his weight loss plan.

"You rest for the night ahead while I buy something to eat." He walked out the door. It clicked behind him.

She scanned the room for something to help her escape. Maybe Scott would take a long time or be in a car accident. With all the different shades of blonde hair colors, he might not remember the one he liked. Kidnapping her had to be Scott's last ditch effort.

Megan had never been able to get out of the handcuffs. Ben had told her if a man could break his thumbs, he could squeeze his hands out of the cuffs, but Ben didn't explain how to do that. She waited until Scott's car drove away and then screamed so loudly, for so long, her throat hurt.

Giving up, she let the tears fill her eyes. She wished Scott had taken her to the house. Then Ben and George would have found her. They'd never locate her in a cheap motel off a main road.

Since she'd left Scott and spent time with counselors and the Grants, she learned that Scott's mistreatment of her hadn't been her fault. Scott chose to torment her. In the past she had tried so hard to be a perfect wife but had failed. It had always been up to her to be so good, Scott wouldn't be bad. But it wasn't up to her. Unless Scott wanted to change, he would always be hurtful.

Was it wrong to leave her husband when God had put them together, till death do them part? It would have been worse to stay with him and let him kill her for that would only be more bad publicity for Christians.

She thought of Ben and smiled. His tenderness for her proved there were decent men.

CHAPTER FORTY-SIX

Ben ran his hands through his hair. Scott was so desperate, he'd kidnapped Megan in broad daylight in front of an older woman. His reckless behavior bordered on psychotic putting Megan in greater danger.

And Ben didn't think Scott Collins had ever accepted Christ as Savior. A born-again Christian would never treat his wife like Scott had. He could only be a wolf in sheep's clothing, who would rip Megan to death.

Lord, protect her, keep her safe and warm.

Ben turned to his mom and buttoned up his jacket. "It's going to freeze again tonight. I hope she's not outside without a coat. Eileen convinced the news station to show Megan's pictures taken after Scott beat her. We'll find her, but will we reach her in time?"

George gripped Ben's shoulder. "We placed her in God's hands and we're praying. Megan's intelligent, and you've been giving her tips on how to escape tight places."

"Has your computer expert located any places that Scott might use to confine Megan?"

George shook his head. "Scott owns no property, except their house and his three cars. I've checked with the Sparks to find out if anyone in the church has a cabin or country home. The few people that do have never loaned it to Scott."

"There are lots of places he could hide her in a twenty-mile radius."

"Scott has influence and knows everyone in the community. He probably paid off a judge and who knows how many others."

Ben called Eileen. "Can you find out where Scott is right now through the ankle bracelet?" He ended the call and turned to George. "She'll phone back."

When the cell rang, Ben pressed the button, listened, and nodded. Then he put the cell in his pocket. "Scott's at the hospital praying for the sick. Let's follow him and maybe he'll take us to Megan."

*****

Megan had been unable to get out of the handcuffs. Her heart pounded faster when a car trunk slammed. Her husband had returned. She looked toward the door and waited for the lock to click. Scott stepped into the motel room, switched on the overhead light, and marched toward her. Megan caught a tantalizing whiff of enchiladas, chili, and cumin from the take-out orders Scott carried. Her mouth watered.

He set the bags on the desk and glared at her. "I suppose you have to use the bathroom."

She nodded. "Yes, please."

Scott unlocked the cuff attached to the iron leg of the bed and put his own wrist in it. He clamped it closed and ordered. "Let's go."

After Megan had eased herself, Scott snarled. "I've put you on a strict diet. No food or drink for a week so you'll be ready for the broadcast."

Washing her hands at the sink, she wondered what television program he talked about. She knew better than to ask.

Scott bolted the bathroom door behind him and unlocked the cuffs. "Your appearance disgusts me. You're fat. Take off your clothes and get in the shower."

She twisted the water taps. After undressing, she stepped in the old bathtub and pulled the curtain. Leaning over to adjust the faucet, she scooped several handfuls and swallowed. After soaping up, she let the blast of water rinse her. She kept her mouth open, gulping down as much water as possible.

He screamed, "Hurry up."

She turned off the taps and stepped out of the shower. Then she reached for the towel he held out to her. She kept her head lowered as she dried off and wrapped the towel around her.

With a pinched expression, he scowled. "I can hardly stand to look at you." His eyes narrowed. "After I color your hair, I want you to put on a lighter shade of makeup."

Megan had never questioned why he changed her hair, her makeup, size, and clothes. Why didn't he like anything about her? And why had it taken her so long to realize she'd never be good enough?

"You'll have to put your clothes back on because the ones I bought are too small for you. On second thought, you won't need anything to wear the rest of the night." He snapped the handcuffs back on her wrist and pulled her toward the bed.

When he finished with her, he lifted the take-out order from the bag with his right hand cuffed to her left one. He was ambidextrous so could do whatever he wanted without hindrance.

Megan caught a whiff of food, but she wasn't too hungry yet. With the little water she'd gulped in the shower, she might last longer than other times. She looked away and prayed.

Trust in the Lord with all your heart. Lean not to your own understanding.

She searched the room again for a way to escape. Ben's voice ran through her head. *Watch where he keeps the keys and look for something to knock him out.* Scott had kept the keys in his pants pocket which were on the other side of the room.

After he'd eaten his enchiladas, he yanked her to the dresser to put the leftover food on it. He picked up the remote to the television and clicked through the channels. He stopped at the photo of her beaten face but moved on to the next station which also showed a picture of her.

Scott let out a stream of vulgarities. "Why have they put your picture on every channel? You're not important. No one has any business in our marriage."

The anchorwoman announced. "If anyone has seen Megan Jane Collins, please contact the authorities. She was taken by force from the home of Edna Steel at noon. Her husband is wanted by the police for the disappearance of over six million dollars, violation of the restraining order, assault on his wife, and kidnapping charges. He is considered dangerous."

Hearing the word dangerous, Megan shuddered. He was about to explode with rage and violence.

Scott hurled the remote against the set. The screen shattered. "Why do you make me lose my temper?" He pounded the wall. "I'll have to practice restraint. You can't have any bruises or cuts on you when we go on national television."

Megan kept her head lowered and mouth shut.

He growled. "At least have the decency to answer me."

"I'm sorry." She whispered.

"Is that all you can say?"

Megan was familiar with that response. No matter what she said or did, he'd take his fury out on her. She braced herself for the inevitable blows, but they didn't come.

"Here's the deal, Megan."

It was out of character for him to offer her a trade. It meant she had something he wanted badly.

"You must be in shape and beautiful by the end of the week, so you'll look gorgeous for the camera. You'll confess to taking the missing funds from the church, running away with Benjamin Grant, and having an affair with him. You can't stop yourself from stealing, which is why you're committing yourself for psychiatric treatment."

Tears filled her eyes and ran down her cheeks. She wanted to ask him. *If I don't do this, what will you do?* But she knew what he'd do. Heartlessness glared from his stony eyes. She would go along with him.

"After the broadcast you'll have an unfortunate accident or commit suicide. If you don't do exactly as I say, I'll kill your boyfriend, Benjamin Grant. After he is out of the way, I'll take care of his mother."

She nodded, but her stomach churned. Ben didn't know Scott as well as she did. She crossed her arms and rubbed the goosebumps. She was afraid for Ben and his mother.

Megan passed a horrible night handcuffed to the monster in bed.

*****

Ben and George drove to the hospital, but they couldn't find Scott. They talked to several patients. Scott should have visited them, but he hadn't been there all day.

He phoned Eileen and asked her to check out the man watching the monitoring screen for Scott's ankle bracelet.

She returned his call. "The man viewing the screen was called away and a loop of Scott at the hospital played over and over again."

"How did that happen?" Ben asked.

"Scott must have paid off someone. Have you checked out every square inch of the house, including the basement?" Eileen asked.

"Basement? Megan never mentioned that. We didn't find one in the house. Could Scott have taken her to another house with one?" He turned to George. "Did Megan ever talk about a cellar where Scott hurt her?"

George shook his head. "Let's call the county clerk and check out the house plan."

Eileen secured the plan and sent it to them. They studied the layout, but there was no basement.

They secured a search warrant to look through Scott's house again. More officers joined them to hunt for a basement. Half of the law officials looked outside for the cellar door while the other half searched inside the house.

Ben tapped on walls, moved bookcases, and pulled out drawers peering behind and under them. "I've a gut feeling, there's a basement."

"It wouldn't be anywhere near the main rooms." George opened a cupboard.

A young female officer approached them. "I have an idea. Will you follow me?"

In the garage, she turned to them. "Maybe he's using the door of the basement to leave without us knowing it. Let's move Mrs. Collin's car."

When the men pushed the vehicle out of the way, Ben spotted a trap door. He tugged it open and pulled out his gun. George had taken out his weapon and nodded at Ben, who raced down the stairs.

Seeing the barber chair with handcuffs, Ben flinched. Duct tape, ropes and more handcuffs were spread on the table next to it. He pulled out a pair of gloves to pick up the Taser. He closed his eyes to stop the tears as he sent up a prayer for Megan.

George tapped the walls. "Scott's been here every day, so Megan can't be far away. We'll find her. There might be a secret chamber. Let's look for a way from this basement into the house."

Ben spotted a loose piece of sheetrock and moved it to the side. He pulled open a lopsided door and started up the uneven steps with

George right behind him. Ben pushed open an old wooden door, stepped into a tiny closet, and slid another door to the side. He went into another closet that opened under the stairs to the second story.

"That is a twisted way to an underground chamber, but it would be the perfect hiding place." The young female officer had followed them. "The historical society believed the house had been used in the Underground Railroad. They wanted to search it a few years ago, but Rev. Collins refused."

Taking a deep gulp of air, Ben turned to the group of officers. "Let's look around the yard and see if there are any freshly dug graves. We'll need search dogs."

Several hours later, an officer approached Ben. "The hounds didn't pick up her scent outside the house and there are no newly dug graves."

Ben shook his head. Where was Megan?

CHAPTER FORTY-SEVEN

After a week, Megan could scarcely stumble from the bathroom to the end of the bed. Too bad the iron leg was the only secure place to handcuff her while Scott was gone. Her dizziness slowed her thinking. Were it not for the gulps of water from the shower, she would have already passed out from dehydration.

The words of the Lord ran through her head and gave her strength and courage.

Scott carried shopping bags into the room and opened them. Most of the anger had left his face. He pulled out clothes and spread them on the bed. "Let's go in the bathroom so you can use the mirror to make yourself beautiful for the camera." He unlocked the cuffs.

Would he drag her down to the station and expect her to be quiet? Questions always angered him, so she had learned to say nothing. With the Lord's help, she might survive. Megan's hand trembled as she put on her mascara. She lifted her free hand to steady the wand.

When she finished, he pulled her into the bedroom. Having been starved for a week, she might be able to fit into the small outfit. *Lord, please let the dress fit.* She stepped into the blue dress and slid her arms in the sleeves. He stood behind her and started to zip it up. The garment fit snugly. "Take a deep breath, Megan."

She did.

And he finished zipping it. "Turn around and let me look at you."

Megan pasted her plastic smile on her face. "Do you want me to wear earrings?"

"You look and sound like your old self, Megan."

Her old self had long gone. She had pretended to be the perfect slave, as she searched and hoped for a way to free herself. Why would a man want a wife who only obeyed him as a servant and responded to him exactly as he told her? She gave him another fake smile. He kept her under his control by not giving her any shoes or a coat. She'd be a fool to run off in freezing weather in February.

Scott moved the chair in front of a plain wall. "Sit down." Then he handcuffed her to the iron frame of the chair.

He went outside. The car door slammed, and then the trunk banged. He marched back inside with a professional camera.

"Let's practice your confession before I film it."

She opened her mouth and presented another synthetic smile. Talking was difficult with her parched throat, but she'd do her best to save Ben and his mother. Scott had mistreated her far less over the last few days than he ever had. If Ben was already dead, maybe she could still rescue his mother.

"I would like to confess. I stole over six million dollars from the church and ran off with Mr. Benjamin Grant. We've been having an affair for a long time. I've sinned against God and hurt my husband. I've been depressed and am voluntarily committing myself to a psychiatric facility."

"Great job." Scott adjusted the camera. "You always were a good actress."

And he'd never noticed that she'd been acting most of their marriage to please him.

"Now for the real thing, sweetheart. Say it again with more sincerity."

As Scott filmed her during the final shot, she slowly lifted her cuffed wrist as far as it would go. *Lord, please let the camera catch a glimpse of it. Don't let Scott notice.*

"Not bad." Scott grinned. "I'm going to run this down to the station." Before going to the door, he handcuffed her back to the iron leg of the bed. "When I come back we'll celebrate."

She licked her lips and tried to swallow her saliva, but her mouth was dry. Scott denied her food and water not only to make her lose weight but keep her weak so she wouldn't have the strength to escape.

But she thought only of running away. She scanned the room again for anything. If Scott had left a knife she might have whacked off her hand and left it with the cuffs, just to get away.

Do not fret because of evil men. For like the grass they will soon wither. Trust in the Lord and do good. Commit your way to the Lord. Trust in Him. Be still before the Lord and wait patiently for him.

So she waited.

*****

She shuddered when Scott returned about an hour later.

He grinned. "They'll put it on the evening news."

After handcuffing her to the chair leg, he turned his back on her. A pill bottle popped open. His elbows moved as if he prepared something. He could only be mixing a drug, so it would look like a suicide.

When he turned back to her, he had a large tumbler in his hand. "You must be thirsty. I've poured you a nice cool lemonade."

"Thank you." With her free hand, she took the drink and pretended to sip on it. "I'm going to take my time and savor every drop. I appreciate it."

He came close to her and ran his fingers through her golden hair. "Oh, Megan, I've missed you." He took the glass from her hand and set it on the table. "Would you come back to me of your own free will?"

With tears in her eyes, she looked at him. "I could try."

Lie. Lie. Lie. Big lie, but she needed to put on another act to avoid the drugged lemonade. She'd prayed to die so many times during his torture over the years but having had a taste of freedom, she wanted to live.

He started to pull her to her feet but the handcuffs stopped her. Leaning over, he unlocked the cuffs and wrapped his arms around her. He kissed her and she returned his caresses. He unzipped her dress and let it fall. After taking off the rest of her clothes, he pulled her to the bed.

For the first time, she was out of the cuffs. As she gave her best performance in bed, she thought only of escape.

Thank you, Jesus.

When he finished with her, he beamed. "I've missed this, Megan."

Then he went into the bathroom.

She was free. Her heart thudded faster. God gave her a chance to run.

Run Jane. Run.

With shaking hands, she grabbed the bedsheet, wrapped it around her, and tiptoed to the door, not stopping to dress or pick up her discarded clothes.

Scott stepped out of the bathroom and stared at her with disbelief. He yelled, "I trusted you." His expression quickly turned to rage. Shrieking expletives, he slapped her face. She had braced herself for the strike but hadn't been prepared for the burst of pain.

A blow with his fist knocked her to the floor. Blasphemies spewed out of his mouth.

If only she could have reached the door and run to the office. Freezing to death would be better than what Scott would do to her now. He was angrier than she'd ever seen him. Hitting and kicking her, he lost his balance and crashed against the desk.

From the floor, she looked up and yanked the leg of the writing table hoping to spill the drugged lemonade. It tipped over. Then the desk wobbled and crashed on top of her.

*****

Ben and his mother watched the national news. Megan's confession mesmerized Ben. She had to have been drugged, or she'd never have said what she did.

His mother shook her head. "How could that sweet girl claim she left her husband to have an affair with you? You and Megan were never alone in this house, and she never went out with you."

"Her husband must have threatened to hurt her."

After Ben made a phone call, he reached for his jacket and kissed his mom. "I'm going to the television station. Keep the doors locked."

Ten minutes later, Ben met George in front of the building. They went inside and showed their credentials. Ben asked to speak with the news director.

When he arrived, Ben shook hands with him. "I've been working on the Megan Collins kidnapping case. I'd like to see the digital recording of her confession."

The director nodded. "I'll have someone make a copy of what we aired, but I'll have to charge you for it."

"That's fine." Ben pulled out his wallet.

"Do you want to look at it here or take it with you?" The newsman asked.

"Here please, and as soon as possible."

He escorted Ben and George into Editing Room B.

"I'll bring a copy and call the technician." The news director left.

When it was ready, the recording played.

Ben cocked an eyebrow. "Look in the lower left hand corner," he pointed to the tiny part of the metal. "Can you enlarge her wrist?"

"It looks like a bracelet." The technician wrinkled his brow.

"No, it doesn't to me. George, what's it look like to you?"

"Handcuffs."

"Go ahead and enlarge it." Ben took a ragged breath.

As it played for them again, he caught the slow movement of Megan lifting her arm slightly and tugging it a little. "Enlarge it some more."

Ben's stomach knotted when he saw it for the fifth time. "It's obviously handcuffs. She's being held against her will. Let's take this copy to the authorities."

Fifteen minutes later, Ben and George walked into the police station and arranged for the lead detective to see the recording. As they watched again, Ben leaned closer. "Let's compare the wall and the chair to furniture in local motels."

Lord, let us reach Megan in time.

CHAPTER FORTY-EIGHT

The following morning, Ben received a call from one of his colleagues. "We matched the inside of the room in the film clip to a Majesty Motel at 3456 Franklin Boulevard. The police are on their way there."

Ben and George met the officers at the motel and asked to see the register.

They looked over the list of guests. The name Dan Fuller jumped out at Ben. "Do you remember this guy?"

The manager shrugged. "He wanted a room with privacy for their honeymoon."

"Did you see his wife?"

"No. She must have waited in the car."

Ben remembered the license plate number. "Can you take us to the room?"

The manager led them to the far side. "His car is gone."

Ben pounded on the door. "Open up, Rev. Collins."

Silence.

A police officer hesitated. "We don't have a search warrant."

"I have reason to believe that Megan is in imminent danger of serious bodily harm." Ben's voice wobbled. "A warrant will take too much time. We should go in now."

The manager pounded on the door. "Mr. and Mrs. Fuller, open up."

Silence.

The manager removed a key and unlocked the door, Ben and George slid out their weapons and followed the officers into the room. Ben headed straight to the form wrapped in a bedsheet on the floor. He knelt beside Megan while George and the officers checked out the bathroom and closet.

An officer shouted, "I called an ambulance."

Ben found a faint pulse on her neck. "Megan."

Her right eye was swollen and her face bruised. Her left hand was handcuffed to the iron leg of the bed. "George, help me unlock these cuffs."

Hearing the ambulance approaching, Ben didn't check under the bedsheet for knife wounds and bleeding. A few minutes later, the paramedics rushed into the room and went to Megan. After taking her vital signs, they started an IV and gave her oxygen.

Ben spoke to the police officer. "Scott Collins is using Dan Fuller's name and car. Here's the license number." He turned to the paramedics. "I'd like to go with you. I'm concerned the guy who did this may come to the hospital to finish the job."

"Sure, come on." The EMTs slid the stretcher into the back of the ambulance.

After Ben jumped inside, he glanced at George. "Meet me at the emergency room."

Ben sat next to the stretcher and held Megan's hand. "Lord, please touch her, heal her."

When the vehicle pulled into the hospital, Ben followed the paramedics inside.

Her eyelids fluttered open and closed again. Then they stayed open. In slow motion, she turned her head from side to side. Her eyes stopped at Ben, and she whispered, "Are you okay? How's your mother?"

Ben held her hand. "We're fine. How are you?"

Megan had been beaten and in pain, but she was only concerned about him and his mother. She understood God's love, lived it, and let it flow through her to others.

"Better now." She whispered, "May I have some water, please?"

A nurse returned with a cup and straw and handed it to Ben, who held it to Megan's lips.

When she began to gulp it down, Ben pulled it away. "Not so fast."

"I'm so thirsty."

"I know, but you need to take it easy."

"Scott got angry when I tried to escape." Tears filled her eyes.

Ben put the straw to her lips again. Then he looked at the doctor, who had come into the room. "How is she doing?"

"I can't tell you without the patient's permission."

"You have it." Megan groaned and nodded. "I want to know, too."

"I started pain medications and antibiotics. I'm running tests. You need x-rays and an MRI."

"How long will I be here?"

"If there are no complications, we can release you today. If there are internal injuries or broken bones, we'll keep you longer. We won't know until the results come back." The doctor looked at his clipboard.

"Mom's been praying for you, so I need to call her." He put the phone to his ear. "Good news. We found Megan in time. She's in the hospital but in bad shape. Her husband hurt her again." Pause. "Okay. I'll see you later. I love you."

Megan tried to sit up, but fell back on the bed. She whispered. "Ben."

He leaned closer. "I'm here. Lie still."

"I'm sorry," she whispered. "Please forgive me for saying that I left Scott to have an affair with you. He threatened to kill you and your mother if I didn't say it. I didn't want anything to happen to either one of you."

"If it makes you feel better, I'll say I forgive you, but I was never upset with you. I suspected Scott threatened you. I hope he'll be sent to jail for a long time."

"Have you talked to Eileen and Cindy?" Megan asked.

"They called me right away after you were kidnapped. I've kept them updated on our progress."

"Do they have a place for me to go?"

"I talked to Mom. She and I want you to stay at her house. We've missed you."

"I missed you, too." Her eyes closed.

"Megan?"

No answer. His heart lurched. He reached for the pulse on her wrist.

The nurse moved closer and checked her heart. "Severe dehydration causes sleepiness. It'll take some time for her to recover her strength."

Ben nodded. "I understand."

Lord, heal her and let her be alright.

CHAPTER FORTY-NINE

Scott clenched the steering wheel. He should have killed Megan instead of leaving her handcuffed to the bed. He had used all the sleeping pills in the lemonade that she spilled and didn't have time to get more tablets. His informants told him that Benjamin Grant was too close. Scott's associates were being watched so he wasn't able to hire anyone to go back to the room and make it look like suicide.

He hated Dan's old car, but no one would ever suspect an important man like Scott of driving such a clunker. He turned off the interstate and went down a secondary road heading north to the Canadian border.

Scott was a free man. Megan had taken the blame for stealing the missing money, and her boyfriend would be busted for beating her. Laughing, he rubbed his ankle. His fans were foolish for trusting him. His own parents had never trusted him. He had misled everyone because most people were stupid.

His deacons and church elders were the most irresponsible of all. They never asked about the money he had collected. A few did, but they believed what he told them. The government had never found the fourteen million he'd taken from members. He had less than half of that now after paying off everyone, but it was enough to start all over again. Roaring with laughter, he sped down the road. He had outsmarted them all.

No one suspected he'd kept all the money in his house. Over the years, he'd hidden the cash right under everyone's eyes. None of the authorities had learned his home had two secret chambers, both used in the Underground Railroad. He'd installed several safes in the second hiding place and managed to save the money in hundred dollar bills. He hadn't taken time to stack and attach the last batch together, so he had tossed the loose currency into the suitcase which he put in the backseat. He had jammed the rest of the money into a duffle bag and stuffed it in the trunk.

Scott hoped Dan's old car would last until Scott reached Canada. A freezing wind blew through the broken glass in the back window. He shivered.

Wailing police sirens startled him. They must be after someone else. No one would ever arrest him, not since Megan confessed to his crimes. The blue lights behind him blinked as they came closer. He slowed to let the vehicles go around him, but they didn't. Maybe a tail light was out on Dan's old car.

Why did they keep following him? Sweat broke out on his brow. He pressed down on the gas. His heart raced faster than the car. Another police vehicle roared past him and halted a thousand yards in front of him to block the road.

Something had gone wrong. Why were they after him? It didn't matter, but he couldn't let them find the money. So he veered off and drove into a deserted field. The old vehicle bounced over the ruts. He glanced in the rearview mirror. A patrol car followed him. He flattened the accelerator to the floor to drive as fast as the old car went. Bam! Bump. Bump.

Were they shooting at him? No, it felt like a flat tire. Where could he go now? He couldn't surrender. No one would ever understand. He deserved the money because he was smarter than everyone else.

As the car bumped along, another tire exploded. Bam! Bump! Bump! Scott didn't give up. He swerved away from more patrol cars. Seeing the end of the field ahead, he kept his foot on the gas to reach the opposite side.

When the police cars stopped, Scott sighed in relief. They were letting him go. He was free. But his foot mashed down hard on the accelerator and the car zoomed forward. A click from the back seat distracted him, and he looked over his shoulder. The lid of his suitcase had popped open and money blew out the window. He couldn't lose everything he had worked for all those years. A stream of blasphemies shot out of his mouth as he unfastened his seatbelt and reached back to close the luggage.

Then he turned back to the steering wheel, screamed, and cursed God.

His car flew off a cliff and plummeted.

*****

Ben ran into the living room. "There's a special newscast we need to see."

His mother picked up the remote and turned to the local broadcast.

A female reporter stood next to a crumpled car. "During a fast-paced police chase, Rev. Scott Collins drove off a cliff and plunged to his death."

Megan paled and leaned closer to the television.

Ben left and returned with a glass of water. "Drink this." He sat next to her.

With shaking hands, Megan took the water and sipped it.

The newswoman looked into the camera. "The police retrieved over six million dollars in cash from inside the car."

Mrs. Grant turned off the television. She came and sat next to Megan. "This proves he stole the money all the time."

Ben asked, "Can I do anything?"

"It's a shock." Her lips quivered. "If I saw his body, I might be able to find closure."

"Are you strong enough? You've only been out of the hospital for twenty-four hours."

"I'm weak, but I can do it."

"I'll call some people and set a time to take you to the morgue."

"Thank you."

His phone rang. "Yes, Eileen. She's right here." He handed his cell to Megan.

She leaned forward. Then she raised her voice. "Married?" There was a long pause. "Legally." Another long pause. "Funeral?" When she ended the call, she turned to them. "Eileen talked to one of Scott's lawyers. I'm still his legal wife because he never signed the divorce papers. We didn't have time for a judge to grant the divorce." She sniffed. "As Scott's wife, I should make funeral arrangements. It would be a good Christian testimony."

"We'll help in any way we can." Ben put an arm around her shoulders.

CHAPTER FIFTY

Several days later, Megan sat in the front row for Scott's funeral. She'd been shocked at how dead and beaten up Scott had looked in the morgue. Probably as battered as she'd been for fifteen years. Cuts, gashes, and dried blood clots marred his once handsome face. Seeing him like that had given her a strange peace. He'd never hurt her again. Had death been the only way to stop him from hurting her?

Megan leaned closer to Ben and whispered. "I'm surprised how many people have come."

"Most are here out of curiosity."

After a hymn, Megan walked to the front. "No one knows what's in another person's heart. The truth is that Scott was a cruel and sadistic husband. After I escaped, he blamed me for his own criminal acts. We're all sinners, including myself, but I asked God to forgive me. He sent his Son to die an agonizing death on the cross so that I could spend eternity in Heaven with Him. He wants me to forgive Scott, too. It's hard, but I have been able to forgive him."

Tears streamed down Megan's face. "What hurts me most is that Scott may have died without Christ. If he never repented of his sins, it is now too late for him. What about you? Are you ready to meet God if you die today?"

After the funeral, Ben walked his mom and Megan to the car. Photographers and news men with microphones rushed toward them. Megan had told Ben she didn't want to comment.

So Ben turned to them and held up his hands. "Please respect Mrs. Collins. She doesn't wish to make a statement." He opened the car door for his mom and Megan.

After they were in the car, Ben smiled. "People spoke well of your talk and were touched by your powerful testimony."

Mrs. Grant took Megan's hand. "I'd like you to stay with me as long as you want."

Tears filled Megan's eyes. "My mother abandoned me. So my grandmother raised me. I'd like to stay with you, but I need to learn to be independent."

*****

For two weeks after the funeral, Ben and his mother helped Megan go through Scott's house and pack the property Megan wanted. Ben carried several loads to a storage shed Megan had rented. After the house was secured and Megan signed all the necessary papers, she packed to leave.

Ben walked Megan to her car. He didn't want her to go, but he couldn't ask her to stay. She needed time and space.

"I'm going to miss you." He took her hand and put his free arm around her shoulders. "I know it's too soon, but one day I'd like to get to know you better. I care deeply for you. When you're ready, would you consider going out on a date with me?"

"So much has happened." Tears ran down her cheeks. She wiped them away. "I need time."

"Yes, I understand."

Could he let her go without telling her? What if something awful happened and she never knew?

"Megan, I love you. I've loved you for months, but love is patient. You take all the time you need, no matter how long it takes to sort through everything, I'll wait for you. I'll be here."

She smiled and nodded.

He opened her car door, and she slid inside. He had to surrender her like God wanted him to do. She deserved peace and freedom. As he closed her door, his heart squeezed shut. When she drove away, his shoulders shook with sobs. Letting her leave had been harder than any battle he'd fought in the war.

*****

Megan wept as she drove down the road. Why was she leaving unconditional love, a love that endured? The greatest love she'd ever known since experiencing Christ's love.

Ben never ordered her to submit and obey. He would never punish her or beat her. Ben had been a pillar of love and strength. He had stood by her side and in front of her when necessary to protect her from harm. He loved her unconditionally.

She had learned to relax in the depth of his love. It wasn't proud. Never once did he boast about anything he did for her. He went about his life and work with quiet humility. He never asked for thanks or favors from her. Ben never kept a tally of kind acts to remind her of them later. Nor did he pull out a list and claim that she owed him for a favor.

First Corinthians, chapter thirteen came to her mind. Love never insisted on its own way. Ben had never forced his will on her and he'd never become angry with her. She'd seen frustration and disappointment on his compassionate face a few times, but he'd never demanded anything from her.

His love was as faithful as a sunrise coming up each morning. Always there, strong and powerful, like God's love. How did Ben do it? He let God's love fill him and flow through him. Ben breathed, lived, and walked love.

Why was she driving away from the sweetest and truest love she'd ever known?

Megan didn't need time. She needed Ben's love. She didn't want to go anywhere. She wanted to live with Ben's mother, work in a hospital as a pediatric nurse, and get to know Benjamin Grant better.

She wouldn't make the same mistake she did with Scott. She would do it right this time. She'd learn everything she could about Ben. Marriage could wait and so could she.

Pure love was never in a hurry. Lust passed and was gone, but love lasted forever.

She applied the brakes, stopped the car, and swerved into a U-turn. As she drove back, her breath came out in ragged gasps.

Seeing Ben's Honda still in his mother's driveway, she jumped out and ran up the sidewalk.

Run Jane, run.
Run to real love.
Run to proven love.
Run to the man who loves you.

Ben stepped out of the front door and went to her. "What happened?"

She saw sincere devotion, unconditional love.

Tears streamed down her face.

"Did someone try to hurt you?" With his fingertips he wiped the tears off her cheek. Then he reached out for her hand.

"I want to stay and go out on that date, and learn all about you because I love you."

He pulled her into his arms and held her close to his chest. "We'll go slowly and date for as long as we need, two years, five years or ten. Love waits. I'll wait. I love you."

THE END

Did you enjoy this book?
I hope so.
Would you take a quick minute to leave a review?

https://www.amazon.com/review/create-review?ie=UTF8&asin=B0177Y2AJ0&channel=detail-glance&nodeID=283155&ref_=cm_crdp_wrt_summary&store=book/

It doesn't need to be long. Just a sentence or two telling what you liked about the story.

Thank you for your time.

Made in the USA
San Bernardino, CA
30 December 2016